NO END TO THE JOURNEY

NO END TO THE JOURNEY

A NOVEL

S. SHANKAR

STEERFORTH PRESS
HANOVER, NEW HAMPSHIRE

Steerforth Press L.C.
25 Lebanon Street
Hanover, New Hampshire 03755

Library of Congress Cataloging-in-Publication Data
Shankar, Subramanian, 1962–
No end to the journey : a novel / S. Shankar. — 1st ed.
p. cm.
ISBN 1-58642-093-3 (alk. paper)
1. Retirees — Fiction. 2. Older men — Fiction.
3. Parent and adult child — Fiction.
4. Conflict of generations — Fiction. 5. India — Fiction. I. Title.
PS3569.H332614N6 2005
813'.54–dc22
2005010190

ISBN-13 978-1-58642-093-2

FIRST EDITION

FOR UJAY

PART ONE

walk. He had been propelled into the practice by the death from heart trouble of one of his two best friends.

Striding along at this well-rehearsed pace, Gopalakrishnan passed the shadowy, soundless houses of his sleeping neighbors. He came to the tall doors of the temple and took, as he always did, the branch to the right. Here another feeble lamp flung its illumination desperately into the street. The meaner houses that lined this portion of Meenakshisundareswarar Temple Street remained veiled in the darkness to which — Gopalakrishnan was pleased to note — a dead quiet had returned. For a moment Gopalakrishnan could fantasize that the village had been abandoned and he was alone. He kept close to the temple's red-and-white striped wall as he walked, for this branch of the street was full of potholes and even the little rain of the previous night had filled them with water. He picked his way carefully over the drier ground along the wall, shaking his head at the sorry state of the street. He thought for a moment that he should write to the authorities — he would have to find out to whom exactly — about the potholes and began composing a letter of complaint in his head. *Dear Sir/Madam: Subject: Terrible Potholed Condition of Meenakshisundareswarar Temple Street. It is only after the most careful thought that I am writing this letter. I am a retired civil servant living in Paavalampatti, my ancestral village, after more than forty years of distinguished service in the Ministry of Information and Broadcasting in New Delhi. I happily returned to be with my respected mother, who is now old, about a year ago. Complaining is not to my liking, but I would kindly like to bring to your valued attention the big potholes in Meenakshisundareswarar Temple Street behind temple . . .*

As he was composing this letter, it occurred to Gopalakrishnan that these potholes were really no affair of his. He did not live here, in this wretched portion of Meenakshisundareswarar Temple Street. If those who did — those who had to step into these potholes every time they went anywhere — could not be bothered by the state of the street, why should he? Why should he waste his time? He was rethinking his letter when his sandal added its own angry squelch of grumbling. He had, despite his care, stepped into a patch of mud. He commended himself for having folded his veshti out of harm's way and it was only this pleasure at his foresight that lifted him a little out of his exasperation.

The final house in this branch of Meenakshisundareswarar Temple Street belonged to Sundaram, named no doubt for the presiding male deity of the village. Gopalakrishnan did not know Sundaram well. He was even older than Gopalakrishnan and lived by himself. He was a tall, thin, hollow-cheeked man who liked his privacy. To Gopalakrishnan's mind, his house fit him perfectly — the modest house had not been painted in decades and had faded into a nondescript gray color. The steps leading up to the thinnai were chipped and broken. The warped wooden shutters of the windows were always shut. Now the whole village was dark and silent, but darkness and silence were the permanent condition of Sundaram's house. Gopalakrishnan had never seen a light in the house, nor heard a sound from it. He averted his eyes as he passed.

Beyond Sundaram's house the street faded into a trail that ran under some coconut, mango, and banana trees before reaching the Tamarabarani River. Gopalakrishnan entered the trail and found it easier to traverse, trail though it was, than the sorry, potholed apology for a street he had left behind. The distance to the river was short, but when he emerged from under the trees it seemed to him that the slab of darkness with which the night had covered up the village had been pried loose a little by the rising sun. A gray light filled the air. Gray clouds hung heavy from the sky. The grayness of the day seemed to have seeped into the very river. The trail met the river where it bent and formed a little beach. Over time industrious hands had supplemented the beach with stone steps. As he left the trail and descended the steps to the river, it seemed to Gopalakrishnan that the river curved lifeless before him in the dim light. But when he dipped his foot in it to wash the mud off his sandal, he found the water flowing and alive and refreshing.

Crouched there, on that wet stone step by the water, Gopalakrishnan noticed the rocks in the middle of the river, the very rocks around which he had learned to swim as a young boy. He vividly remembered one time — he was perhaps five or six — when his father, a thin white towel wrapped around his waist, had waded out to the rocks with him. The little river was in spate. He had clung to his father's neck, the cold water rising slowly up his bare legs and filling the pockets of his shorts as the two of them went deeper and deeper into the water. The flowing green water came up to his father's stomach. The current pushed and pulled against the two of them, making his father's towel float ghostly just under the surface of the river. His father had leaned against one of the rocks and reached up to pry Gopalakrishnan's hands loose from around his neck. "No," Gopalakrishnan had whispered, terrified. His father's small and narrow face was implacable in the steady brightness of the afternoon sun. "Swim. You know how to swim," his father had said in his unwavering voice, his voice that never rose in anger or fell in doubt. "Are you a girl that you are shy to swim in the river?"

A lifetime ago. His father was now dead.

Gopalakrishnan returned to the trail, which now followed the river around the bend. The trail was broad and flat near the beach and Gopalakrishnan strode along thinking of his boyhood. His arms swung in rhythm by his sides and his delicate chin was thrust firmly forward. Because it had rained, there was a crisp freshness in the air that appealed to him. This was his favorite part of the morning walk. The trail took him away from the village rapidly. The stand of banana and coconut and mango trees through which he had come was now between him and the village. The houses of Meenakshisundareswarar Temple Street were more and more lost behind the trees. Then he had rounded the bend and even the few glimpses of the houses that he'd had could not intrude themselves upon him. For a good while now he would encounter no one. He was little more than a good shout away from the village but he might as well be the only man around for miles. The trail grew narrow now and the terrain wilder. Depending on the surroundings, the trail approached the river or abandoned it. In one place, the trail diminished so much the tall weeds brushed against his bare legs. The furry touch of the wild vegetation made Gopalakrishnan wonder what his wife, Parvati, would think of his presence in this place at this time. She did not know his morning walk included this trail. Snakes, he decided with amusement, she would think of snakes. Parvati was terrified of them.

Snakes . . .

Gopalakrishnan wished he had not let the creatures come slithering into his mind. He had been walking this trail for months and never had the thought of snakes entered his head. A rustle sounded in the wild undergrowth to his left. He was reassuring himself that he had only imagined the sound when it was repeated. It seemed closer now, more ominous. Involuntarily he quickened his pace; the undergrowth was suddenly full of menacing sounds. How was it that this rustling and hissing and slithering had not been audible to him before? Something long and sinuous darted swiftly across the trail in front of him. Gopalakrishnan hurried down the trail, trying not to run. Ahead was the familiar hulk of the white-painted bridge on which the highway that connected the village to Thirunelveli Town, the closest town of any size, crossed the Tamarabarani. The trail left the side of the river as it approached the bridge, rising up the embankment of the highway to cross over to the other side. This was where Gopalakrishnan customarily left the trail to continue his walk along the highway. He scrambled up the embankment. A white bird sitting on the cement wall of the bridge turned its head alertly at his approach. The bird watched him for a moment and then, as if unable to bear his undignified rush upward, rose into the air with three or four strokes of its wings. Gopalakrishnan was puffing and panting by the time he had gained the top.

Standing by the highway, Gopalakrishnan took great big breaths of air. He was surprised at how breathless he felt. O his heart, his heart, his sorry, sixty-five-year-old heart! He ruefully seated himself on the low wall abandoned by the bird to rub his chest. He was embarrassed at the way he had rushed down the trail. A man of his age! Stampeded into a mad scramble at the thought of snakes! He quickly glanced around to see if anyone had observed his unceremonious flight. Only the bird drifted up above, a white patch moving lazily against the gray canvas of the sky. He calmed down as he sat on the wall, the day brightening moment by moment around him, his amusement at his behavior also growing moment by moment. When his breathing had subsided sufficiently he rose from his perch and resumed his walk in his customary fashion, along the highway, back toward the village. But, still, the hollow feeling that had quietly opened up inside him at this reminder that he was getting old persisted. His steps did not falter. His feet rehearsed instinctively the lesson of decades. But, still . . .

Paavalampatti lay at a little distance now, beyond the wild expanse through which he had hurried a moment before, on the other side of the trees that veiled the village. At this distance, the only visible signs of the village were the satellite dish (a black upturned umbrella of wires and rods listening for invisible communications from the sky) and the newly painted gopuram of the temple. Were it not for the satellite dish and the brightly colored gopuram, it would have been as if the village did not exist. Both of these upward emanations of the village had managed to raise themselves above the mass of trees. They marked the rough location of Meenakshisundareswarar Temple Street. Paavalampatti was certainly much larger than that Y-shaped street; indeed, the greater portion of the village lay on the other side of a railway line. From Gopalakrishnan's present vantage point, the only sign of this railway line, which like the highway connected Paavalampatti to Thirunelveli Town, was an almost imperceptible indentation in the mass of trees. Somewhere in that indentation, as he well knew, were two railway tracks, and by their side a little railway station made up of two tree-shaded platforms of cement and a little yellow-painted building that contained both the stationmaster's office and the ticket office. But railway station, railway line, and what lay beyond the line were all obscured from Gopalakrishnan's view as he made his way along the highway.

The other side of the highway was cultivated land. Green rice fields, patterned into squares and rectangles by brown banks of mud, stretched away to the distance, where hills rose to the sky. Beneath the green of the rice plants the water in the rice fields reflected the leaden sky above. In places the mud banks were so broad and so solid that coconut trees grew out of them, making Gopalakrishnan think of giants with green shaggy heads picking their way in single file through the rice fields. As he watched, two less singular beings crossed the highway up ahead and descended to one of the paths through the rice fields. The man walked in front; the woman followed with a basket on her head. The man, smaller in size than the woman, turned now and then as he walked to fling loud words back at the woman.

"Do you know how far it is?" the man shouted. "Two miles. Early in the morning you want us to walk all that distance to save a few paise!"

The woman did not say anything.

"And when we get there, is your father going to welcome us?" the man persisted. "When have I ever been given the respect due to a son-in-law in your house?"

Still the woman did not speak.

"I am telling you," the man said. "If your father does not give us money for bus fare when we return, there will be no one more angry than me. I am letting you know this right now. Don't complain to me later that I made a big scene in your father's house."

"Look ahead and keep walking," the woman said, provoked at last. "Don't waste your energy turning around to shout at me."

The couple walked on through the rice fields, flinging words back and forth. In the time since he had set out on his walk, Gopalakrishnan saw, Paavalampatti had forsaken mat and mattress. He was thankful when the voices of the couple faded into the distance. He would be alone in the new day for at least a few moments longer.

Soon Gopalakrishnan arrived at the place where Station Road connected to the highway. The macadamized surface of Station Road had long since worn away. Only a few patches showed here and there in the narrow road. If he were to turn into Station Road he would pass Paavalampatti Railway Station before returning to Meenakshisundareswarar Temple Street. But Gopalakrishnan did not turn into Station Road. He was not done — not even close to being done. He continued on to the red-and-white metal railway gates, whose purpose was to guard the highway from the tracks. The gates were open because there was still an hour before the morning train to Thirunelveli Town thrum-thrummed its way into Paavalampatti Railway Station. By then the gates would be closed and masses of cars and Tempo vans and bicycles and pedestrians would be waiting on either side. At this early hour, however, there was no one at the railway crossing. Gopalakrishnan crossed the tracks and came to the row of shops that stood along the highway on the other side of the gates.

Super Haircutters and Jyothi Tailoring were yet shut, but Ramu, a dark stocky fellow who was the proprietor of Paavalampatti Provision Store, was flinging back the green wooden doors of his shop. A musty smell of spices and talcum powder and gunnysack wafted in Gopalakrishnan's direction from the gloomy interior of the shop, in front of which a boy, perhaps ten years old, waited for Ramu with some money in his hand. Gopalakrishnan knew Ramu well because he, like virtually everyone else in the village, shopped at Ramu's store. But he did not recognize the boy, who was jingling the coins in his hand and idly watching Gopalakrishnan striding down the highway. The boy did not live in Meenakshisundareswarar Temple Street.

Gopalakrishnan was almost past the shops when a shout rang out — "Gopalakrishnan-Sir, O Gopalakrishnan-Sir."

It was Ramu. Gopalakrishnan wondered why the shopkeeper was calling out to him so loudly. He always settled his monthly account with Ramu promptly. It couldn't be anything to do with money. Why then was Ramu calling out to him so rudely this early in the morning? Probably something trivial. Probably Parvati had sent a message yesterday asking for something or the other from Ramu and Ramu wanted clarification about it from him. But what did he know about lentils and coffees and varieties of rice? What could he tell Ramu about whether Parvati wanted this brand of appalam or that? He would have to stop if he were to respond to Ramu. He did not want to stop. He did not like interrupting his brisk morning walk. So Gopalakrishnan pretended he had not heard Ramu and kept going down the highway, making sure not to let Ramu's impertinent shout make him falter in his precise strides. Ramu could send someone home if he wanted clarification about something.

Behind him, Gopalakrishnan heard Ramu's voice say loudly, "Can't hear a thing. That's what happens when you get old. Your hearing begins to go." That made Gopalakrishnan feel embarrassed and guilty. Perhaps he should have stopped. Too late now. He was already too far away, and he could hear the waiting boy laughing sympathetically at Ramu's words. It was impossible to go back.

Beyond the shops, Gopalakrishnan passed a banyan tree in a little clearing by the highway. Its branches were like a roof overhead, the many aerial roots sprouting from its branches like the pillars of a hall. The clearing in which this tree stood was where the private and government buses that roared up and down the highway, to and from Thirunelveli Town, stopped. The vehicles could be sleek video coaches with air-conditioning or ancient contraptions patched up and reeking of diesel fumes. Under the banyan tree, between two of the largest aerial roots, was a little stall with a thatched roof whose purpose was to cater to the men and women who came and went on the buses. In front of the stall two kerosene stoves had been set on a wooden table, their blue flames hissing and crackling in the morning air. Over one flame water for coffee boiled in a battered aluminum kettle; over the other a flat black frying pan warmed as a woman rubbed it with a cloth soaked in oil, preparing it to make dosas. Cigarettes and biscuits and bananas and sundry other edibles were arranged on shelves inside the stall. Outside, in front of the stall, two silent men — one young, the other much older — sat on wooden benches and sipped frothing brown coffee from glass tumblers. They were both dressed in faded khaki uniforms with a symbol over the shirt pocket that Gopalakrishnan recognized as the logo of a chemical factory in Thirunelveli Town. Probably waiting for a bus to take them into town. From the resemblance in their worn faces, already so tired so early in the morning, Gopalakrishnan surmised they were father and son. Father and son drank their coffees thirstily, sitting in the same way on the bench, with their knees apart and leaning forward a little. The aroma from the tumblers made Gopalakrishnan think of his own morning coffee, thick and milky, waiting for him at home. He lengthened his strides a little.

Now the village, as if forsaking its former shyness, stepped out from behind its veil of trees and came right up to the highway. Gopalakrishnan passed the little, forlorn library of the village, which no one visited. Since his return to the village Gopalakrishnan had been inside it just once. There were two bookshelves with a scattering of Tamil pulp fiction and English *Reader's Digest* condensed books on them. There was a single wooden table with four folding chairs, one broken, around it. On the table popular Tamil weeklies and monthlies lay scattered. One glance was enough for Gopalakrishnan to comprehend the nature of the library. There was no reason for him to return. Next to the library was the village school, which usually compensated for the library by its busyness and cacophony. Now it too was silent and forlorn, waiting for the day to begin, for the students to throng the classrooms, the verandas, the staircases. Gopalakrishnan saw that the rain had turned the playground that fronted the school, usually pebbly and brown, into a stagnant pool of black water.

Behind the library and the school were the houses that made up the village this side of the railway track. Immediately behind were the houses of some upper-caste Pillaimars and just one or two Brahmins, and Gopalakrishnan seemed to remember that a handful of other castes, Chettiars and Naickermars, too, had houses there. Beyond them was the main Pillaimar section. The Pillaimar were the biggest landowners in the village. Some of the largest houses of the village were in this section. The Muslim houses were farther down the highway; the houses and huts of the Paraiyars and Kuyavars even beyond them, as if to reflect their generally abject status in the village. Or so Gopalakrishnan thought. There was a time when it could have been said with greater certainty that the Pillaimars live here, the Paraiyars there, and the Muslims in yet another part. But year by year each part had been seeping into the others. Consider the Pillaimars — and even a Muslim! — who were now living in Meenakshisundareswarar Temple Street. Unthinkable not so long ago. He did not mind that they were. In fact he approved of it. But the changes made him less certain who was where. Part of the reason was that he had been gone from the village for such a long time, working in Delhi and coming back only for visits. He had returned to live here only a year before — his retirement had made it possible and his father's death had made it necessary. On the other hand, no doubt things were still mostly as he thought they were. Paavalampatti had certainly changed, but it could not have changed that much. It was still, after all, only a village.

Musing in this manner, Gopalakrishnan came to the extreme southern boundary of the village, marked by an Amman temple. The Amman of the temple was called Kizhaku Vaasal Selvi because that is what the goddess did — she guarded the southern threshold of the village. The temple was maintained by the well-to-do Pillaimars of the village, who had made it grow, decade by decade, from a little stone idol standing by itself under a tree to a respectable-sized cement structure safe behind a low cement wall. It was not common for Brahmins to worship in the Amman temple, but Gopalakrishnan had been in it a number of times over the decades — partly out of curiosity and partly because of his mother, who had often insisted he pay his respects to the Amman too before returning to Delhi after a visit.

Opposite the temple, Gopalakrishnan turned into a path running along a narrow canal that took water to vegetable gardens. Low shade trees lined the canal, separating it from the fields of spinach beyond. On the other side of the path was the Muslim section of the village, which was large, taking up many streets. Some of the Muslims of Paavalampatti owned land, others were in various trades related to construction, like carpentry and plumbing. One of them — one A. R. Rahim, the richest of them, so rich that even Gopalakrishnan knew of him — had a brick factory in a neighboring town. Gopalakrishnan had heard Vasu, his neighbor in Meenakshisundareswarar Temple Street, complain that money from places like Kuwait was pouring into the Muslim section of the village and that it was growing in size year by year. But as far as Gopalakrishnan could remember there had always been many Muslims in Paavalampatti.

Gopalakrishnan came to the village's mosque — a little white-painted building with a modest hint at a minaret in one corner. Some men were sitting on a circular cement bench under the tamarind tree in front of the mosque, drinking their morning tea and coffee. A few wore colorful checkered lungis wrapped around their waists, others shirts and pants. One or two, perhaps the more devout among them, wore white skullcaps. Gopalakrishnan could hear their desultory conversation as he came up the path.

"You can't be too careful. I'm telling you. Anything can happen even here."

"Fatima won't listen to what I say."

"What will you do about it?"

"What can I do? I'll ask her mother to talk to her."

"Children. You bring them into the world. You raise them. And what do you get for your trouble? More trouble."

"It won't rain today."

"How do you know?"

"Why won't I know? This is a body that has lived on this soil all its life. If I don't know, who will?"

"I had a letter from my uncle."

"The one in Dubai?"

"Yes."

"What did he say?"

"He is coming on a visit."

There was a stir of interest.

"When?"

"He is already in Madras. He said he will come maybe in a week."

"Long time Hassan has been gone."

"Four years."

"Just you see. He will be fat as a buffalo."

"Dubai!"

The men noticed Gopalakrishnan's approach and stopped their conversation. His appearance was not unexpected, for invariably Gopalakrishnan would pass by on his daily walk when the men were gathered under the tree. At such times, it was customary for the man who had been speaking of his uncle arriving from Dubai, a young man with glasses and a serious manner about him, to raise his hand in friendly greeting to Gopalakrishnan. He did not fail to do so now. And Gopalakrishnan, who did not know the man's name (for that matter, which Muslim neighbor's name, other than A. R. Rahim's, did he know?), also did not fail to return the friendliness with a wave of his own hand, as he did now. Unfortunately for Gopalakrishnan, at this very moment of his distraction a bicycle passed him at great speed along the path, throwing muddy water all over his white veshti. "Ay!" Gopalakrishnan shouted out, but the man on the bicycle fled down the path toward the Paraiyar houses without even a backward glance. Gopalakrishnan reviewed the damage to his attire. The veshti was soaked through. Beneath it his bare legs were dripping with mud. He noticed the men in front of the mosque observing him silently. Stiffening his back and lowering his head, he hurried down the path, turning quickly into the street that would take him back across the tracks, back into Meenakshisundareswarar Temple Street.

As he entered his street, he saw his neighbor Vasu standing bare bodied on the thinnai of his house — the third house on the left, three or four doors down from his. Vasu was scratching his hairy back, raking his sacred thread up and down from his left shoulder to his waist. His eyes were closed, his mouth was open, and his pudgy face was quivering with pleasure. When he heard Gopalakrishnan approaching, he stopped, opened his eyes, and shouted in Gopalakrishnan's direction, "Not at your studies? You haven't begun your reading of the Ramayana yet?" And then his voice grew more concerned when he noticed the filth with which Gopalakrishnan was covered. "What happened?" he asked. "Look at your veshti! Did you fall down? Did you have an accident?"

Gopalakrishnan was sure he could hear barely suppressed delight in Vasu's voice. How the man exulted in his every discomfiture! He passed on to his own house without an answer. The ground in front of his house had already been swept, sprinkled with water and decorated with a kolam. Today Parvati had used the rice flour to draw a bird in the middle of squiggly concentric rectangles. The design was more complicated than usual and were it not for his besmirched condition Gopalakrishnan would have paused to admire his wife's handiwork. The front door that he had quietly shut behind him when he had left on his morning walk now stood ajar, letting the fresh morning air into the house. He left his sandals by the door and passed rapidly through the dark passageway until he came to the central space of the house, open to the sky but secured by an iron grill above. As he hurried through this courtyard, his wife Parvati called out to him from the kitchen: "Have you returned? Your coffee is ready." But he continued on to the back of the house without paying her any mind, passing through the door leading to the enclosed yard with the bathroom on one side and the well on the other. Beyond this yard was another, smaller, enclosed yard that contained empty cow stalls and the flush toilet that Gopalakrishnan's father had added to the house some twenty years previously. Gopalakrishnan went into the bathroom, took off his shirt and veshti, and turned on the shower to test the water. The shower gurgled loudly but no water came out. Parvati had again forgotten to switch on the motor that pumped water up to the overhead tank!

First the mud on his sandal. Then the snakes on the trail. Then the little incident with Ramu. Then the mud all over, just all over him! And now this. Would nothing go right this morning? He slapped his forehead in frustration and came out of the bathroom in his loose underwear. He thought of going into the kitchen to yell at Parvati. But what was the use of that? He stood by the well, leaning helplessly against its wall, his legs itching from the slime coating them.

The well's metal bucket stood on the wall, next to the pipe that led from the well to the overhead tank. A thick coir rope was tied to its handle. On an impulse, he threw the bucket into the well and watched it plunge down, the rope singing loudly as it passed through the metal pulley dangling from the crossbeam over the well. The bucket struck the water with a loud thud, tipped over, and began to fill. He let it fill to the top and then, as it began to sink, pulled on the rope. The bucket rose slowly, swinging from side to side, splashing a little water back into the well. The coir was rough on his hands, but he liked feeling the heft of the bucket in his arms and shoulders. When the bucket emerged he lifted it out and let the water pour over his legs, washing away the mud and the slime. He flung the empty bucket back into the well and leaned over the wall to watch it go hurtling back down to the water.

"Is that a good idea?" Parvati said to him, standing in the doorway leading back into the house, his coffee in her hand. Her sari, her white hair, her long face — they were all still disheveled from sleep. She had not yet had the time to have her bath. She would not have it until much later. If Gopalakrishnan had his morning duties and rituals, then so did she. After nearly forty years together, the morning of one fit the morning of the other like a foot in a well-worn sandal. Or, at least, that was how it should have been. Sometimes a sharp pebble could lodge between foot and sandal. Gopalakrishnan noted that the loud hum of the water pump now filled the air. He ignored Parvati and waited for the bucket to fill; and then he pulled on the rope to lift it out of the well, enjoying again the feeling that the exertion produced in his shoulders and his arms.

"You might pull a muscle," Parvati warned him.

This time he raised the bucket high over his head, took a deep breath, and let the water pour over him. It was cold, cold enough to make his body shudder.

It had been years since he had bathed by a well like this, with water drawn directly from it. He had done it now and then when he was a boy, by this very well, though not of his own volition. His father, Paavalampatti Krishnaswamy Iyer, had forced him to do it whenever some incident or the other had made him reflect on his young son's developing character. The next morning, the irksome incident still fresh in his mind, his father would summon him to the well, pull up the weighted bucket, and pour the cold water over him. "I observe you every day," he would note firmly, over his son's cries and entreaties. "You are growing up lazy and self-indulgent."

Bathing by the well had been a form of education. Gopalakrishnan had done it often enough, though it was more customary for his mother to heat water for him on the wood-fired stove in the kitchen and for him to then bathe with bucket and mug in the small bathroom outside. There were also days — days his mother had successfully subverted his father's will — when he was meant to bathe by the well but did not. On such mornings, when his father himself could not be present to supervise Gopalakrishnan's bathing, water for Gopalakrishnan would be put on the kitchen stove the moment his father had left the house. As the water came to a boil, his mother would warn Gopalakrishnan not to tell his father what she was doing. It would be their secret, one of many they came to share against his father. Her tender face would be serious and trusting as she made him understand that he could not betray their secret. Gopalakrishnan could not imagine doing so.

Paavalampatti Krishnaswamy Iyer, fair man that he was, never used hot water himself. He always bathed by the well, pulling the bucket up with quick, practiced movements and flinging it over his small and compact body without a thought for its coldness. There had been no overhead tank in those days when Gopalakrishnan was a boy, nor any pump to bring the water up from the well. But Gopalakrishnan's father had continued to bathe by the well even after tank and pump had been installed. By that time Gopalakrishnan had been living in Delhi for many years. In Delhi there had been neither father nor well.

Gopalakrishnan threw the bucket back into the well and waited for it to fill.

Gopalakrishnan had spent more than forty years, by far the greater part of his life, in New Delhi. He had gone there a young man; he had returned from there an old one. Maybe not old, exactly, but he certainly felt himself edging in that direction. He was sixty-five — seventy did not seem so far away now. His father had died quite unexpectedly the year before at the age of eighty-seven of (the doctors surmised) a heart attack. By that arithmetic he had a good twenty years or more — twenty years to spend in Paavalampatti, to which he had returned to be with his mother, abandoning his well-ordered, retired existence in Delhi. On the other hand, it was worth considering that only his mother stood now between him and death. His mother, Kamala, was no longer the strong woman she had been when he was a boy. Far from it. Her hair, once upon a time thick and long as a rope when braided, had gone short and white and wispy. Because she had lost so many of her teeth, her face had crumpled and fallen in on itself. Each passing year had opened more and more breaches in her body, so that she seemed now the very sum of her ailments. Whenever he looked at her, Gopalakrishnan, too, felt himself under assault from death. How differently from his father, outwardly well till the very day of his death, was the process of aging treating his mother!

Paavalampatti Krishnaswamy Iyer had retired as headmaster of a primary school more than a quarter of a century before his death. The school was in Chinnapettai, a neighboring village now only two stations away on the railway line. He had started as a teacher of Tamil. This was well before Independence, when there was no railway station at Chinnapettai. A bicycle would have helped in his daily going back and forth, but he had had to save a little money from his salary month by month to buy one. If his father had really wanted to, he surely could have found the money for a bicycle for his son; but as always happened when it came to money, Paavalampatti Krishnaswamy Iyer's father had raised the issue of his daughters. The marriages of Paavalampatti Krishnaswamy Iyer's three sisters remained to be arranged. Until Paavalampatti Krishnaswamy Iyer's acquisition of the bicycle, his only way of reaching the school was by foot or by hitching a ride in a bullock cart from under the great banyan tree where the buses now stopped.

Both alternatives required him to set out before daybreak, either walking through the paddy fields in the predawn darkness or else jolting his way in a bullock cart smelling of straw and the carter's sweat.

Many months went by before Paavalampatti Krishnaswamy Iyer had saved enough money to buy a secondhand bicycle. A wealthy zamindar, one of the biggest owners of land in the district, who was clearly more indulgent than Paavalampatti Krishnaswamy Iyer's own father, had imported the bicycle from England for his own son. Restless and fickle as a monkey, the youth had quickly tired of the bicycle, for which he really had no use, and moved on to another shiny toy, a gramophone player. Paavalampatti Krishnaswamy Iyer had gotten the bicycle — a black-painted Hercules with a leather saddle and an oil lamp in the front — for an unbelievable price.

This bicycle was brought to him at his school one afternoon by one of the zamindar's men. Watched by curious pupils and his fellow teachers, Paavalampatti Krishnaswamy Iyer climbed shakily onto the bicycle and slowly rode it home. He did not as yet have much practice riding. When, on the way, he came upon a large patch of mud he could not circumvent, he got off the bicycle and hoisted it onto his shoulder so that the tires would not get dirty. The leathery smell of the seat, now pressed against his face, was intoxicating. Past the patch of mud, he climbed back on the bicycle and rode unsteadily into Meenakshisundareswarar Temple Street to find his father coming down the street from the opposite direction. His father had been to the temple and his forehead was painted white with sacred ash. Father and son met in front of the house.

"What is that?" Father had asked in his loud voice. In his prime, Paavalampatti Krishnaswamy Iyer's father had been a tall man as strong as a bull. Though he had already entered upon his time of sickness when the incident of the bicycle happened (he eventually died of lung cancer), he still towered over his son.

"A bicycle," son had replied.

"No. That. Do you know what that is?"

Paavalampatti Krishnaswamy Iyer saw what his father was indicating. "A seat."

"A seat! That is leather. Skin of a dead animal. Are you fit to call yourself a Brahmin? This bicycle will not enter the house."

But the bicycle — a bicycle Paavalampatti Krishnaswamy Iyer had bought with his own money, with no help, no help whatsoever, from his father — had entered the house. By the time Gopalakrishnan was of an age he could remember, the bicycle stood, always shining and well oiled, on the veranda at the front of the house. Despite his father, Paavalampatti Krishnaswamy Iyer had found a way to keep the bicycle.

That was the kind of man Paavalampatti Krishnaswamy Iyer was, at least in his own eyes, for he told the story often. In fact, Paavalampatti Krishnaswamy Iyer told many such stories, though in his telling they were not stories so much as fables or moral anecdotes, intended mostly for Gopalakrishnan or his sister, Gauri. Sometimes they were reiterated for Gopalakrishnan's mother, who would listen quietly with her head bowed, continuing with whatever it was that she was doing. Her broad face with the large eyes that could, at other times, be filled with such emotion would remain expressionless.

"Did you hear what I said?" his father would say when he was finished.

Then his mother would nod her head without raising it and say, "Yes. What was I doing but listening to you?"

Another story Paavalampatti Krishnaswamy Iyer loved to relate concerned his kudumi. When he was a boy, Brahmins had still commonly worn the little tuft of hair at the top of the head. According to the fable, Gopalakrishnan's grandfather had once happened upon Paavalampatti Krishnaswamy Iyer sound asleep with his head on his desk when he was supposed to be engaged in doing some accounts — some simple addition and subtraction of rupees and annas and pice — for his father. Gopalakrishnan's grandfather had become enraged. He had immediately hunted out a long coil of strong twine and returned with it to tie one end to a rafter and the other to the boy's kudumi to ensure that Paavalampatti Krishnaswamy Iyer would not nod off in the middle of his review of his father's account books. Every time that his head sleepily lolled to one side or the other the twine was sure to jerk it painfully back. As long as his head was bent dutifully over the account books in just the right position, he was fine. The moral of this fable? Paavalampatti Krishnaswamy Iyer always told the story as accompaniment to some punishment that was being meted out to Gopalakrishnan and his sister and the context of its telling made the moral perfectly clear: This is how I was taught my lessons; see how easy you have it.

Unlike Gopalakrishnan, his sister remained unmoved by their father's stories. Gauri was the kind of child who could patiently listen to the fables, endure whatever punishment had been devised, and return, with an equanimity far beyond her age — she was after all only a year older than Gopalakrishnan — to her busy social life with her friends. She was an immensely popular child. "I don't even listen to his stories anymore," she had once said to Gopalakrishnan in response to his complaints. She was standing with her hands on her hips, seeming very much a woman though she was at this time only eleven years old and still wearing her long black hair in two well-oiled braids that dropped down her back. "Learn to ignore it."

Gopalakrishnan could not do that. Perhaps it was because Gopalakrishnan was the object of his father's attentions in a way Gauri — was it because she was a girl? — never was. Gopalakrishnan was led to brood often on his father's fables and when he was old enough to consider them critically he found exactly the opposite moral to the one intended by his father in the story of the kudumi: Always do unto your children what your own father has done unto you.

There was the time his father had made him go to school without breakfast for many days as reprisal for his wasteful eating habits; and yet another time when, after an especially poor school report, his father had not spoken to him for a whole week. In place of direct communication, he had taken to referring to him as "that lazy fool" to his mother, as in "Tell that lazy fool I want to see his clothes put away right now," or "Has that lazy fool eaten? I will eat after him. I have no desire to eat with fools." Neither Gopalakrishnan's father nor his grandfather seemed to have much patience for those they considered fools. Over time Gopalakrishnan came to recognize the shadow of his grandfather in his father.

The recognition came slowly. It would not have been easy for those without intimate knowledge of the family to see the similarities between his father and his grandfather that were apparent to Gopalakrishnan. Never had a lock of Gopalakrishnan's hair been tied by twine to a rafter, never had he had to struggle with all his will over a bicycle with a leather seat. The two men were in many ways vastly different personalities. Gopalakrishnan's grandfather was a big man, with a rotund fleshiness that belied his physical strength. He owned much land around the village and spent all his life living off it, which meant managing it and overseeing it while others tilled and sowed and harvested. He had been to school but despised book knowledge. He had not been able to bring himself to finish high school. Because he owned so much land and because he was so temperamental — friendly and generous one moment, angry and spiteful the next — he was feared as well as respected in the village.

Paavalampatti Krishnaswamy Iyer, on the other hand, prized education above all else. He was as quiet and small as his father was loud and big, as inclined to be reading a book as his father was to be guffawing with his friends. He had not only finished school but had traveled the hundreds of miles north to Madras to attend Madras Christian College. This was in the late twenties, when the college was still in its George Town location in the heart of old Madras, in premises centered on the steeple of Anderson's Church. Facing the college, across broad and busy Esplanade, were the red Indo-Saracenic minarets of the high court. The narrow alleys of George Town were all around, bustling with lawyers and traders, sailors and students. Over it all the smell of the sea hung constantly, like the rumor of an even larger world beyond Madras.

There was no sea in Paavalampatti. Madras was nothing like the village but Gopalakrishnan's father kept very much to himself. He was in Madras to get an education, not lose himself in the distractions of the city. His disappointment was fierce when he found himself unable to earn a degree because his father had fallen sick and he had to return home. That same year he started, against his father's will, as a schoolteacher. It was his way of expressing his resentment at his recall. Also that year, this time against his will, he was married off when he was barely nineteen. This was his father's way of letting him know what he thought of his resentment. The next year, Gauri had been born, and the year after, Gopalakrishnan.

Throughout his boyhood, Gopalakrishnan witnessed the great struggle between his father and his grandfather. His grandfather was jealous when it came to his authority, and he fought to preserve it despite his progressive decline into a series of illnesses, culminating in the finality of lung cancer. Gopalakrishnan had never really known his grandfather in his prime. He had only heard tell of his great booming voice and his great appetite for food and the way he had once with his bare hands forced a rogue bull rampaging through his fields down to its knees. The grandfather he had known was fading slowly from life. When the lung cancer took hold, the decline became more precipitous. First, there was the uncontrollable coughing and the blood on the pillow in the mornings. Still his grandfather made himself get up and do some work. Then the cancer spread to the liver and there was jaundice. Gopalakrishnan remembered his grandfather lying in his bed, his skin and eyes a frightening yellow. His grandfather was fatigued all the time now and found it hard to get about. He was confined to the house, and finally to his bed. Through it all he waged a losing campaign with his son for sway over the house.

The outcome of the contest was as inevitable as night succeeding day. By the time Gopalakrishnan's grandfather died after years of sickness, Paavalampatti Krishnaswamy Iyer had married off his three sisters to bridegrooms he had chosen and sold much of the land against his father's wishes. Gopalakrishnan's grandmother was a timid, quiet woman who had not been able to resist her husband and now had no desire to resist her son. Until her own death many years later, she remained a shadow in her own house. Slowly control of the house had passed from Gopalakrishnan's grandfather to his father and the latter had begun more and more to show himself, in his own particular way, as the same unbending man that the former was. He had erected a shelf in the very room in which Gopalakrishnan's grandfather lay sick (it really was the most convenient room) for his Tamil and English books of literature and history — Shakespeare and Kamban, Gibbon and Tagore, even a copy of Subramania Bharathi's revolutionary nationalist poetry. Paavalampatti Krishnaswamy Iyer was not political — he simply saw no reason *not* to read Bharathi, like him a Tamil Brahmin from Thirunelveli District, simply because the British seemed to find him threatening. He had also added English as one of the subjects that he taught his students, and had risen to the position of assistant headmaster. And still he went to school on the same Hercules bicycle he had bought years before.

As soon as he was old enough to consider such possibilities — just fifteen and learning to shave — Gopalakrishnan resolved to get away from Paavalampatti.

It was 1947 and India was becoming independent in a shuddering paroxysm of violence and hope and hatred and celebration. Fanatical religious riots tore through the country, especially far in the northeast and the northwest, where Pakistan was being partitioned out of India. Meanwhile, Gopalakrishnan was still in Paavalampatti under the supervision of his father, who made him, over and above his school homework, memorize entire passages from Shakespeare, Tagore, Shelley, and Bharathi. The times were militant, but his father was immovably catholic in his tastes. Each week Gopalakrishnan — Gauri was not subjected to this improving exercise — would have to memorize and explicate a passage or a poem that his father had chosen from his growing library. One week it was "Friends, Romans, countrymen" from *Julius Caesar,* the next a section from "Modern Woman" by Bharathi. Yet another week it might be a passage from that new fiction writer Puthumaipittan, or else

Wordsworth's "The World Is Too Much With Us," picked out of Paavalampatti Krishnaswamy Iyer's much-consulted copy of Palgrave's *Golden Treasury*. An anthology of "the best songs and lyrical poems in the English language," *The Golden Treasury* was a favorite of his father's. Gopalakrishnan came to detest heartily both Palgrave and the shallow-chested flute-playing naked youth — his legs were crossed demurely — depicted on the title page of the book. Many were the passages Gopalakrishnan had memorized out of the book to present on the appointed day, when his father would summon him into his room, fold his concise frame into his easy chair, close his eyes, and gesture to him to begin his recitation of the selection, in English or in Tamil as the case might be.

On the day it was Wordsworth's "The World Is Too Much With Us," Gopalakrishnan had recited the sonnet with the hated Palgrave gripped firmly in his hand for confidence. He tried not to rush through his recitation or to stumble over words difficult to pronounce, like *wreathed* or *sordid*. At the end of the recitation, his father had opened his eyes and looked at him for a long moment.

"What does the poet mean by 'the winds that will be howling at all hours'?"

"Nature?"

Gopalakrishnan was able to see his guess was right.

"What do we call it when the poet writes something like 'bares her bosom'?"

This was a familiar question, the kind of question his father had asked before. Gopalakrishnan had prepared for it. Striving mightily to drive out of his mind the distracting, vivid image of a woman baring her luscious bosom, he had said: "An alliteration."

More questions followed and Gopalakrishnan answered them adequately. He was beginning to think this week had gone well when his father asked suddenly, "How can the world be too much with us? What does the poet mean by this?"

"Too much with us? Too much with us . . ." Gopalakrishnan had looked at the text of the poem for a clue but found no help there. "I haven't thought about it . . ."

"Why not? It is the title, isn't it? It is the main thing in the poem, isn't it? Think about it for next week. First thing next week I will ask you what the great poet means by that. There is much you can learn about the world from this poem, Gopu. Or have you decided to be a fool the rest of your life? Think about what the poet is saying in that second line about wasting our powers. Think about it."

As Gopalakrishnan left his father's room — the very room in which his grandfather had died — at the end of this catechism, he saw his father with the retrieved Palgrave in his hand, his lips moving soundlessly as he read Wordsworth's poem to himself. What could it be that his father saw in this poem about somebody called Proteus rising from the sea and somebody else called old Triton blowing some horn? Why ever would he want to read this obscure English poem yet again? But there his father had been, oblivious to the world, his narrow face bent over the book, reading with concentration. Bewildering. Incomprehensible. So bewildering, so incomprehensible, that the moment had stuck in Gopalakrishnan's mind.

In this fashion, Gopalakrishnan read widely and memorized widely. He also forgot widely. He never ceased to be surprised at how quickly the memorized passages vanished from his mind. What remained were not the passages but a deep familiarity — it could not be called love — with books and reading.

It was not until 1950, when he was eighteen years old, that Gopalakrishnan finally managed to leave Paavalampatti. His sister, Gauri, had married and gone to her new home in Madras. Now

Gopalakrishnan followed her there to study at the same Madras Christian College his father had attended some twenty years before. By this time the college had been moved to a new campus — situated in a veritable forest — far outside the city in Tambaram. Getting to Madras by train was an expedition. The atmosphere on the campus felt monastic. His father, who came with him to see him set up in his residence hall, was pleased with the new location of the college.

"No diversions here. No cinema houses to waste your time in. You will be able to concentrate on your studies far away from the city," Paavalampatti Krishnaswamy Iyer had said approvingly.

With his father back in distant Paavalampatti, Gopalakrishnan promptly set about finding ways to get to the city. Gauri lived in the heart of Madras, in lively Mylapore, no more than a good shout from the Kapaleeswarar Temple. Sometimes, when Krishna and Natarajan, his closest friends from college, were also in the city, he went to the cinema house, to the Roxy or to the posh and glamorous New Elphinstone on Mount Road. Both Krishna and Natarajan were, like him, from villages far in the south. He even went with them to while away his time on Marina Beach, where they would lie on the sands and eat groundnuts and watch the crowds wetting their feet in the restless ocean. They would do nothing at all but waste their time by talking. Sometimes, especially when a pretty woman went by, they were quiet and awkward.

"Did you see her? Did you see her?" Krishna would cry the moment the woman was out of earshot.

Natarajan would hiss back at him: "Quiet! Somebody will hear you!"

Madras was full of such unknown experiences and awkward moments. At the end of his three years at Madras Christian

College, Gopalakrishnan found himself with a decision to make. His father had inculcated enough discipline in him that he proved himself a passable student in earning his B.A. in history. Krishna and Natarajan were both returning to their villages, before they decided what it was they wanted to do with the rest of their lives. Gopalakrishnan hesitated to go back to Paavalampatti. If he returned home with his bachelor's degree, no doubt his father would have been able to find him a teaching position in a school. He had a feeling this was what his father expected. But he thought of his father at his desk with a book. He thought of him setting out for his school — he was by now headmaster — on his bicycle. He thought of how quickly and surely his father's hands moved on the rope of the well as he drew water up in a bucket. He imagined himself doing these trivial, humdrum things in his turn, as he succeeded to his father's position in life. He could not. These were not difficult endeavors. He might not love books like his father but he had read enough of them in his time. And he knew how to ride a bicycle and to draw water from a well. Why then could he not see himself in Paavalampatti doing these kinds of things? He did not know the answer to the question, but he was certain that he could not.

What then was he to do? Where was he to go?

Such was the problem confronting Gopalakrishnan at the end of his college years. The quandary resolved itself when his brother-in-law, Prakash, informed him of a job at a Tamil newspaper based in Madras. He applied and was hired as a reporter, a job description that meant very little to him. On receiving the news of his employment, his father wrote a long, carefully composed letter setting out the responsibilities of a journalist. Gopalakrishnan saw from the letter his father had thought long and hard about what it meant to be a reporter. Gopalakrishnan left Tambaram and Madras

Christian College and moved in with his sister and her joint family in Mylapore.

In the house were Gauri; her husband, Prakash; their three children; and Prakash's aged parents. At the center of the household was Gauri. She it was who ran the little house in Mylapore, deciding who was to eat what and what was to be done when. Physically, she had taken after her father and was small and compact. She had had her three children in quick succession but had not lost her firmness of body and quickness of manner. She was a presence in Mylapore and in Kapaleeswarar Temple, where the priests all knew her. Prakash worked for Indian Bank and it was already clear that he would go far in his profession as a banker. Gauri was determined that he would.

Gopalakrishnan entered the professional world of the newspaper with trepidation. He had a desk in a room he shared with five other employees in the newspaper's offices on Mount Road, not far from the New Elphinstone Theatre, where he had watched so many movies with Krishna and Natarajan. In this room there were two ceiling fans, gray steel cupboards along the white walls, a clay pot of water with a tumbler over it in a corner, and green bamboo shades over the windows. One of the five men he shared the room with was another reporter roughly his age named T. R. Murthy. His full name was T. Ramamurthy Iyer, but he had let go of the caste identification at the end of his name and reduced the "Rama" to an initial.

Murthy was nothing like Krishna or Natarajan or anyone else that Gopalakrishnan had ever known. He smoked cigarettes and ate meat. He dressed neatly in a white shirt and black trousers and wore a carefully groomed moustache on his upper lip that Gopalakrishnan later discovered was inspired by the Bombay film star Raj Kapoor. One evening soon after he had begun working,

Gopalakrishnan found himself invited by Murthy to India Coffee House, a little distance away on Mount Road. In the busy first-floor premises of the restaurant, clamorous with the sound of stainless steel trays and tumblers, Gopalakrishnan asked for a dosa while Murthy ordered an omelet.

"Have you been here before?" Murthy asked, sitting expansively with his legs crossed at the ankles and one arm flung on the back of the empty wooden chair next to him.

"No."

"One of my favorite places to eat. What do you think of the Daily Fat Stomach?"

"Daily Fat Stomach?"

"The newspaper. The Daily Fat Stomach."

Gopalakrishnan saw that it was a clever pun on the name of the newspaper for which they both worked. When he made a noncommittal answer, Murthy only smiled and asked another question, "What do you think of this business of making Hindi the official language of India?"

"I have not thought about it."

"You should. It will be a big issue in years to come. The people in the South will never accept Hindi. We all have to think about it as citizens of our country."

"Do you know Hindi?"

"No. But I don't care about the issue so much. I can learn Hindi if I have to. My thinking is like Nehru's on this. The first thing we must do is develop the country. If the country will develop by promoting Hindi, fine. If not, then let's not do it. Nehru has the right ideas for India. We are lucky to have him as prime minister."

The time in India Coffee House convinced Gopalakrishnan that Murthy was a modern man. He fell quickly into Murthy's company.

They spent so much time together that it became a joke around the offices of the Daily Fat Stomach. Gopalakrishnan did not care. He too dropped the Iyer at the end of his name. He too took up cigarettes, keeping up with the habit long after Murthy had given it up. But he hid both these innovations from his father, judging wisely that Paavalampatti Krishnaswamy Iyer would not find them to his liking. He never smoked on his visits home to Paavalampatti and always included the Iyer at the end of his name in letters that he wrote to his father. It was only after many years, when he was married and in New Delhi, that the pretense regarding the name was quietly allowed to lapse. The one area in which Gopalakrishnan could not bring himself to follow Murthy's radical example, though, was meat eating. After one or two tentative forays into the world of dead flesh, he returned sheepishly to his original diet.

Gopalakrishnan did not work at the Daily Fat Stomach very long. The Daily Fat Stomach was a relatively new newspaper. An industrial house based in Madras had started it only five years before. There were older Tamil newspapers like *Dinamani*, which had a most venerable reputation, and newer ones like *Dina Thanthi*, that wanted to speak the language of the common man. The Daily Fat Stomach wanted to be neither the former nor the latter — or rather it wanted to be both. A man who had worked for years at *Dinamani* was editor but he had been hired to make the Daily Fat Stomach more like *Dina Thanthi*. The Daily Fat Stomach was deeply dissatisfying to Murthy, who despised the newspaper for its muddleheadedness, for the meager salary it paid them, even for the very fact that it was a Tamil newspaper. He never referred to it as anything other than the Daily Fat Stomach. "No matter how long you work here, a fat stomach is all you will get," he often declared. He pointed out to Gopalakrishnan that most of their senior colleagues had substantial paunches. Seeing the newspaper through his eyes, Gopalakrishnan too came to regard it as a small, provincial thing. The luster of the job — the first job of his life — faded a little.

And then there was the evolving situation at home. Murthy was right: The small salary the newspaper gave him was not enough for him to be able to live by himself in comfort. Gopalakrishnan contributed financially to the household, of course, but now Gauri had another child and space in the little house was becoming precious. He was Gauri's brother and so nothing was being said — yet. Once or twice Gopalakrishnan felt he had interrupted Prakash and Gauri in a conversation about him. He had walked into the room and his sister and her husband had fallen abruptly into silence. Prakash's parents were increasingly cold to him. How long would it be before Gauri too changed? She was his sister but she was married and had a family of her own to consider. He knew it was unseemly that he had been living with Gauri for nearly a year. Despite the friendship with Murthy, despite the thought that he was, like Murthy, a salaried man in an urban center, despite the growing conviction that he too was one of the new men of what Murthy liked to call the New India — despite all this, Gopalakrishnan began to feel the limitations of his current life.

One day Gopalakrishnan was in the office of the Daily Fat Stomach, laboring at a story on a new development scheme for Madras that would convert portions of Guindy Park into hospitals and educational institutions, when Murthy sauntered over to his desk with a sheet of paper. Gopalakrishnan could tell from the way Murthy placed the sheet in front of him that this was important, that Murthy was excited.

"What is this?" he asked, glancing up at Murthy curiously.

"Read it and you will see, Gopu," Murthy replied. He stroked his moustache with finger and thumb in a gesture Gopalakrishnan had come to recognize as expressing impatience.

It was copy for a Government of India advertisement that was to appear in the Daily Fat Stomach. All India Radio was looking for Tamil newsreaders — "staff artistes" they were called. The nature of the job was described. Requirements and a deadline were mentioned. The vacancies were in New Delhi.

"So what?" Gopalakrishnan asked, leaning back in his chair bemused.

Murthy shook his head in disbelief. "Think about it! We should apply. If they select us, we will be in Delhi. Think of that — working for All India Radio in Delhi!" He looked expectantly at Gopalakrishnan.

Gopalakrishnan considered the advertisement again, reading it over carefully. "Delhi? I don't know . . ." he said.

Murthy took back the sheet of paper. "I am definitely going to apply!" he declared as he walked briskly back to his desk, which was across from Gopalakrishnan's. For the rest of the day the sheet of paper sat there on Murthy's desk, pinned down by a paperweight, fluttering in the breeze from the ceiling fan like a bird desperate to take flight.

That day and the days after Gopalakrishnan mulled over Murthy's proposal cautiously. New Delhi. All India Radio. In an atlas, he looked up how far New Delhi was from Madras. It was the other end of the country, more than a thousand miles away. It seemed impossibly far. Days, not hours, in a train! People spoke Hindi there. He knew no Hindi. People said English wasn't as prevalent as in Madras and that people in Delhi wanted to make Hindi the official language and didn't like it if you couldn't speak it. Could he adjust to such a strange city? He thought of something else. He did not know how to cook. Who would cook for him? What would he do if he did not like it after he went there? He would no longer have his job at the newspaper, at the Daily Fat Stomach. On the other hand Murthy was busily preparing to apply. Gopalakrishnan had no doubt that Murthy would be successful. The Daily Fat Stomach would not be the same without him. The thought of Murthy gone from the little office with the green blinds and the six desks was disheartening. There would be no more trips to Higginbothams Bookstore with Murthy or long conversations about the New India at India Coffee House. And how long could he continue to live with Gauri? The All India Radio position would definitely be a step up from his current newspaper job. A salary on the central government pay scale! It was not a prospect to take lightly.

Gopalakrishnan applied for the position at the last minute. He got his application done on time only because Murthy helped him. Both Murthy and he were selected as candidates for an interview and a voice test to be held in New Delhi. The coincidence was not surprising. They both worked for one of the more prominent Tamil newspapers of the time; they both had excellent qualifications for the job. It was January when they traveled together on the Grand Trunk Express to New Delhi, where Murthy had an uncle with whom they would stay. It was the longest distance either one of them had ever traveled. The country that went past them in the windows of the train on the first day seemed familiar to them. It was a rural landscape Gopalakrishnan knew from Paavalampatti: a dirty green scrubland interrupted now and then by rice fields and coconut trees and temples with gopurams. They heard Tamil and Telugu in the stations. The hawkers brought coffee, muruku, and vadas for them to buy. Murthy was voluble and observant, his excitement palpable.

The second day the languages grew more alien to their ears. Was it Marathi that they were hearing? Or was it Hindi? They had no way of telling. Gopalakrishnan noticed that the trees and the plants had changed. And was that building a temple? It looked like a temple, but where was the gopuram? Murthy had brought a map of India with him. He pored over it to locate the stations as they passed them, directing a running commentary toward Gopalakrishnan as he did so. On the station platforms the faces transmutated, shaping themselves to unfamiliar molds from a different history.

On the third day, Murthy too grew silent. He followed Gopalakrishnan's example and pulled on a sweater, because it had grown cooler. They were not far from New Delhi now. When Gopalakrishnan looked out into a station at which the train stopped, he was desolated to see how changed everything seemed. He saw men in their Nehru topees and shawls drinking tea from little brown clay pots and speaking their strange language. The language had to be Hindi by now. Or was it Hindustani, whatever that was? The women all had their heads covered. One such woman appeared suddenly at the window carrying a basket of rotting bananas in her arms. Her teeth were stained red from chewing paan and there was a touch of green in her eyes. She spoke again and again to Gopalakrishnan in her strange language, evidently trying to get him to buy bananas. A faint odor of mustard oil and sweat wafted from her into the coach. Gopalakrishnan could only stare back at those eyes touched with green, helpless with ignorance of her language. Finally the woman stalked away, throwing a word that sounded very rude back at him.

All these strange people, they too were Indians.

And so, at last, after its long journey up the peninsula of India, the engine of the train pulled into the dim light of the station in New Delhi and came to a halt with a great expulsion of air that sounded very like the machine's sigh of relief. Murthy's uncle was waiting for them on the platform, searching for them over the heads of red-jacketed coolies with metal armbands diving for customers in the sea of passengers beginning to pool on the platform. When he saw them, he shouted out nonchalantly in Tamil over the commotion, "What? You managed to get here without getting lost?" Gopalakrishnan saw at once the family resemblance between Murthy and his uncle. The resemblance was not just physical. He could discern it in the voice, in the easy posture of the body, in the expression on the face.

"How was the journey?" Murthy's uncle asked, striding up to them with no mind for the people around him. He beckoned with a finger the coolie he had already engaged and spoke in rapid Hindi to him. The coolie proceeded to arrange around him the luggage that Murthy and Gopalakrishnan had brought with them.

Looking at uncle and nephew greet each other amidst the daunting chaos of the station, Gopalakrishnan told himself that he would not take the AIR job even if he was successful in the interview — which was, he quickly assured himself, unlikely.

The interview with the All India Radio Selection Board was in Broadcasting House on Parliament Street. The building was built like a shallow V with cylindrical structures at the tips and at the center. It seemed to Gopalakrishnan unusual, modern, very New

Delhi. "Do you know?" Murthy said in a whisper as he and Gopalakrishnan entered the building together. "This is where Nehru spoke on August 15, 1947. This is where he declared India free over the radio." Gopalakrishnan was impressed by the information. He followed Murthy down one of the verandas to the office at which they were to present themselves, feeling even more unfit for the ordeal ahead.

Gopalakrishnan was the first to be called to the interview. When he walked into the room indicated to him by the clerk, five men were seated behind a wooden table, drinking tea and laughing uproariously. One of them noticed him hesitating at the door and waved him in, "Don't worry. It is not about you, Mr. Gopalakrishnan. You are not the reason for our merriment." The man was Indian but his accent was very English.

When calm had returned and Gopalakrishnan was in the chair meant for the job applicants, the man who had waved him in asked him a question about Nehru's efforts to establish friendly relations with China. Indo-Chinese relations had recently been much in the news and Gopalakrishnan's interrogator wanted his opinion on the manner in which All India Radio had covered the issue in a recent news broadcast. Gopalakrishnan knew little about Nehru and China and even less about the right way to handle such an issue in a radio broadcast. Still nonplussed by the hilarity that had greeted him on his entrance into the room, he fumbled at an answer to the question and ended up admitting ignorance. The admission was received in silence. Then another man asked him about his experiences at the Daily Fat Stomach and still another wanted to know about his education, and before he knew it the interview was over. He proceeded then to the voice test in one of the studios in the building and it was not until Murthy too was done — Gopalakrishnan waited for

Murthy in the shaded portico downstairs where cars and rickshaws and cycles came and went — that he and Murthy were able to compare their interview experiences. Murthy was bubbling with confidence. He felt he had done very well in his interview. Gopalakrishnan shared with him his misgivings about the question on China. When he saw Murthy's face grow annoyed, he felt satisfied. Didn't he know of the new alliance of ex-colonized countries Nehru was trying to form? Murthy demanded with irritation. Secretly Gopalakrishnan rejoiced at his impending failure.

But when Gopalakrishnan returned to Broadcasting House on the appointed day to consult the notice board on which the names of the successful candidates were posted, his name was first in the alphabetical list, two names above Murthy's. With a sinking feeling he saw that he had not, evidently, done as poorly as he had thought. Murthy was delighted they both had been selected. Confronted with Murthy's enthusiasm at their dual success, Gopalakrishnan was thrown into a quandary. Murthy was right — it was a good job. On what grounds would he refuse the job? To go back to his position at the Daily Fat Stomach? Laughable! Murthy would be kind but he would treat that choice with the disdain it deserved. He could not bear the idea that Murthy would secretly scorn him. He knew Murthy well enough to know that he would not understand how Gopalakrishnan felt; and, for that matter, did he, Gopalakrishnan, himself? Could he say why he felt this great trembling within at the thought of New Delhi and the AIR job? He could find no rational answer to the question. And so when Murthy clasped him firmly by the shoulder and said, "Come! First order of business, a letter of resignation to the Daily Fat Stomach," Gopalakrishnan could not refuse him.

Gopalakrishnan and Murthy wrote identical letters of resignation to the Daily Fat Stomach and solemnly shook hands with each other before sending the letters on their way at the post office. Gopalakrishnan did not tell Murthy, but he felt ill when he thought of his letter making the return journey he had expected to make. As a man of the New India, he was ashamed of the feeling; but he could not deny it — he did feel ill. Later, he also wrote letters to his father and sister, telling them he had decided to stay in New Delhi. There were only a few days before they were to start at All India Radio, and he would not be able to travel all the way to Paavalampatti and back. He conveyed his regrets. He would come on a visit as soon as he could.

Reluctantly, Gopalakrishnan began to set up household with Murthy in New Delhi. With the help of Murthy's uncle, he and Murthy searched for a place to live. Gopalakrishnan showed no enthusiasm for the search, but finally they found a little two-room barsaati reached by climbing an exposed, external staircase. The barsaati was in Sunder Nagar, near India Gate. Gopalakrishnan had to admit that the barsaati was charming. It had two rooms instead of the usual one. The best part of it was the large adjoining open terrace, skirted by a gray cement wall. From the terrace Murthy and Gopalakrishnan could watch the activity of the street below in which all kinds of people passed — the neighbors and their bawling children, the charpoy man twanging his tool loudly to let people know he was available to tighten the strings of their cots, the collector of old newspapers and bottles singing out his high-pitched cry, the man with the monkey on his shoulder beating his little drum. During the day, the street was a medley of sounds. They learnt to recognize a few of the Hindi words that they heard — a *charpoy* was a stringed cot, *seedha* was "straight," *achaa* was "all right."

Also visible from this terrace was the yard of the house. Since it was still winter, the landlord's wife would take in the afternoon sun in the yard below. She would sit on her charpoy, sometimes gossiping with a neighbor, sometimes knitting a sweater or picking through lentils for stones or dirt. The landlord, Sharma-ji, was only a little older than his two tenants and his wife was young, with wonderful soft cheeks and striking eyebrows that were a single line above her eyes. The first time that Gopalakrishnan and Murthy noticed her presence in the yard below they watched her self-consciously, too shy to mention her presence to each other.

The barsaati was close enough to Broadcasting House on Parliament Street that Gopalakrishnan and Murthy could use bicycles as their main means of transportation. Gopalakrishnan would cycle to work daily past the white arch of India Gate. From India Gate he would go up Rajpath, with the green lawns and red dirt lining its sides, towards Rashtrapati Bhavan, which had once been the palace of the British rulers of India and now was home to the president, a man from Bihar named Rajendra Prasad, who had been an associate of Mahatma Gandhi's. Over time he came to know the green dome and light-colored stone of the building well. When he arrived at work he would see in the distance the circular Parliament Building, also of light-colored stone, that was the real seat of political power in independent India. Connaught Place, with its shops arranged in rings, Teen Murti House, where Nehru lived, the Reserve Bank of India building — these too he passed as he wandered about in the company of Murthy, learning his way around the city. The avenues were broad, the roundabouts wide and spacious. He came to know the names of streets, to get a sense of the people, and slowly the city began to take shape in his mind. New Delhi did not have the commercial bustle of Madras. When Gopalakrishnan pointed this out to Murthy, Murthy replied, "So what if you don't see so many businesses and shops and things like that? What can shopkeepers do? This is where the real power is, Gopu."

New Delhi was still mainly a political city, a city of civil servants. People like Murthy's uncle, who had been in Delhi a long time, talked of the changes the city was going through because of the recent migration of refugees from Pakistan. The violence of Partition had thrust into the city countless uprooted families, who now lived in slums and in hastily constructed housing and in homes of friends or relatives. They were transforming New Delhi. Murthy's uncle, who worked for the Home Ministry, complained about the changes that were being wrought by these new entrants who lived between and behind the monuments. But what would Murthy and Gopalakrishnan know of these changes? The modern monumentality of New Delhi was what impressed Murthy, and Gopalakrishnan, under the influence of Murthy's enthusiasm, could not remain immune to it.

And then there was the work itself. Every time Gopalakrishnan went into the sealed sanctum of the broadcast studio to pronounce gravely into the mike dangling before his face he could not help but marvel at the notion that his voice, spoken so softly here in Broadcasting House, was being heard thousands of miles away, even perhaps in Paavalampatti. It was an amazing, amazing thing! The very idea of it! And so Gopalakrishnan slowly let himself be seduced by Murthy's passion for New Delhi. In a few months he seemed to have forgotten his initial misgivings about the alienness of the city, even that he had ever had them. Which man of the New India could remain immune to New Delhi?

In those months, Gopalakrishnan often wondered what his father thought of his new job. He did not find out until his visit to Paavalampatti more than a year later that his father had invested in a radio. Paavalampatti Krishnaswamy Iyer did not say he had bought the radio because of his son's recent appointment as a staff artiste in AIR. Perhaps his decision to buy a radio at this very time was truly only a coincidence. In any event, one day he disappeared suddenly to Thirunelveli Town on his trusty bicycle to inspect a secondhand Philips radio he had heard someone was selling. Two days later, the radio had arrived on Kovalu's bullock cart. It was a monstrous thing with a scratched wooden cabinet and chipped white knobs on a glass panel. Four stars and three wavy lines adorned the net covering the speaker on the front of the cabinet. It had taken two men to carry the radio into the room in which Paavalampatti Krishnaswamy Iyer slept and in which he had his books. He had already cleared a space in a corner for it. The morning after the radio's arrival, when it was time for the Tamil news bulletin, Gopalakrishnan's parents and neighbors gathered in the room. Paavalampatti Krishnaswamy Iyer switched on the radio. First there was music and then, as luck would have it, instead of Gopalakrishnan somebody called N. Karthikeyan had read out the news. It was two days before Gopalakrishnan's voice, immediately recognizable, welled out of the box — "This is P. Gopalakrishnan, reading the news . . ."

"Ay! Gopu! Gopu is speaking!" Gopalakrishnan's mother exclaimed, forgetting herself and excitedly clapping her hands. Her large expressive eyes glowed at the sound of Gopalakrishnan's voice.

Paavalampatti Krishnaswamy Iyer turned to glare at her. "Let me listen to the news!" he said in his quiet but firm voice.

It became a daily ritual in Paavalampatti — one of which Gopalakrishnan in New Delhi had no inkling — to listen to the morning Tamil news bulletin to see whether or not Gopalakrishnan's voice came out of the enormous box that was the radio. Sometimes it did but most times it did not. Gopalakrishnan's father and mother had no way of knowing when Gopalakrishnan was to read the news. His mother never failed to exclaim when she heard his voice and Paavalampatti Krishnaswamy Iyer never failed to glare at her and tell her to shush so that he could listen to the news. It was, truly, a ritual, especially to Gopalakrishnan's mother. Despite Paavalampatti Krishnaswamy Iyer's many impatient but meticulous and teacherly explanations, Gopalakrishnan's mother never did understand the science of radio broadcasting. She knew it was not magic but nevertheless there was something magical about it. There was sorcery certainly in the way it changed how she thought of her son. She had borne Gopalakrishnan and raised him. She remembered him as a boy — how she remembered him! — and now he had become a being in whose creation she seemed to have played very little part, perhaps even none. She had always been close to Gopalakrishnan. Gopu had been not only her child but her ally and her refuge. Now as she listened to his voice on the radio — her broad forehead furrowed in concentration and her hair, once so long and thick, gathered up in a bun atop her head — she felt him slipping away from her.

In New Delhi, Gopalakrishnan too felt himself changed. It was the city, it was his work, it was the constant company of Murthy — now that he had forgotten his initial misgivings he felt quickened, fired up. Now he was elated that he had decided to join AIR. He thought back to the Daily Fat Stomach days with relief and fond amusement. Gopalakrishnan and Murthy had nine or ten colleagues

— staff artistes like them — in the Tamil section of the News Services Division. They translated into Tamil news that came to them in English, and then read it out to the world from one of the studios in Broadcasting House. They worked in shifts. The busiest was the morning shift. The four or five staff artistes assigned to that shift would arrive at three and begin translating the news into Tamil as it came to them. At six, one of them would go into the studio to read out the translated news. And then the men could go home until it was time for them to return for another shift, often later that same day. It certainly helped that Gopalakrishnan and Murthy were living close enough to Broadcasting House to cycle back and forth. The barsaati they had found had been a stroke of good fortune.

Gopalakrishnan began to develop a social circle, at first among other Tamil staff artistes. There was Karthikeyan, who was older and the most experienced of them all. He was kind and helpful and was their leader as far as work went. Sometimes he would join Gopalakrishnan and Murthy for a chat over a cup of tea at the stall outside Broadcasting House. But he was a family man and kept very much to himself when it came to life outside Broadcasting House. Shanmugam and Govindarajan were good not only for tea but for a movie between shifts. They too were single. Shanmugam had been in New Delhi and at All India Radio for some time. Govindarajan was new to the city, having been hired at the same time as Gopalakrishnan and Murthy.

And then there was Ganapathy. Ganapathy had been working as a staff artiste for a few years and generously devoted himself to initiating both Gopalakrishnan and Murthy into the mysteries of radio broadcasting. Ganapathy was short and rotund, with fleshy pockmarked cheeks and large, bulging eyes that were always darting hither and thither. He loved to linger in the verandas of Broadcasting House even when it was not his shift. He had a favorite place by one of the columns lining the verandas and there he was often to be found turning a newspaper around in his hands and waiting to ambush someone with his words.

"O Chatterjee," he might call out to the bespectacled man hurrying down the veranda, "Did you see what the paper here says about your beloved Calcutta?" Mr. Chatterjee was a serious fellow and would keep rushing by with a mumbled response. Ganapathy did not mind. Someone else would stop and soon a loud and jocular group would be gathered around him. There was no topic and no person beneath Ganapathy's interest.

Ganapathy had lived in Delhi for many years and knew both Hindi and the city well. He was considerably older than Gopalakrishnan and Murthy but not married. When he discovered that the two of them had never been to Old Delhi, he cried, "But that is the best part of Delhi!" and offered to introduce them to the city Emperor Shah Jahan had built centuries before.

"When exactly?" Gopalakrishnan asked.

Ganapathy did not know, but Murthy immediately said, "Sixteen hundred something . . . Do you know? Shah Jahan was the man who built the Taj Mahal." He added that he wanted to see the Red Fort and the Jama Masjid.

"Soldier and God," Ganapathy noted with a laugh that made the flesh in his body shake. "But when we are done with them I will take you to eat such food you will forget soldier. Try not to forget God."

They went on their expedition to Old Delhi the next weekend. Gopalakrishnan and Ganapathy dutifully trooped behind Murthy to the broken fort of red sandstone, after which they went to the grand mosque, with its three white onion domes floating above a structure that was also made of red sandstone. In between fort and mosque lay the narrow gallis of Old Delhi, and it was into this warren that Ganapathy led his two new friends when Murthy had pronounced himself satisfied. If Ganapathy was to be believed, this part of the city had been filled, in the time of Shah Jahan, with glittering shops and the mansions of noblemen. Chandni Chowk it was called, after a pool in the area into which the moon cast its reflection at night. No doubt those shops and mansions had deteriorated long ago, for the flood of history had coursed through Shah Jahan's city with particular violence. Most recently the riots of Partition had hit here badly and many of the original Muslim residents, those who had not been murdered, had fled to Pakistan. In turn, Hindus and Sikhs who had escaped the murdering and rioting in Pakistan had come to Chandni Chowk. Many of the shops Gopalakrishnan passed had signs declaring OF LAHORE, indicating that the owner had come from what was now Pakistan. Only the cracked elegance of an arch here or the junk-filled dignity of a courtyard there gave hint of the lost days. Two years earlier the clock tower that had stood in the area had collapsed and had not been rebuilt. Shah Jahan's imperial city was becoming a district of warehouses and tenements. The pool of water into which the moon had flung its reflection once upon a fabled time was long since gone from Chandni Chowk. Only memory lay pooled there now.

"But look," Ganapathy philosophized, "in the midst of death there is life." The gallis might be narrow and mean but they were thronged with people. Ganapathy led Gopalakrishnan and Murthy through the gallis, calling out with zest to shopkeepers. It was clear he was well known in the area. They came finally to the roadside dabba of a dear friend of his named Amjad Ali, near Turkman Gate.

Amjad Ali served naan and tandoori chicken and dhal and masala tea to truckers. It was here that they had their lunch.

In this fashion, Ganapathy led Gopalakrishnan and Murthy to the city behind the monuments. He would take them to other little-known eateries around Delhi, or show them where the greatest bargains for food and clothes were to be had, or invite them to obscure little cultural events that no one else knew about. He was a surprisingly good amateur actor, in some demand among drama troupes, and through his involvement in the amateur stage he knew a wide variety of people. At AIR, he was always trying to insert himself into some radio play or the other with mixed success. He was given some minor roles but not any of the important ones that he really wanted. "It is because I am Madrasi," he observed to Gopalakrishnan and Murthy, but there was no rancor in the observation. He was not a resentful man.

Ganapathy's association with Amjad Ali, the origins of which remained shrouded in mystery, had made him a good cook. He had learned the finer points of North Indian Muslim cooking from Amjad Ali and, perhaps spurred on by his success there, had also begun consulting that indispensable bible of Tamil Brahmin cooking, Meenakshi Ammal's *Samaithu Paar*. His range of dishes was great. His sambhar and aviyal and rasam were as delicious as any that Gopalakrishnan, the only vegetarian of the three, remembered his mother making. Both Gopalakrishnan and Murthy found Ganapathy's love of cooking a little strange. Was it normal for a man to relish such an activity so much? Gopalakrishnan and Murthy discussed the question with some amusement. Meanwhile, the two of them, knowing no cooking whatsoever, were subsisting on bread and jam and greasy restaurant food, which was expensive and, after a while, unappetizing. So when Ganapathy — who, for reasons they only understood afterward, was perpetually looking for accommodations — proposed that he move into the barsaati with them, they both accepted eagerly. It would help with the rent and it was understood Ganapathy would take over the cooking.

Murthy had the back room of the barsaati, into which he had moved a cot that his uncle had given him. In a corner of the front room, Gopalakrishnan had a mattress that he rolled up every morning. Another corner of this room had been given over to a kerosene stove that Gopalakrishnan and Murthy had been using to make coffee and one or two other simple things they felt they could manage. This corner would now be Ganapathy's responsibility. Ganapathy moved his trunk and mattress into a third corner of the front room. On the trunk, which he used as a shelf, he set out a striking picture of Krishna. In the picture, the blue-skinned god was standing in front of his white cow, his flute to his lips, a resplendent peacock at his feet. A peacock feather adorned the crown on his head, which was ringed by a halo. Ganapathy's was the only divine picture in the barsaati. Ganapathy was devoted to it. He never failed to start the day without paying it respect. When Murthy teased him about his piety, he smiled sheepishly and said, "Each to his own life." He did not pray the way Gopalakrishnan's father did. He rang no bells; brought no flowers to the picture of Krishna. He would only light an oil lamp and stand silently for a long time in front of the picture, his head bowed over his clasped hands, praying.

Before long the front room had become what Ganapathy called an *adda*. Gopalakrishnan and Murthy learned the meaning of this important Hindi word. It could mean "headquarters," and it could mean "den" or "social gathering." The front room was where Ganapathy entertained. All manner of people came to see him here

— really, to see him perform, for he was the kind of man who was always on the stage. Often they were people that Ganapathy knew from his activities in the theater world. Sometimes Govindarajan and Shanmugam from AIR would come over. Sometimes the "friends" were really mere acquaintances, or even complete strangers who had come with someone else. At these gatherings (Gopalakrishnan and Murthy were always included, of course), Ganapathy would cook and pass cigarettes around and "arrange" for some foreign whiskey. There would be sonorous singing of songs, loud laughter, unending arguments. Almost invariably it was his own money that Ganapathy spent on these occasions; he would never dream of collecting money from his guests. And rare was the guest who would insist on making a monetary contribution to the festivities. So when, some months, he could not come up with his share of the rent on the appointed day, Gopalakrishnan and Murthy did not mind.

There were also nights when Gopalakrishnan would retire to Murthy's bed because Murthy would be sitting up and talking to Ganapathy late into the night. Snatches of their conversation would drift to Gopalakrishnan as he lay on the bed, trying to sleep. They would talk of films and film stars and the latest film music. Sometimes their conversation would be about Ganapathy's religiosity, of which Murthy liked to make fun. When religion was the topic, their conversation could grow heated. Gopalakrishnan would be woken up by Murthy's loud voice and harsh laughter. If he went into the front room to investigate, he would find Murthy towering over Ganapathy seated on a mattress. In the dim yellow light from the naked bulb above, Ganapathy would be quietly but firmly shaking his head in response to Murthy's teasing harangue:

"You are right. Religion has done all the things you say it has. But that is not all religion is. To me, God is a gentle friend who likes to play. He is my goal. My worship is my journey. Why can't I think of God this way? Who says I can't do it?" Often Murthy and Ganapathy went off on their own because Gopalakrishnan did not have the boundless energy that the two of them seemed to have. Murthy liked to accompany Ganapathy on his outings with his friends from the theater world. These friends of Ganapathy intrigued, scandalized, and amused him. Soon they and their lifestyle had become another topic with which to tease Ganapathy.

Though Murthy and Ganapathy spent a lot of time together, it was with Gopalakrishnan that Ganapathy seemed to establish a special bond. Every now and then Ganapathy would make it a point to make a particular dish that Gopalakrishnan had enjoyed the last time he had made it. Gopalakrishnan was touched by this attentiveness. He grew fond of Ganapathy, whose humor and good nature he learned to appreciate. Ganapathy would speak intimately of things to him that he would never share with Murthy. Gopalakrishnan learned Ganapathy had grown up in Bombay. He asked about Ganapathy's family.

"I don't have any family. My parents are dead," Ganapathy said.

"Excuse me for asking."

"It's all right. It's a long time now."

"You don't have any brothers and sisters at all? Not even cousins?"

"Two older brothers. But I don't consider them family. I don't keep any contact with them."

"Why? What happened?"

"There was a house that my father had built in Matunga. Do you know Bombay? That is a part of Bombay where many Tamil people live. My brothers cheated me out of my share of the house. They said they would take care of the selling and all the legal matters. I trusted them, and before I could blink my eyes they had arranged things in such a way that I got nothing. They did not like me. They thought I was a loafer and a wastrel. That was when I left Bombay and came to Delhi."

Gopalakrishnan felt embarrassed that he had elicited these confessions from Ganapathy. To make amends, he told him of his own family, his mother and father in Paavalampatti and his sister in Madras. When he had finished, Ganapathy said wistfully, "I already like your family. They seem so nice."

"Yes," Gopalakrishnan said. "I am very close to them."

Gopalakrishnan went on a visit to Madras and Paavalampatti after more than a year had gone by — he had come in the winter, slogged through the desperate heat of the summer and enjoyed the welcome relief of the monsoons, and now another winter and half of another summer had passed. When he returned, he realized he was now a Delhi man: riding in the rattling bus from the station through the now familiar Delhi streets he felt a sense of homecoming. It was the period before the monsoons — the monsoons had already broken in Kerala and it was raining a little even in Paavalampatti, which lay over the hills from Kerala. But Delhi was yet so shrouded by the summer cloud of dust, the heat over it so unforgiving, that it made you wonder at the folly of men who had chosen to build such a great city so close to a desert. Nevertheless, Gopalakrishnan realized in the bus, he was content, even proud, to call it home. Ganapathy and Murthy were happy to see him and he to see them. He settled cheerfully back into his routine of Broadcasting House, the barsaati, and frequent evenings out with his good friends Murthy and Ganapathy.

One day, when many more months had passed by, Murthy said to him quietly, "Do you remember? You didn't want to stay when you first got here." It was evening. He and Murthy were sitting out on the terrace smoking cigarettes. Through the two windows of the front room, the busy sounds of Ganapathy cooking could be heard. In the yard below, Sharma-ji, unaware of their presence on the terrace, was making loving noises with his wife on the charpoy. Gopalakrishnan was taken aback at Murthy's comment. He had almost forgotten his initial misgivings about Delhi. Had he really wanted to go back to Madras? And had his desire been so evident to Murthy? It could not be . . . He made no reply to Murthy but he marveled to himself that life in Delhi had arranged itself so to his satisfaction. Murthy too remained silent, as if lost in some deep reflection.

No doubt it was the contentment into which he had fallen that caused Gopalakrishnan to be unprepared when Ganapathy suddenly said to him a few weeks later in the barsaati, "Murthy wants me to move out."

"Why?" Gopalakrishnan asked, shocked. Recently Murthy had been very busy and Gopalakrishnan had seen less of him than usual. Had Ganapathy and Murthy had some kind of a fight? He could not imagine the gentle Ganapathy in a fight with anyone.

"I don't know. I saw him in the newsroom today and he said to me, 'Ganapathy, how long is it that you are going to be with us?'"

"What did you say?"

"I was surprised. I asked him what he meant."

"So, what did he say to that?"

"He wouldn't give me a proper answer. Do I have to leave? I don't know what I am supposed to do."

"Did you two fight?"

Ganapathy shook his head solemnly. "No. He has been very busy, and I haven't even seen very much of him."

"I'll talk to Murthy," Gopalakrishnan said.

"Stay out of it," Ganapathy said. "Why do you want to get involved unnecessarily?"

Murthy denied he had asked Ganapathy to leave, but he would not meet Gopalakrishnan's eyes as he did so. When Gopalakrishnan pressed Murthy to speak his mind, Murthy said, "His friends are always in our rooms, day and night. He never pays his share of the rent on time or in full." Yet he insisted that he had not asked Ganapathy to leave. Before the conversation ended, he blurted out: "You should be careful about being always with Ganapathy. People will think you too are like him."

"What do you mean? What are you trying to say?" Gopalakrishnan asked, frowning.

"I am speaking as your friend," Murthy said, but would not explain himself further.

Almost overnight the barsaati was changed. Where it had been a place of easy companionship and shared life, it became now a simmering cauldron of brooding resentments and unspoken bitterness. In his good-natured, expedient way, Ganapathy carried on as if nothing had changed, but Murthy withdrew more and more, first from Ganapathy and then from the barsaati. He was hardly ever home, and given how close the three friends had been in the past, Murthy's absences were themselves a resounding, unignorable judgment. Gopalakrishnan began to feel caught between the two most important people in his life. Ganapathy and Murthy were his best friends — his only friends really; the other people he knew were mere acquaintances. Gopalakrishnan was not good with languages. Though he had learned Hindi he was not comfortable in it. This had become a barrier in his cultivating friendships with people who were not Tamil or did not know English well. Murthy had, as always, a certain justice on his side in his criticisms of Ganapathy; but were they not already familiar with the kind of creature that Ganapathy was? Why this sudden intolerance? He gathered Ganapathy had borrowed money from Murthy and had not yet returned it all. But Ganapathy was always borrowing money and not returning it all. What had happened to make Murthy so exacting? What had caused him to become so unforgiving, so judgmental, of Ganapathy's extravagant conviviality?

Gopalakrishnan did not find an answer to these vexing questions, but the impossible situation resolved itself suddenly one day when Murthy announced he was leaving All India Radio and also moving out of the barsaati. This time it was Gopalakrishnan and Murthy who were alone in the barsaati. Ganapathy was on his shift at Broadcasting House. Murthy was packing his things even as he made the announcement. His red metal trunk was lying open in the middle of the room and he was rapidly throwing his things into it. Three bags had already been filled. On the terrace outside the barsaati two coolies waited to be summoned.

Gopalakrishnan, who had just returned to the barsaati from a visit to the market, was so stunned by the announcement he was unable to make any reply. He stood with the cloth bag of vegetables still in his hand and listened to Murthy's words as if he were a stranger. Murthy had landed a job as a sub-editor at a prestigious English daily and his parents had persuaded him to get married. They had arranged his marriage to a good, carefully selected girl who was a Tamil Brahmin like him. Murthy glanced over at Gopalakrishnan and laughed as he shared that final bit of information. The combination of developments meant it was time for him to leave the barsaati. He was moving to a new area of the city, to an apartment more fitting to his new position. Murthy did not exactly say "more fitting," but Gopalakrishnan felt he heard it in Murthy's words.

When Murthy had finished packing and looked over at his friend, he saw that Gopalakrishnan was still standing with the bag of vegetables in his hands. He noticed the way Gopalakrishnan's lips were pressed together and the way his eyes were hard. He and Gopalakrishnan had been inseparable for the past four years, from the time they had been together at the Daily Fat Stomach in Madras. "Look, I am sorry I am telling you like this," Murthy said, looking away. "My uncle has found a flat. I have to take it immediately. You know how good flats are here in Delhi these days. If you don't say yes immediately, the flat is gone. I would have told you earlier if I had known. I will pay my share of next month's rent of course." He looked at his narrow wooden cot, the only belonging of his still remaining untouched in the room. He had rolled up his mattress and tied it with a cord. The large red metal trunk and the three bags had been gathered in the middle of the room. The room in which he had lived for nearly three years was bare of his things. "You can have my cot," he said. And then he indicated his things to the coolies and was gone.

When Ganapathy returned from Broadcasting House, Gopalakrishnan was sitting out on the terrace, waiting for him in the gathering gloom of the evening.

"Murthy is gone," Gopalakrishnan said to Ganapathy as he came onto the terrace from the staircase.

"Gone?"

"He has taken his things and left."

"For where?"

"He is not living here anymore. He is getting married. He has found a flat."

"He did not say a word about this all this time!"

"He is leaving AIR."

"You mean he is going to resign?"

Gopalakrishnan nodded his head. Ganapathy was silent as the news sank in.

"He is going to be a sub-editor at a newspaper." Gopalakrishnan mentioned the name of the newspaper Murthy had joined.

"Nice job to have," Ganapathy said. Then he saw how it was with Gopalakrishnan. He said to him, "Murthy must have had his reasons for having to tell you like this, all in a hurry, right before he left. I am sure there was a reason."

Gopalakrishnan stood up abruptly and said, "What do I care for his reasons? I just thought you would want to know that Murthy is no longer living here." He went down the staircase and out into the street, leaving Ganapathy standing on the terrace in the darkness.

A few days after Murthy's departure an envelope arrived for Gopalakrishnan at the barsaati. Inside was a pink and yellow invitation to Murthy's wedding in Madras and with it a letter containing Murthy's new address. Gopalakrishnan did not go to the wedding. Nor did he send a telegram or even a letter of congratulations. Many weeks later yet another letter arrived. Gopalakrishnan showed Ganapathy the letter. Murthy was married and back in Delhi. He wanted Gopalakrishnan to visit and meet his wife, Lakshmi.

"Will you go?" Ganapathy asked him. If Ganapathy was hurt

that Murthy had not written to him, he did not reveal it.

Gopalakrishnan shook his head: "Why should I? I don't have the slightest desire to meet Mr. Murthy and his wife, Mrs. Murthy."

"You are angry still."

"I have reason to be."

Ganapathy was silent for a while. "Anger is a waste of time," he said finally.

"I can't be a philosopher like you," Gopalakrishnan sneered. He wanted to add that Ganapathy had not shown himself so forbearing with his brothers in Bombay.

"Murthy has written you two letters. He is trying hard to make amends with you."

"Two letters — do you think that is all it will take to make amends?"

"Don't be like this, Gopu," Ganapathy said. "Good friends are hard to get." He spoke as if from experience.

After Murthy's departure it was only Gopalakrishnan and Ganapathy in the barsaati. Murthy had not been much of a roommate the past few months; nevertheless, his departure was an event of some consequence. The barsaati felt empty without his things in it. Moreover, Ganapathy had begun spending much time downstairs in the Sharmas' home. He had become good friends with Sharma-ji, whose wife was pregnant. Gopalakrishnan, who had moved into Murthy's room and taken over his cot, often found himself alone in the barsaati. On such occasions he thought about the absent Murthy, whom he had known so well for so long. Perhaps Ganapathy was right; perhaps Murthy had made a sincere effort in writing the two letters. Lying on Murthy's cot, Gopalakrishnan found himself thinking that if Murthy had been in the wrong, then so perhaps had he. After all, he had not bothered to go to the wedding of his oldest and best friend (yes, Murthy was that) or even to send a telegram congratulating him on the day of his wedding. It was not that he had not remembered. He had, but had deliberately chosen not to send a telegram. Who was to say that he was not quite as much at fault as Murthy? Yet Murthy had written him a second letter, hadn't he? Gopalakrishnan went over the events that had transpired and came slowly to the conclusion that it was not easy to assign blame. And then there was curiosity about Murthy's wife. What kind of a woman had Murthy married?

So Gopalakrishnan relented and called Murthy at the newspaper where he now worked. If Murthy was surprised to hear from him, he did not show it. Gopalakrishnan, too, was matter-of-fact on the phone, as if nothing worthy of note had occurred between them. They arranged for Gopalakrishnan to visit for lunch on Sunday. During the week, Gopalakrishnan went to a curio shop in Connaught Place and spent a lot of money buying a wedding gift for Murthy and his wife — a replica of the Taj Mahal made out of white stone that glowed softly when a light bulb inside was switched on. On Sunday he carried the Taj Mahal in a bag to Murthy's apartment in Defence Colony. Gopalakrishnan was impressed by the apartment's posh location but the apartment itself was modest — a little two bedroom carved out of a grand house. The entrance to the apartment was at the back. To Gopalakrishnan's dismay, a Taj Mahal like his, only much larger, was already sitting in Murthy's living room. Murthy was gracious about the unfortunate coincidence. "Your Taj Mahal is just the right size for this room," he said, removing the other Taj Mahal to make room for his. The drawing room was sparsely furnished but the cane chairs, the side tables, the pictures on the walls all had been chosen with care.

The harsh Delhi sun filled the room with its bright light. Murthy sat across the room from Gopalakrishnan, next to his wife. Gopalakrishnan saw that Lakshmi was very beautiful, so beautiful that he was afraid to look at her in case she noticed how beautiful he found her. He focused his attention on Murthy and they spoke reminiscingly of the Daily Fat Stomach and All India Radio. Gopalakrishnan mentioned Ganapathy but Murthy showed no interest in him. They talked of other friends and acquaintances while Lakshmi listened quietly, a fixed smile on her face. She looked up every now and then and glanced into the adjoining dining room, as if she wanted to escape them and their talk. She showed no interest in this regurgitation of the past. Did she care about the life her husband had lived for the past four years? It did not seem so. Gopalakrishnan thought she had the aloof manner of a woman who knows she is beautiful. At last she indicated the clock on the wall and said, "I will go get lunch ready."

Murthy's eyes followed her into the dining room. When she disappeared into the kitchen, he looked at Gopalakrishnan and said, "Did I tell you? She's a B.A."

Gopalakrishnan was impressed. A wife who was a college graduate!

Murthy's eyes returned to the dining room. Lakshmi had come back from the kitchen with dishes of food on a tray. "In music," Murthy added, when she had once again disappeared into the kitchen. "She has studied Karnatic music. She sings very well. She has given public performances in Madras."

Gopalakrishnan watched Murthy follow his wife with his eyes as she prepared the table for lunch. He felt a sudden rush of fondness and jealousy for his friend.

Lunch was an all-India affair. There was a variety of dishes from the different parts of India, each better than the other. There was vegetable rice and rotis and aloo chole and green beans in grated coconut and pitlai. There were two kinds of homemade pickles and fried appalam. For dessert there was both vermicelli payasam and gulab jamun. Even the gulab jamun had been prepared at home.

"I haven't eaten like this in years," Gopalakrishnan said and meant it, for it was clear that Lakshmi was a better cook even than Ganapathy.

Lakshmi raised her eyes from her plate and said in perfect English, "Thank you. I am proud of my cooking." Her voice was soft and melodious, the voice of a trained singer. Murthy, sitting next to Lakshmi, beamed as if he himself had done the cooking. Gopalakrishnan thought to himself: The stories I could tell her about Murthy if I really wanted to! The stories!

Gopalakrishnan was glad he had renewed contact with Murthy, but he came away from his visit restless and dissatisfied. The sudden and enormous changes Murthy had made in his life dislodged Gopalakrishnan from the bog of routine into which he had sunk, setting him rolling in new directions. He began to look at his life anew. There was the question of whether he was going to be a staff artiste all his life, the way Ganapathy was likely to be. Ganapathy remained unchanged. He was as always — mild, affectionate, undependable. But now that Gopalakrishnan was alone with him in the barsaati, his erratic rent paying and his addas were no longer quite so amusing. Gopalakrishnan was attached to Ganapathy, was very fond of him, but was he going to live the rest of his life with him in the barsaati? Was that what life had in store for him?

Gopalakrishnan's parents had been importuning him for some time to get married. They had already found an appropriate girl in a neighboring village — a Tamil Brahmin like him, of course —

known to friends of theirs. The horoscopes matched and so did the two families' subcaste and their social and economic status. Gopalakrishnan's father was keen on this alliance and now Gopalakrishnan, too, felt it would not be bad to explore it. Ganapathy's food, tasty as it was, could not compare to Lakshmi's. No doubt Parvati, the girl his parents were considering, would make an improvement to the material circumstances of his life in the way Lakshmi had in Murthy's. Gopalakrishnan resolved that he too would make changes in his life — he too would get married and find another job.

First came the job. He took the appropriate Union Public Service Commission examination and did passably enough to join the Information and Broadcasting Ministry as a section officer. He would no longer be a staff artiste at AIR; he would be part of the permanent civil service. His office was now in a new building that had been built to accommodate the growing branches of the central government in New Delhi. His prospects were immeasurably better. He was given a government flat and, only a few months after Murthy, he too had moved out of the barsaati. Ganapathy helped him move his few things in a cycle rickshaw to his new flat, which was in Sector Four of R. K. Puram. The identical blocks of white government housing — fading to gray now — were far different from Sunder Nagar. The buildings were grouped in threes, one in the middle and two flanking this middle building, facing each other across a common maidan. Each building had four flats. Gopalakrishnan's was on the first floor of his building. In the maidan, as they arrived, boys were playing cricket with a pile of bricks for wickets.

"You are one of the sahibs now, Gopu," Ganapathy said after a tour of the two-bedroom flat. It was a typically generous exaggeration. A section officer was not very high up in the civil service hierarchy and the flat was really not that big. Nevertheless, compared to the barsaati, the flat was immense.

"You will be alone now in the barsaati," Gopalakrishnan said in response, because he felt unaccountably guilty.

"Don't worry about me," Ganapathy said.

"You should look for another job. What will you get by being a staff artiste at AIR all your life?"

"I want to concentrate on my acting now. That is what I am going to do."

"Be serious," Gopalakrishnan pleaded. "For once be serious."

Ganapathy was taken aback at Gopalakrishnan's vehemence. "All right," he said. "Very well. You want me to look for another job? I will do it." But both he and Gopalakrishnan knew he wouldn't.

Fresh from his employment success Gopalakrishnan went to Paavalampatti. The day after his arrival, still tired from his long train journey, he went by bus with his parents to "see" Parvati. A few chosen relatives and Gauri, who had come for the occasion from Madras, accompanied them.

Parvati's village was smaller and less prosperous than Paavalampatti. The Brahmin street was short and nondescript. Her house too was small, modest. A great crowd of relatives and village elders had squeezed into the little front room of the house. Gopalakrishnan was given a comfortable sofa chair to sit in, but the chair was located right beneath a high window through which the afternoon sun beat down on him with especial violence. He felt dizzy and sweaty. He looked around the room and felt disconnected from everyone in it. When Parvati came in to be presented to him and his family, he did not look at her. What was the point? He had seen a picture of Parvati. The girl in the picture had a long face and protuberant cheeks. It was not a remarkable face except for the steady eyes and the thick, curly hair. He had already decided he was going to get married and this was the girl his father had selected. What else was there to do? He kept his head down and his eyes on the floor in front of him. After Parvati had retreated again to the interior of the house the conversation continued around him as if he had nothing at all to do with what was going on. Parvati's mother began describing to Gauri the jewelry and kitchen utensils and clothes and furniture that were to be given as part of the dowry. Gopalakrishnan was reminded of something that he and Murthy had often talked about. He suddenly said, "I don't believe in dowries." He had not meant to speak. And then he added, "Nor do I believe in horoscopes." He had not meant to say that either.

The silence that followed was long.

"Modern boys," Parvati's father, a quiet man with a perpetually worried expression on his face, said at last. "The ideas they have!"

There was relieved laughter.

In the bus returning to Paavalampatti, Gopalakrishnan's father raised his voice above the murmur of the passengers around him and said to his son, "Haven't you learned anything about how to talk? Who is interested in your ideas about dowries and horoscopes?"

"Yes," Gauri said, for once taking her father's side against him. "That was not the right way to behave."

"Just remember one thing," Paavalampatti Krishnaswamy Iyer said. "We have given our word. Your marriage to the girl is certain."

Gopalakrishnan did not say anything. Why had he made the remarks about dowries and horoscopes? He began to regret them now. He had never meant to raise questions about his marriage to this girl called Parvati.

After giving his assent to the alliance, Gopalakrishnan returned to Delhi, to his new job at the Information and Broadcasting Ministry. He was, in fact, eager for the wedding, although it was still many months away. It was decided that the engagement ceremony would be held the day before the wedding so he would not have to make another long journey from Delhi. In Delhi, he deliberately left his new government flat unfurnished so that Parvati could fill it with things she wanted. He slept on a mattress on the floor and ate out. Often he went to the barsaati to have dinner with Ganapathy.

The wedding, which was in Parvati's village, was a blur made up of the priest's Sanskrit chants, the smell of sandalwood paste, the smoke from the ritual fire, the rustle of silk saris, the never-ending commotion of men and women and children. Gopalakrishnan barely remembered Parvati by his side.

It was not until Gopalakrishnan and Parvati had come to Madras, spent a day with Gauri, and finally were by themselves in the train to Delhi that Gopalakrishnan was able to scrutinize his new wife. Sitting next to Parvati on the train racing toward the north — she in a silk sari and he in his fine new shirt and trousers — he saw that her picture had not lied. Though her face was a little long she was not unattractive. He liked the way her wide mouth was quick to smile and the way her voice sounded when she was frightened. Gopalakrishnan had done the long train journey to Delhi so many times by now he had forgotten how he himself had felt the first time he had made the journey. They were close to New Delhi, passing stations sounding with the cacophony of Hindi, before it occurred to him that Parvati was moving to a strange city far from her parents with a strange man. It was then he said to her, "We will be in a new flat in Delhi. I haven't bought any things for it. I want you to buy the things."

"You mean there is nothing there?"

"A few essential things. But mostly you have to fill it with your things."

Parvati was silent for a while and he realized that he had only succeeded in frightening her even more with the idea of filling an empty flat with things. "We will do it together," he said.

"Yes," she said humbly. "I think I will need help."

The confession was strangely pleasing to him.

Gopalakrishnan and Parvati spent their first few weeks in Delhi setting up the flat with furniture they bought and with the things that had been sent on by Parvati's father as part of the dowry. Their furniture was simple — a sofa, a dining table, a bed, a radio. The radio and the bed were part of the dowry. On top of the radio, Gopalakrishnan placed a Taj Mahal like the one he had given Murthy. When Gopalakrishnan felt the flat to be presentable, it was his turn to invite Murthy and Lakshmi to lunch. Murthy's wedding gift was a small music box from Germany whose top opened to reveal a couple standing stiff in all their European finery. Gopalakrishnan could not recognize the music that emanated from the box when the lid was lifted, but Murthy said it was by a famous German composer.

Lunch was nothing exceptional. Parvati had made an effort but, as she herself admitted, she knew few dishes. During lunch, Parvati was voluble. She knew only Tamil and was grateful to find Tamil speakers other than Gopalakrishnan to speak to. She was like a traveler through a desert who stumbles on an oasis. She drank thirstily of the social occasion. She carried on with little artifice about herself, her father, to whom she was very close, and her prior life in a village near Thirunelveli Town.

"What subject did you do in college?" Murthy asked her during a pause in her flood of words.

"I didn't go to college," Parvati replied. "Appa needed help at home, so I stayed back."

Murthy nodded his head and said, "I know how that can be. But I think it is so important that women also get the same chance to go to college as men."

"Have you been to college then?" Parvati said to Lakshmi artlessly.

Before Lakshmi could reply, Murthy said, "She has a B.A. in music. From Madras."

Lakshmi, who had been mostly silent through lunch, lifted her soft eyes from the plate of food on which she had kept them fixed and said to Parvati, "If my father had needed help, I would have done exactly as you did."

After that Parvati was silent and it was Murthy who did the talking. Gopalakrishnan tried not to look at Murthy. He felt for the first time since the wedding that perhaps he had not married well. Disappointment insinuated itself into his mind. He tried to shake it away, ashamed of himself for feeling as he did.

In all the long decades of his married life that followed Gopalakrishnan was careful never to express disappointment with Parvati as a person. Certainly, he sometimes yelled at her or disregarded her opinions, but never did he let her feel diminished as a person. He knew he hadn't because — from the day Murthy and Lakshmi had visited, when he had felt the subtle stir of regret within him — he had always been careful, so careful, not to betray disappointment. It was not love for his wife that occasioned this care in him; he would have been embarrassed if someone had asked him whether he loved his wife. It was not love because there was no longing in it, and it was not kindness because there was no self-approval. It was not even loyalty, for it was an attachment that went so deep, was so fundamental, and at the same time so unthinking, that Gopalakrishnan could really imagine no way of abandoning it. Was there a word for it? Perhaps, but Gopalakrishnan had never thought to ask himself that question because he only felt it, and lived it. He did not know what he felt and lived. He was not the kind of man for that kind of knowledge. Life with Parvati — a life of such unarticulated commitment — was what it was.

Parvati adjusted quickly to Delhi. She did not like the city but her nature was such that she came to make herself much more at home there than Gopalakrishnan. She was good with languages and soon knew Hindi much better than he did. She joined a ladies club in R. K. Puram. She became active in the Tamil Sangam. On a winter afternoon, she would often sit out on the maidan on a charpoy with women who lived in neighboring flats, just as Gopalakrishnan remembered Sharma-ji's wife doing in the courtyard below the barsaati. Her best friends were a Bengali woman and a woman from Kerala. None of them liked Delhi but they met every day and gossiped with one another in Hindi. Gopalakrishnan, on the other hand, loved Delhi, but had no friends other than Ganapathy and Murthy.

Life in Delhi included setbacks and sorrows. Much of the sorrow concerned the difficulties Parvati had in bearing children. After many years of trying there was a miscarriage. Gopalakrishnan remembered forever after the green walls and the medicinal smell of the room in the nursing home in which the lady doctor had informed him and Parvati of the loss of the baby. He remembered the way Parvati's face took on that stony expression he had come to know so well. More years of anxious trying and despair followed and, certainly, he grew frustrated with Parvati during that time. A dark time. Was Parvati to blame for their inability to bear children, or was he? How could he be the one responsible? He stumbled from year to year, careened from fear to unarticulated fear. But Gopalakrishnan and Parvati had got through that period of their life, shaken but otherwise intact. Finally, Suresh was born. True, Suresh was difficult. He tested them with his waywardness, his recklessness, his prodigality. Nevertheless, unlike Parvati, Gopalakrishnan did not think Suresh had been very unusual as a child. Which child did not have a little rebelliousness in him? That was not the way Parvati thought. She did not always agree with Gopalakrishnan on the best way to deal with Suresh and that only compounded things. Suresh quickly learned to resent his mother's strictness — if there was one quality in Parvati that Gopalakrishnan felt he could criticize, it was her strictness. Such unnecessary strictness. After all, hadn't everything worked out with Suresh in the end?

All that time of trial had passed. By the time he had left New Delhi to return to Paavalampatti, Gopalakrishnan's difficulties were long behind him. So he had observed to Parvati when they were preparing to move to Paavalampatti. He and Parvati were in the midst of suitcases and boxes, packing up the apartment in New Delhi in which they had settled after his retirement. He had been inspired by the solemnity of the occasion to say to her in a voice full of emotion, "Parvati, it is forty years since I came to Delhi. Imagine that! I cannot say everything has been easy here. But I can say this. Life here did not beat me down. Was it luck? Maybe. But I think I have done at least a little to deserve what I have. Have I not struggled with Suresh to bring him up right? I worked hard at my job to make a success of it through my diligence and enterprise. Even in concerns of health, where so much depends on things one has no control over, I have been conscientious. Haven't I for years and years gone walking every day without fail? That kind of discipline matters. It surely matters."

In the thirty years and more Gopalakrishnan had spent in the Ministry of Information and Broadcasting, diligence rather than enterprise was the quality most often singled out in assessments of his work. Deputy Secretary Shetty, under whom he had worked for many years, had often said, "If you want a job done promptly and well, give it to Gopalakrishnan. There is no one more persevering." Of course, this same Shetty had taken credit for work Gopalakrishnan had done on a rural information campaign during the heady days of the Green Revolution in the sixties. In due course, Gopalakrishnan had, during the seventies, become a deputy secretary himself, leading (as he well knew) ungenerous colleagues of his in the ministry to pooh-pooh his achievement and say behind his back that he clung to his industriousness like a drowning man to a rope and this was why it had taken him so long to become deputy secretary. Gopalakrishnan did not think he did. And even if he did, how could that be a bad thing?

Soon after becoming deputy secretary, Gopalakrishnan had met Murthy at a symposium for prominent journalists organized by his ministry at Shastri Bhavan. Murthy had gone from achievement to spectacular achievement, becoming a very visible and public figure in journalism. At the end of the symposium, at which Murthy had been one of the featured speakers, Gopalakrishnan had gone up to Murthy to say hello. He was proud that Murthy, who was his friend, had been given such a prominent place in the program.

"I hear you are now a deputy secretary," was the first thing Murthy said in Tamil when Gopalakrishnan came up to him. He was standing with a glass of cold lemon juice in his hands. There was a strict rule that there was to be no alcohol at government events. "You will be secretary by the time you are done!"

Unlike Gopalakrishnan, who was beginning to gray, Murthy's hair was still jet-black. Parvati thought he dyed it. Gopalakrishnan felt Parvati had a tendency to be suspicious of Murthy.

"Maybe," Gopalakrishnan said in reply to Murthy, also in Tamil. "Who can play the games you have to play to rise so high? I will do my work as well as I can. Let the rest take care of itself." But secretly he felt proud of Murthy's prediction. What did it matter what was said of him by his colleagues in the ministry, who neither knew him nor understood him?

And then he had added, "Do you know what I hear? You are next in line to be editor."

He could see Murthy was pleased he had heard of his impending success.

"I have my own column now," Murthy had said. "TR Talk. Have you read it?"

Of course Gopalakrishnan had. TR Talk was a regular and avidly read column in which Murthy offered his opinion on every political issue of the day.

Over the years, Gopalakrishnan had fallen into what he regarded as an easy and comfortable friendship with Murthy. They saw each other rarely — perhaps once or twice a year, and then for the most part by accident at some symposium or professional affair. Nevertheless, Gopalakrishnan continued to regard Murthy as one of his closest friends. Gopalakrishnan had not really made friends in the Ministry of Information and Broadcasting. He had many colleagues and professional acquaintances, but he was content to let them remain so. He had found neither a Murthy nor a Ganapathy during his long tenure there.

Long after Murthy and Gopalakrishnan had moved on, Ganapathy continued to live in the barsaati. The cot that had belonged to Murthy and then to Gopalakrishnan passed on to him. He moved his trunk, with the picture of Krishna still adorning its top, to a corner of the back room. No other changes were made to the barsaati. Ganapathy continued to cook on the kerosene stove. The only "furniture" in the front room continued to be an old mattress with a dirty and torn sheet over it. Empty Johnny Walker whiskey bottles accumulated in a corner because Ganapathy was too distracted by nature to have the batliwallah take them away. The walls, unpainted, faded to a dirty yellow color.

"Why don't you get Sharma-ji to paint the walls?" Gopalakrishnan had asked in exasperation during a rare visit to the barsaati. Sharma-ji had become a prosperous retailer of auto parts.

"Shh," Ganapathy had hissed back. "Isn't it enough that he lets me stay here?"

Though he visited the barsaati rarely, Gopalakrishnan saw a lot of Ganapathy. Often on a Sunday morning Ganapathy would turn up at Gopalakrishnan's flat bearing a small gift of fruit or biscuits wrapped in an old sheet from a newspaper. On his visits he would first sit with Gopalakrishnan for a while. "How are things in your office?" he would ask politely. Depending on what answer Gopalakrishnan made he would be impressed or would commiserate. After an appropriate period of time with Gopalakrishnan, Ganapathy would disappear into the kitchen to help Parvati — to cut some vegetables or to grate some coconut or, after Suresh was born, to take charge of the baby while Parvati cooked. And then would be revealed the true purpose of his visit. Reading his newspaper or listening to the radio in the adjacent room, Gopalakrishnan would soon hear the voices in the kitchen grow louder.

"No!" Parvati's voice would be loud with shock.

"I am telling you the truth, Manni!" Ganapathy always addressed Parvati as if she were the wife of his elder brother even though both Gopalakrishnan and Parvati were much younger than he was.

"I don't believe you!"

"Really! There are such people in the world. They have so much money they cover their pet dogs with gold chains and feed them the finest food from the best restaurants."

"It can't be true!"

"Really! Chicken korma from Oberoi Hotel! You can ask Gopu if you want."

"Chee! Chicken korma!"

Parvati and Ganapathy were well matched in their love of chatter. Occasionally the voices would fall to gossipy whispers — only to be followed immediately by soaring peals of laughter from Parvati. Ganapathy could always make Parvati laugh — he loved to perform for her because she was the most sympathetic of audiences. He was attached to her.

Gopalakrishnan would envy the merry commotion in the kitchen, but he knew he could never be a part of it. Were he to go in there — to get a stainless steel tumbler of water, say, or to collect Suresh so that he could play with him — the merriment would stop immediately. Parvati would turn an inquiring face toward him — could she get him something? — and an expectant silence would descend on the kitchen. If it had been someone other than Ganapathy, Gopalakrishnan might have frowned on the unusual intimacy between Ganapathy and his wife. But who could suspect shabby, sweet Ganapathy of vulgar designs in the kitchen? He was the hapless brother Gopalakrishnan had never had.

Ganapathy's shabbiness was a sign of his decline in fortunes. More often than not Ganapathy's Sunday visits would conclude with a request to "borrow" some money. If Gopalakrishnan declined to make the "loan" — it was of course never returned — Ganapathy would be perfectly cheerful about it. It never ceased to amaze Gopalakrishnan how cheerful Ganapathy remained during his gradual but steady slide into financial difficulties. He worked for AIR as a staff artiste for many years, always living beyond his means, and then left his job suddenly to commit himself to stage acting, which, as he never stopped noting, was his real passion in life. Gopalakrishnan quizzed Ganapathy severely on this decision when he heard of it on one of his visits. Ganapathy would only say, "Leave it alone. I don't want to talk about it. Everything has its time. The time of AIR is finished. Now it is time for me to throw myself into my acting fully. If you cannot live life and enjoy it, can you still call it life? God will take care of everything." Gopalakrishnan was not satisfied. He made some inquiries and heard through his contacts in AIR that Ganapathy had been quietly asked to leave. There had been difficulties with regard to absences. Too often he had arrived for work clearly intoxicated.

When Ganapathy visited next, Gopalakrishnan glared at him as he stepped in through the open front door. Ganapathy noticed the expression on his friend's face and stopped at the threshold. "What is it, Gopu?" he asked. "What has happened?"

"I called AIR."

"Why did you do that?"

"You were asked to leave!" Gopalakrishnan yelled at him. "You were drunk all the time."

"Not all the time," Ganapathy said with a frown. "That's not correct."

"Not all the time? Not all the time?!" Gopalakrishnan could not believe what he was hearing. He could not keep himself from yelling.

Parvati appeared from the kitchen with Suresh at her hip and said, "Why all this shouting? There is no need to shout like this. The neighbors will hear." She hurried Ganapathy into the kitchen.

After Ganapathy had departed, Gopalakrishnan said to Parvati, "Useless fellow. I don't know why I let him come here."

"Don't talk like that. He's your friend."

"What kind of friend is he? He comes only because he wants to borrow money."

"You know that's not true. He is your friend. He is good with the people around him. He doesn't know how to be good to himself."

"What does that mean? 'He is good with the people around him. He doesn't know how to be good to himself.' I have no idea what you have just said. Sometimes, Parvati, you talk nonsense."

For many months after learning of Ganapathy's ejection from AIR, Gopalakrishnan refused to lend Ganapathy any money. Nevertheless, Ganapathy remained his usual ebullient self. If he felt offended, the only sign was the drop in the frequency of his visits. Then one Sunday morning he appeared suddenly after many weeks of absence. He had lost weight and his clothes were unwashed and even more threadbare than usual. Gopalakrishnan was shocked at his condition. It appeared he was earning a little money from stage dramas and odd jobs here and there. But his acting career was not turning out as he had expected. So derelict did Ganapathy seem that Gopalakrishnan had to fight the temptation to say, "I told you so." Over the years he had gone with Parvati to see Ganapathy act once or twice. In his opinion Ganapathy was always one of the better actors in the production. But even Gopalakrishnan knew there is the ability to act and then there is the ability to manage an acting career. Ganapathy may have had the former, but he surely did not have the latter. What, though, was the point in regurgitating all that now? No matter how self-inflicted Ganapathy's present misery — Ganapathy, lost still in his enthusiasms, hardly saw it as such — Gopalakrishnan saw no alternative but to give him some money. He could not bear to see his friend like this.

Ganapathy's finances improved, and then declined, improved again, declined again. He would find jobs, lose jobs, act and get paid, find himself cheated out of money. In this fashion he went through life. It helped that Sharma-ji was prepared to be a little indulgent with regard to the rent. Ganapathy, who was very good with children, was indispensable to Sharma-ji and his wife. If they had to go somewhere, they would leave the children with him. Most evenings he would help Sharma-ji's five children with their mountains of homework while Sharma-ji's wife prepared dinner.

One day, Gopalakrishnan got a phone call in his office from Sharma-ji. The message only said Ganapathy was in Irwin Hospital and that it was serious. Gopalakrishnan immediately canceled his appointments for the day and went to the government hospital on the Lambretta scooter that he had bought a few years prior. Ganapathy was too poor for a private hospital. On the sprawling campus of Irwin Hospital, the oldest in the city, Gopalakrishnan was soon lost. He wandered the yellow corridors thronged with patients, visitors, and hospital employees trying to find the ward to which he had been directed. Finally a bespectacled nurse in white cap and frock indicated to him a hall with two long rows of beds in it. When Gopalakrishnan entered this hall, he found men and women — whether patients or visitors he could not tell — sleeping on the floor by some of the beds. Gopalakrishnan prayed he would not find Ganapathy on the floor. Looking for his friend, he walked down the long aisle between the two rows of beds, past the wan patients and their anxious companions, past the harried doctor bending to hear an old woman's whispered words with an impatient nurse by his side.

Ganapathy seemed asleep on his bed when Gopalakrishnan found him. He was dressed in a white hospital garment marked by brown stains. His mouth had fallen a little open but his eyes were shut. He had long since lost most of his hair. He who had once been full and round — yes, full and round as a question mark on a white page — had long since declined to the gauntness of an exclamation point. His spirit, though, had remained as open and questioning as always — Gopalakrishnan had seen him only the previous week, and he had been heady with news of a new play in which he had been given a role. He was confident this was the role that would make him as an actor. The director of the play thought there was potential for a movie here, not a big Bombay blockbuster of course but a tastefully done art movie. Who knew where this role would take him? That had been Ganapathy only the previous week, eager with the pleasures and opportunities of life, refusing to consider himself done, finished. Now a ward orderly in khaki shorts saw Gopalakrishnan approaching down the aisle and said brusquely, "He is dead."

Gopalakrishnan had come to the hospital ready to find Ganapathy very sick. But dead! He was not yet fifty! The shock of the orderly's announcement made Gopalakrishnan stop abruptly in the middle of the aisle. The orderly was standing next to Ganapathy's bed. On a metal trolley he had collected the array of medical paraphernalia — syringes, vials of medicine, stainless steel trays, all manner of equipment for which Gopalakrishnan had no name — that had apparently been brought to bear on Ganapathy in an attempt to save his life. As the orderly got ready to wheel the trolley away, one of Ganapathy's hands slid off his chest and swung back and forth, back and forth, below the edge of the bed. When the orderly reached over the trolley to lift the hand and place it back on Ganapathy's chest, Gopalakrishnan saw the fingernails were bluish. The skin of the hand had a peculiar pallor to it. Ganapathy dead. Sharma-ji, returning that very moment from taking care of paperwork, saw the expression on Gopalakrishnan's face and said in Hindi, "There was nothing they could do. His heart was finished."

Gopalakrishnan and Sharma-ji took care of the cremation of the body. Gopalakrishnan sent a telegram to Ganapathy's eldest brother in Bombay. He left a phone message about Ganapathy's death at Murthy's newspaper — Murthy was by this time editor. He indicated in both messages when and where the cremation was to be. He heard neither from the brother nor from Murthy. Neither Gopalakrishnan nor Sharma-ji knew how to contact Ganapathy's many other friends and acquaintances. Only the two of them — in a Tempo van Sharma-ji had hired for the purpose — accompanied Ganapathy's body to the cremation ground on the bank of the Yamuna River. During the short trip, Ganapathy's body lay on the floor of the van on a bed sheet Sharma-ji had brought from home. Gopalakrishnan could not bear to climb into the back with him. He sat in the front with the driver of the van, leaving Sharma-ji to ride with Ganapathy. By the time they arrived at the cremation ground it was evening. Ganapathy's body, wrapped in linen, was placed on a pile of wood on a stone platform above the inky waters of the Yamuna. It was then they learned from the officious priest that, according to custom, neither he nor Sharma-ji could light the funeral pyre because their own fathers were still alive. Sizing them up expertly, the priest informed them that there was, as luck would have it, a man who could be hired to do the job. No sooner had the priest spoken than a scrawny man in a vest and white dhoti materialized by their side.

"He is a very good man," the priest assured them as the man grinned and eagerly nodded in assent.

And so it was this stranger who lit Ganapathy's funeral pyre, placing the yellow, flaming torch with ostentatious care by the head of Ganapathy's body. The flames hungrily licked their way along the pyre. The smell of burning flesh and wood rose into the night air.

The following weekend Gopalakrishnan went through the barsaati, sorting through Ganapathy's meager possessions. Most of the things he threw away because they were junk. He mailed only a small box of personal things to the brother in Bombay because he did not know what else to do with them. Out of Ganapathy's things, Gopalakrishnan kept for himself the picture of Krishna and a photo album. Gopalakrishnan was not really religious — he believed in God but was not given to daily prayer — but he could not bear to send Ganapathy's beloved Krishna off to Bombay to a man who had not even bothered to respond to news of his brother's death. He brought the Krishna home and added it to Parvati's shelf of gods. The photo album was filled with pictures of Murthy, Ganapathy, and himself from the happy days when they had all lived together in the barsaati. He felt he had a right to the album.

In the weeks that followed it became clear to Gopalakrishnan how great a blow Ganapathy's death really was. Now that Ganapathy was gone Gopalakrishnan realized how much he had depended on him for emotional sustenance. He thought often of his friend. He did not grieve for him like Parvati, whom he found one day weeping and looking sadly through the photo album. She shut it when she saw him and said, "He was a good man. He was always laughing and happy." Gopalakrishnan could not show his feelings like Parvati, but after Ganapathy's death there was within him a sadness of a kind he had never known, not even at the time of Parvati's terrible miscarriage, and also a strange fear. In subtle and private ways the substance of his life took on a newer, more melancholic shape. It was not the first time he had been close to death. He remembered his grandfather dying in Paavalampatti when he was a boy. But there had not been the same intimacy between him and his grandfather. Now he understood that death was the most iron-willed of directors and when she rang the curtain down there was no actor, no matter how filled with exuberant love for the drama, who could refuse to exit the stage. The discovery should not have been unexpected. It was.

Not long after Ganapathy's death Gopalakrishnan found himself visiting his doctor. He had begun wondering about his own heart. True, Ganapathy had been older than he by five or six years and quite dissolute in his ways. Gopalakrishnan knew he did not live his life like Ganapathy, who had abused his health without a care. Nevertheless, he wished to have himself examined thoroughly. After the checkup, Gopalakrishnan's doctor assured him that his heart was fine. Gopalakrishnan was relieved, but he interrogated his doctor further about what he could do to keep his heart healthy. He would give up smoking of course. What else could he do? What other routine could he devise that would be helpful? Would it help if he walked every morning? Of course, the doctor replied, it certainly would. Daily exercise of that kind could not hurt. In fact, the doctor recommended it strongly.

Gopalakrishnan displayed his usual diligence in committing himself from that day to a daily regimen of morning walking. He started the regimen in Delhi. His return to Paavalampatti did nothing to interrupt it.

Even after his bath by the well, Gopalakrishnan felt dirty, as if the slime that had covered his legs had not washed off. He felt aggrieved. If the daily morning walk went well — if he fell into his rhythm easily and was able to maintain it without mishap until he was back in front of his house — it was an activity to be remembered with pleasure. Today there had been too many unfortunate accidents; aside from the disaster in front of the village mosque, his rhythm had been upset too many times. Then there had been the matter of Parvati and the motor pump and the lack of water in the bathroom. That too had been exasperating. True, bathing by the well had not been without pleasure, but he could not find it in himself to be consoled by that. After all, he had not intended to have his bath in this fashion. And he still felt dirty. No, Gopalakrishnan could not be satisfied with how the morning had gone thus far. He was most definitely aggrieved.

So he sat in his room in his easy chair (originally his father's), frowning, his legs resting on the long wooden arms of the chair, aimlessly turning the pages of his newspaper back and forth. He was finding it hard to concentrate. On the floor by the low-slung chair a steel tumbler of coffee steamed and waited for him. He had not forgotten it. He liked to get his coffee or his tea as hot as could be and let it cool before drinking it. He had explained why to Parvati many times: without doubt, coffee heated thus and allowed to cool had a taste entirely superior to coffee quickened into only half a life.

Parvati did not care enough to argue the point. She was happy to heat his coffee as he wished it.

The room in which Gopalakrishnan sat, the room which was his room now, had once belonged to his father, and before his father to his grandfather. Not only the easy chair but all the other furniture in the room had also belonged at one time to his father or his grandfather. Here, pillow against the wall, was the much-scratched cot of dark wood on which both his father and his grandfather had died. And there, on the other side of the cot, was the desk of the same fine wood, solid and simple in its lines, at which his father had fallen asleep as a boy and been punished by having his kudumi tied to one of the rafters above. And all around were Paavalampatti Krishnaswami Iyer's bookshelves, lining the walls and bearing with stolid patience his yellowing and dusty books. The shelves were of a kind of bamboo buttressed by planks of wood at the back. They looked frail but had lasted more than half a century. Gopalakrishnan could not abide them; they were ugly. But to take down the hundreds of books, many of them ready to follow at the slightest touch their original master into the next world, and replace the shelves with modern substitutes was a task beyond contemplation. So he dusted the shelves, occasionally removed from them books he wanted to read, but otherwise left them alone.

Since his return to Paavalampatti the previous year, Gopalakrishnan had rediscovered the pleasures of reading. At first he had read randomly, picking out from the bookshelves whatever book struck his fancy. More recently, however, his reading had acquired a focus. The desk, which was customarily covered by letters, papers, and bills needing his attention, was now the bearer of different versions of the Ramayana of Kamban, both in the original Tamil and in English translation and retelling. For some time now, Gopalakrishnan had been engaged in a daily study of the Ramayana. Today too he would devote himself to it, but that would be in the afternoon.

It was only mid-morning. Despite the hour, the fluorescent tube light burning high on the wall above the cot cast its white illumination into the room because it was cloudy outside. Even on sunny days, Gopalakrishnan's room, though toward the front of the house, was usually gloomy without artificial light. The house was narrow and long and single storied. It stood cheek by jowl with its neighbors, which too were similarly intimate with their own neighbors. A front veranda — enclosed by a low wall topped by an iron grill painted brown — ran the length of the house facade; doors opened from the veranda onto the thinnai on one side and the house proper on the other. During the daytime, unless both Parvati and Gopalakrishnan's mother had surrendered to an afternoon snooze, these doors were kept a little ajar, so that familiar visitors could enter without having to announce themselves and unfamiliar ones could easily make known their presence at the door. The house had only four rooms, each room taking up a corner of the house. At its center was the customary courtyard, open to the sky but secured by a grill above. A veranda ran the perimeter of the courtyard, so that the house had a kind of interior portico.

Now Gopalakrishnan heard the front doors being opened and bare feet slapping their way quickly to the back of the house. He wondered who it was and leaned forward in his chair so that he was able to look through the window in his room that opened onto the central courtyard. A young woman dressed in a green Nylex sari and carrying a cloth bag in one hand came into Gopalakrishnan's view as she crossed the courtyard. It was Sarala, who lived a few doors up in the direction of the temple. Probably here to use the grinder! Her father owned much land around the village but was unspeakably stingy. When would he get his kitchen grinder fixed or buy a new one? Gopalakrishnan made a loud noise of annoyance and leaned back in his chair to return to his aimless perusal of the newspaper. He lowered one inquiring hand to test the heat of the coffee in the tumbler.

Not quite. But soon.

Sure enough the harsh, coughing cry of the grinder burst into the air in a moment. Something hard — lentils? rice? — was being ground. Of course he had been right in his guess! Didn't he know well the reason Sarala would come scurrying to their house at this time of the morning? The chattering voices in the kitchen disappeared beneath the sound of the grinder.

Now there were many such modern appliances in the kitchen. In the days of Gopalakrishnan's boyhood there had been two pock-marked gray grinding stones (one flat, the other shaped like a bowl) in one corner of the kitchen. If by curiosity a boy — such as he had once been — were to lower his face to the rough surfaces of the stones to sniff them one after the other, the faint smells of the spices and herbs and lentils that had been ground on them would ghost their way up his nostrils. How difficult it was for even hard stone to forget. In those days, baskets hung on a chain from the ceiling in another corner. They were for keeping the fruit and the vegetables safe from rats. And in yet another corner a wood-fired stove had been built into the floor of the kitchen. Gopalakrishnan remembered the stove well — the blackened clay walls, the smell of ash, the smarting of the eyes when it was lit. He remembered waking up many mornings to find his mother bent over it, coughing in the smoke that rose from it to the chute above, her broad forehead beaded with sweat. The stove had been removed long ago. For many years, only a faint circle on the floor marked its prior place in the kitchen. First his father had bought kerosene stoves, and then cooking gas had arrived. Right before his return to Paavalampatti, Gopalakrishnan had had the entire kitchen renovated. He had had a new cement floor laid, a new counter built under which the red cooking-gas cylinders for the stove could be placed, and also new wooden shelves with doors. He had had a sink put in too — a first in the entire village of Paavalampatti, as far as he knew. It was the general practice to wash dirty dishes by the well or in the bathroom in the backyard.

The noise of the grinder finally died away. Gopalakrishnan noted that Amma — she was, and always had been, only Amma to him, but so old was she now that almost all those who could call her by her name, Kamala, were gone — had finished her bath and begun her morning prayers in the puja room. The puja room was the smallest room in the house. A wooden cabinet, filled with small and large pictures of various gods, stood against one wall of the room. At the center of the cabinet was a picture of Shiva with the tiger skin around his waist, his hair knotted, and the snake around his neck. The river Ganga spurted from his hair as he looked out upon the world with ascetic calmness, his right hand raised in benediction. Pictures of Rama and Durga and Lakshmi and Ganesh and Karthikeya were arranged surrounding this picture of Shiva. Also present was the Krishna Gopalakrishnan had inherited from Ganapathy. Parvati's divine pictures had been added to the cabinet in the puja room on their arrival from Delhi. Next to the cabinet was a shelf on which the prayer books, lamps, wicks, lamp oil, matches, kumkumam, and vibhuti were kept. The shelf was stained red and white from the kumkumam and the vibhuti, from all the times the sacred powders had been spilled on the shelf through the decades.

Gopalakrishnan's mother's practiced recitation from her book of prayers, accompanied by the tinny ring of her prayer bell, emanated from the puja room. These sounds would continue to fill the house for some time to come. His mother had always been religious, but since Gopalakrishnan's father's death she had become even more so. Her devotions had begun to take up more and more of her mornings. Though Gopalakrishnan found the chanting emanating from the puja room distracting, he made no attempt to admonish her. The quaver in his mother's voice as she intoned her prayers reminded him that she was now eighty-two years old. How could he make himself a hurdle in the way of his aged mother's piety? That would be neither seemly nor — though, certainly, he did not believe in such things — propitious. In the kitchen, now that the grinder had been shut off, the voices of Parvati and Sarala could be heard again. How Parvati liked to talk! From elsewhere in the street other sounds of the morning — voices in conversation, the ring of a bicycle, children playing — returned to the world. And then he heard Sarala's bare feet slap-slapping their way back across the courtyard. He thought she was making for the front door, but instead she came to his room.

"Uncle," she said, standing at the door to his room.

Gopalakrishnan lowered the newspaper.

"Father said to get the newspaper if you are done with it."

Sarala had just had her bath and her face was glowing and her freshly braided hair was shining black with coconut oil. She was twenty-three years old, but because she was small and slender she looked much younger, as if she were little more than a girl. The bangles on her thin wrist clinked softly as she gently swung the heavy cloth bag she was holding to and fro, waiting for his answer.

First the grinder. Now the newspaper.

Gopalakrishnan felt annoyed but he made himself soften his voice when he spoke. What did Sarala's innocence have to do with her father's stinginess? How was she to blame if her father was a good-for-nothing buffalo?

"I'm not finished with the newspaper, child," Gopalakrishnan said. "I just started reading it." Despite himself he sounded a little sore and whiny. It was the mood he was in this morning.

"It's all right," Sarala quickly reassured him. "I'll tell my father you are not done yet." She turned before Gopalakrishnan could respond and darted away.

Gopalakrishnan heard her go through the two front doors, shutting them gently behind her. He raised himself in his easy chair so that he could see her through the window as she crossed the thinnai on her way to the street. "Sarala," he called out to her. In answer, Sarala's face bloomed behind the grill of the veranda wall. "Come back in an hour," he said.

"All right, Uncle," Sarala said, and disappeared up the street toward the temple.

Sarala had completed a B.A. — in what subject Gopalakrishnan could not remember — at a college in Thirunelveli Town two years before. She lived at home while her parents looked for a suitable boy for her.

Gopalakrishnan would have to focus on the newspaper now because he had no doubt Sarala would be sent promptly by her father. He tested his coffee one more time with his hand and found it just right. He could tell by just how hot the steel tumbler was under the tips of his fingers. He raised the tumbler to his lips and took a long, grateful sip. Then he turned his attention to his newspaper, which was open to the sports pages. The Indian cricket team was once again struggling to win a championship tournament. When was the last time they had won? He frowned, trying to remember, and could not. Useless! he thought to himself. He turned the pages of the newspaper, wondering if he would find something by Murthy. The newspaper frequently carried Murthy's syndicated column, TR Talk. Murthy had recently retired from the newspaper for which he had worked as editor, but he continued to write his column. Today Gopalakrishnan did not find his column in the opinions page of the newspaper, where it usually appeared.

Instead an article about Mani Ratnam's latest film, *Bombay*, caught his attention. He had missed the film when it had come out the previous year. He read through the article and saw that the film was about a romance between a Muslim girl and a Hindu boy. Interesting. He thought to himself that he would perhaps go to Thirunelveli Town to see it if it came back there. It might be worth the trip. In this fashion, he read a story here and a story there and worked his way back to the front page, which he thought he had already read thoroughly. He meant only to give it a quick glance, but it was immediately evident to him when he turned to it that he had not been careful enough. There, in the very middle of the page, beginning right below the "1996" in the date, was this in the boldest headline of all: KASHMIR CONTINUES TO SIMMER, POLICE PURSUE INVESTIGATION INTO CAR BOMBING. How had he missed the story? He read through it quickly. A few days before there had been a car bombing by separatist militants in Kashmir in which two people had been killed; this story was following up on that incident. Things did not look good in Kashmir, the story said. The continuing insurgency was creating tension in India's only Muslim majority state — this could not bode well for Hindu-Muslim relations in the state and indeed in the country as a whole.

Gopalakrishnan thought immediately of the Muslim men in front of the little mosque. He had passed them that morning, had lifted a hand in greeting to them. One of them had replied with a wave of his own hand. He had heard part of their conversation — no mention of Kashmir there. But had these men perhaps discussed the situation in Kashmir after he had left? Or before he had appeared?

Paavalampatti was a peaceful little village. To the best of Gopalakrishnan's knowledge, there had never been a violent incident linked to religion, let alone a car bombing, in the village. What would news of the religious violence in faraway Kashmir mean to these men? Gopalakrishnan tried to imagine how the men might have felt. He could not. The incidents in Kashmir seemed very far away to him; he did not feel threatened by them. But then he was a Hindu and a Brahmin. Did the men in front of the mosque feel similarly removed from these happenings thousands of miles away? He did not know. The world was full of all kinds of people — car bombers and victims, Hindus and Muslims, Indians and Kashmiris, Tamils and Sinhalese. How could one understand them all?

Turning this thought over in his mind, Gopalakrishnan carried the newspaper and the empty tumbler to the Formica-topped dining table — brought back by him from Delhi — which had been placed outside his room in the veranda that skirted the courtyard. The veranda was filled with the smell of cooking wafting out of Parvati's kitchen. Close to the dining table, on a tall stool, was the telephone Gopalakrishnan had had installed the year before, prior to his return from Delhi. There was a time when the only telephone in the village had been in the post office at the end of Meenakshisundareswarar Temple Street. Then, a few years ago, a wealthy Pillaimar family in another part of the village had had a phone installed. Now many houses in the village had acquired the convenience. Next to the telephone, at the head of the dining table, as if a permanent and most honored guest, was a large color television that both Gopalakrishnan's mother and Parvati liked to watch while sitting at the table. The television had been placed on top of Paavalampatti Krishnaswamy Iyer's monstrous radio. When Gopalakrishnan had returned home, he had brought his television with him. For the old-fashioned radio, to which his father had continued to listen till the very end, he had no use, except as a table of just the right height for the television.

Across the courtyard from Gopalakrishnan's room was Parvati's room, which she shared with Gopalakrishnan's mother, who often enough preferred sleeping in the puja room on a mat on the floor. In Delhi, Parvati and Gopalakrishnan had been in one room, but here in Paavalampatti it had felt strange to do the same. Certainly the custom ordaining that after the obligations of childbearing had been fulfilled couples give up sleeping together was much relaxed now. Nevertheless, Parvati and Gopalakrishnan had fallen unthinkingly into the practice on their return. Perhaps it was Amma's presence. Perhaps too there was even an element of relief in their thoughtless succumbing to tradition. Sexual intimacy Gopalakrishnan had never shared with Parvati. If ever that kind of love had had any importance — after so many years Gopalakrishnan could hardly trust what he remembered, but no doubt youth is ever a servant of the body — it had long since vanished.

Parvati came out of her room now. When she saw her husband standing by the dining table, she asked, "Did you see Sarala? She was just here."

"Yes," Gopalakrishnan replied, and then added because he could not resist himself, "Since when has our house become a grinding shop? That girl has only to enter the house and the sound of grinding starts up in the kitchen."

"And then you start grinding out your complaints," Parvati retorted. "The girl came to see me. She had some work with me in the kitchen. What does that have to do with you?"

Gopalakrishnan began to tell Parvati that Sarala was coming back to borrow the newspaper in a little while and then restrained himself. After all, the real scoundrel in the matter was the father. He felt bad dragging Sarala into the discussion.

"She was asking me whether Suresh was going to come home for Diwali," Parvati continued. "I told her no, he wasn't."

"How can he? He has his own business now. He can't be running home all this distance from Delhi fifteen times a year to see his mother."

This was the way Gopalakrishnan and Parvati were. Gopalakrishnan's mother liked to say they were like a snake and a mongoose, the way they picked at each other with their words; she made the comparison often. That was not how she had been with her husband — the number of words Parvati flung at Gopu in a day would have sufficed her for a year, maybe more. So Gopalakrishnan's mother would declare, peering at Parvati from behind her thick glasses. In response Parvati would laugh and ask in a deliberately sweet voice, "Then who do you think is the snake and who the mongoose?"

Were Gopalakrishnan and Parvati, then, natural enemies like the mongoose and the snake? Did they have the same legendary hatred for each other? Or would it be better to compare them to two old wrestlers who know each other's style of play only too well? The wrestlers circle each other, feint one way or the other, and then one lunges for the stranglehold. But the lunge has no ferocity, the hold no real force. If the other succumbs, it is only for a moment. Soon they are back to circling each other with their words. Hostility? If it is there it is conjoined to an intimacy of mutual knowledge going back decades. If Gopalakrishnan and Parvati were natural enemies, they were also bound at the same time by a peculiar form of mutual devotion.

"That's what I told Sarala," Parvati said to Gopalakrishnan, in response to his remark about Suresh. "She was disappointed. I could see it in her face." Parvati smiled with pleasure as she remembered the look of disappointment on Sarala's face.

"I know what you are going to do now," Gopalakrishnan said, sighing. "You are going to talk about Suresh's marriage. It's not that long since his business has put down some roots. Give him some time."

"Give him some time, give him some time! That's all we have given him for years now."

"And what's wrong with that? Everybody takes a little time to settle down. Look at him now. He has a successful business in Delhi. He is earning hand over fist."

Parvati frowned. "You shouldn't speak like that. Do you want the evil eye to fall on Suresh?"

"I don't have any faith in all that superstition," Gopalakrishnan laughed. "If my words had such power, what wouldn't I have done in my life?" But a part of him wished he had not made the remark about Suresh's good fortune.

The pressure cooker in the kitchen let out three shrill whistles, imperiously summoning Parvati back to her work. She picked up the empty coffee tumbler Gopalakrishnan had placed on the table to carry back to the kitchen sink. "Sarala would be a very nice girl for Suresh," she said. "She would be very nice for him."

Immediately Gopalakrishnan said, "I disagree." It was on old topic between them.

"Why?"

"You know why. We have talked about it many times."

"She has lived all her life in the village. Is that the reason?"

"If you know the reason, why do you have to ask?"

"Sarala is a sensible girl. She has a good head and a good heart. She will be a good influence on Suresh. So what if she is a village girl? She knows English. She has a B.A. in home economics. She is a sophisticated girl. She was telling me the other day that they once discussed chicken curry in a cooking class in her college. She had nothing to do with any chicken. But she has the recipe for it."

Gopalakrishnan was amused. "Chicken curry! All you women can think of is food. It all comes back to food always."

"Don't change the subject. Sarala will be good for Suresh. You know it yourself."

"Suresh has lived all his life in a big city. He knows Hindi. He has gone to all kinds of places. Has Sarala even been to Madras? I don't want to say she is a bad girl. She is just not right for Suresh."

"Some places Suresh has been no one needs to go," Parvati retorted.

"Now you are the one changing the subject!"

"All right. You can say what you want. Sarala is good for Suresh.

I too was a village girl. What was wrong with me when you married me?"

And what answer could Gopalakrishnan give to that question? He could only smile sheepishly and hang his head at Parvati's successful maneuver. Parvati stalked off to the kitchen in triumph, bearing the coffee tumbler as if it were a trophy.

Chicken curry! Gopalakrishnan watched Parvati go and laughed quietly to himself. The things Parvati said sometimes!

In the kitchen, Parvati too was amused. She took the pressure cooker off the gas stove, feeling pleased with herself. She thought of her conversation with her husband. How many years had she been married to him? Yes, nearly forty years. Enough time to know how his mind worked. Enough time to know what he thought of villages and village girls and Suresh.

Parvati was twenty-three, already pushing it a little as an unmarried woman by the standards of that day, when she set eyes on Gopalakrishnan for the very first time in her life. It had not been easy to find a suitable boy for her. Parvati's father was part owner of a printing press in Thirunelveli Town. He was the third son and little ancestral property had come to him. He had four daughters and one son. The family was not poor but respectability was a daily struggle. Parvati's father was determined that Parvati, the eldest child and his favorite, make a good alliance. His brothers had promised to help with the dowry and the expenses for the wedding. One day, many months after the idea of the marriage had been broached seriously between the two families and the horoscopes had been seen to match, arrangements had been made for Gopalakrishnan to come with his parents, his sister Gauri, and a few other relatives to see Parvati.

All morning, Parvati's house was filled with the sounds and

smells of festive cooking. Parvati herself spent much of the morning in her mother's room with her mother and her two aunts — the wives of her father's older brothers. The wooden wardrobe with the full-length mirror on its door was in this room. Two silk saris had been selected for the day, one blue with a pattern of gold squares and the other reddish brown with tiny golden mangoes arranged in rows. She tried on the reddish brown one, then the other, decided on the reddish brown, and then, when she was wearing it, changed her mind, because her mother and her aunts insisted it made her look darker than she really was. It was true that she, like her father, was dark. The reddish brown sari accentuated her dark skin by its dull glow. The blue sari, on the other hand, imparted its brightness to her face. Parvati loved the reddish brown sari. She consented to the blue reluctantly, wondering resentfully to herself what it mattered whether she appeared dark or fair.

Once the sari had been chosen, there were arguments about how much jewelry Parvati should wear. Her mother thought she should wear less, her aunts — perhaps because most of the jewelry had been borrowed from them — more. There was pride on both sides. It was difficult to make a diplomatic decision, one that would be disrespectful neither of her mother nor of her aunts. She put on and took off jewelry and stared in the mirror at her face with the prominent cheeks and wide mouth. Was she attractive? Would the man coming to see her find her attractive? In the midst of all this, her father stepped into the room thrice. The first two times he quietly watched her adjusting the jewelry around her neck as she bravely tried to adjudicate between mother and aunts, and then turned around and left without speaking a word. The third time he fingered the edge of his silk veshti and asked, "Are you happy, Paru?

Are you happy with this alliance?" His thin face with the too-large ears looked care-worn.

Before Parvati could reply, her mother, whose life was one long resentment of her husband's modest fortunes, said in the harsh voice she used customarily with her husband, "What kind of a question is that? Is that a question to ask a child like her? What does she know about what will make her happy? We should be grateful that Paavalampatti Krishnaswami Iyer is agreeable to this alliance. His son works in New Delhi, no less. Parvati, remember all that I have told you. Make sure you are respectful to everyone in the room. You don't want the boy saying no to you because of your behavior."

What was there for Parvati to say to her father after her mother's remarks? She remained silent and her father returned to his pacing on the thinnai.

The party from Paavalampatti was due to arrive by bus at an auspicious time in the afternoon. When the moment of their arrival was near, Parvati's brother went to the bus stop to wait for them. Dressed and ready, Parvati sat in her mother's room with her youngest sister. She could see through the window of the room that it was a bright, sun-soaked afternoon. She felt her life turning on a pivot but was calm within. She knew how anxious her father was. She was determined that everything go well. She knew it would go well. The party of visitors arrived. She heard them being received in the front room.

"Welcome! Welcome!"

"Come. Let's sit down."

"It is hot isn't it?"

"How was the bus ride?"

"A little water would be nice."

"What a pretty child."

"When Parvati was this age she looked just like this."

So the polite conversation went. Then the voices were lowered and she could not hear what was being said. When finally the summons came for her, she went accompanied by her youngest sister so that there could be no misunderstanding who the prospective bride was.

The visitors, her parents, her uncles and aunts, other important elders, and sundry curious children of the village had all squeezed into the small front room. A little space had been left in the very middle for her. After touching the feet of the elders (her mother had given her careful instructions regarding in what order she was to do this), Parvati stood quietly in this spot with her head bowed, hot and uncomfortable in her blue Kanchipuram silk sari and jewelry. About that moment she remembered most the light, the bright white light pouring in from the outside through the two high windows. The dear room in which she had spent so many lazy hours lying on the floor reading a novel or a popular magazine seemed bleached of all the familiar colors. For what seemed a very long time she stood as her mother had taught her, with her right hand holding her left arm, while the light grew whiter and whiter around her, and the people and the things in the room grew more and more distant from one another and from her. A peculiar sensation. As if the shape of reality had changed, stretched out, thinned. She felt herself diminished, distanced from them all. She was asked to bring from the kitchen the savories and sweets that had been prepared. When she had returned with them on a tray, she sat in the little space that was hers with her head bowed. The conversation ebbed and flowed around her as if at a great remove. Through the meaningless murmur she could feel the visiting party looking at her. Was her prospective husband looking at her too? She was asked to sing and she sang a devotional song in her tuneless voice. At last, her mother released her with the prearranged signal. She made her obeisances and took the opportunity before leaving the room to steal a quick glance at her future husband.

Dressed in a clean white shirt and dark trousers, Gopalakrishnan was sitting on the sofa chair, his gaze fixed unwaveringly on the floor in front of him. She noticed that his bare feet were enormous. He was seated immediately under one of the windows and the light came flooding down on him directly, casting shadows over his face, which was broad under the thick black hair combed back straight from his forehead. He seemed withdrawn, tired. There were dark circles under his wide-set eyes. She knew he had arrived from Delhi only the previous day. He seemed even more remote from her than the others.

Later one of her sisters brought Parvati some news with a mixture of amusement and shock and scandal: her future husband had spoken only once during the visit, to announce in a quiet voice that he had no belief in either a horoscope or a dowry. Of course, Parvati's sister reassured her, the elders in both the families had dismissed his declaration, though with much indulgent laughter. When Parvati heard this news, Gopalakrishnan seemed to recede even farther into a distance. What manner of man was she getting ready to spend the rest of her life with? And what if he made similar, sudden declarations and demands during the wedding?

Parvati need not have worried about the wedding, which was held in a marriage hall in Thirunelveli Town and was preceded by the engagement ceremony the previous day. Both engagement and wedding went off without incident. On the day of the wedding, her father worked hard to make sure everything was tasteful, impeccable in its adherence to proper custom. Through most of the day she waited in a room that had been set aside for her, surrounded by her sisters. She tried to be happy. She *was* happy. She saw little of her father, who was needed here, there, everywhere. But her future father-in-law, Paavalampatti Krishnaswamy Iyer, sat by her future husband through the whole ceremony with a stern expression on his face. When summoned from her room to fulfill her obligations in the ceremony, she was grateful for Paavalampatti Krishnaswamy Iyer's presence, for she felt he would be a restraint on the unpredictable man she was marrying. She sat by her future husband in front of the ritual fire as he patiently poured every spoon of ghee into the fire when indicated and enunciated every Sanskrit sloka as perfectly as he was able. He made no shocking declarations, rejected no ceremony as superstition.

Parvati was appreciative of Paavalampatti Krishnaswamy Iyer's reassuring presence during the wedding ceremony, but in the days and months and years that followed she came to dislike and fear him — she found he was aloof, obdurate of manner, and made silent but incessant demands of the people around him. He was very different from her own gentle and easygoing father. Of course she could not reveal her feelings. She was ever the dutiful daughter-in-law, but her aversion to Paavalampatti Krishnaswamy Iyer was one of the first things to draw her closer to Gopalakrishnan. She saw early how it was between father and son and found it easy to be sympathetic to her husband because she shared his resentment of his father. She could never tell him so, of course, because it was clear to her that he had never articulated to himself his own feelings. Suddenly her husband did not seem so remote, so daunting, anymore. She saw that he was only a son, confused and hurt and vulnerable. This knowledge, this conviction, found repeated confirmation in the ten years between the marriage and the birth of their first and only child, Suresh. Those years — full of anxieties, self-doubt, and guilt about her inability to bear a child — were not easy. It might have seemed that she was the one who needed protection from the imputations and the questions provoked by her apparent inability to give birth to children successfully; yet it was she who found herself a buffer between Gopalakrishnan and his father. In one sense it was easy for her to be such a buffer — she was blamed anyway.

When Parvati did not get pregnant immediately after the marriage, it was first put down to changing times. It was assumed Parvati and Gopalakrishnan were waiting like other young, modern couples. But then two years passed and still there was no announcement of an impending child. On a trip to Paavalampatti, Gopalakrishnan's mother said in a studied voice to no one in particular, "You know what people say about a woman who is unable to have a child. Something that she or her ancestors did is affecting her. Otherwise what reason is there for a woman to be barren? Things don't happen without a reason. Everything in this world is connected. Who knows what terrible secrets may lie hidden in the woman's past?" This was soon after Parvati and Gopalakrishnan had arrived from Delhi. They and Gopalakrishnan's parents were gathered on the veranda around the courtyard of the house. Parvati saw her husband's face change. He remained silent and sullen through the rest of the visit.

But it was when Paavalampatti Krishnaswamy Iyer began to interest himself in the matter that Parvati saw her husband grow truly dispirited. As if their own anxieties were not enough, blue Indian Postal Service "inland" letters began arriving from Paavalampatti at the R. K. Puram flat in Gopalakrishnan's father's cramped, correct handwriting — English on the outside for the addresses, Tamil on the inside. Paavalampatti Krishnaswamy Iyer had never before written letters so regularly. The letters were brief. They ended always with a sentence asking why there was not yet any "good news" about Parvati. After one of these letters, her husband would descend into a black, irascible mood that could last for days. When Gopalakrishnan and Parvati went home to Paavalampatti on vacations, Parvati had to deal not only with her mother-in-law's increasingly direct comments but also with the way her father-in-law's eyes followed her around the house with an accusation in them.

And that was how she interposed herself between her husband and his parents — by offering herself up during these visits as the vessel into which all the corrosive juices of their collective disappointments could flow. When her husband made no reply to his mother's increasingly pointed questions about what was wrong with his wife or chose to ignore his father's cold behavior toward her, she did not butt in — as she very well could have — with any of the information she had learned from her lady doctor in Delhi about men and women and pregnancy and childbearing. These were not easy topics. For her, the subject was delicate. But, still, sooner or later, she could surely have found the way to defiantly state some of what she had learned to her husband's mother. She did not, because she realized that as long as she was blamed her husband was not.

And Gopalakrishnan? Was he to be considered disloyal to her because of his silences? He did not make accusations of her himself, and in the flat in R. K. Puram they were more companions in their unhappiness over the childlessness than mongoose and snake. Nevertheless, Parvati did wonder sometimes why he could not say to his parents what she herself was always leaving unsaid.

The answer she gave to herself always came back to this — Gopalakrishnan might be husband to her but he was still only son to his father and his mother.

When Sarala did not come looking for the newspaper, Gopalakrishnan went looking for her father. The newspaper had sat on a corner of the dining table all through lunch like an incriminating object. After lunch he had rearranged the furniture in Parvati's room, as he had promised to do many days before. Parvati wanted the steel Godrej almirah moved from one corner to the other. How this would improve things Gopalakrishnan could not fathom. It was whim, plain whim. But what could he do? He had committed already to the task, so there he was for most of an hour, emptying the almirah of Parvati's lesser treasures (silk saris, costume jewelry, handbags, photo albums, and other items that were neither so precious as to deserve a bank deposit box nor so trivial as to be stored in any old cupboard), maneuvering it around the two cots and the chest of drawers also in the room, and then putting all the contents back where they belonged. When, finally, he came out of Parvati's room, the newspaper was still where he had left it. Sarala had not come to claim it. He felt sorry that she had not and also annoyed. How undependable the girl was! He picked up the newspaper and impulsively set out for Sarala's house.

It was afternoon but the sun was nowhere to be seen. Clouds still filled the sky, heavy and brooding. Though showers had seemed imminent all day, it had not rained. Carrying the newspaper in his hand, Gopalakrishnan went up the street in the direction of the temple. Against the dull sky, the newly painted gopuram over the entrance of the temple was vivid. The tower was not tall but the fresh colors — the new coats of red and green and blue paint — had breathed such life back into the statuary of the gopuram that it seemed very impressive to Gopalakrishnan. Directly above the lintel of the temple's door, forming the base of the gopuram, was a representation in stone of Parvati in her incarnation as Meenakshi, standing next to her consort, Shiva, in his guise as the decently clad Sundareswarar. No matted hair, no tiger skin around his waist, no snake around his neck. This was Shiva the Beautiful, not the ash-covered ascetic God of the Cremation Ground, nor the God of the Dance of Destruction. It was Shiva in his domestic guise, standing tranquil by his wife, Parvati. Above these statues of Meenakshi and Sundareswarar the gopuram rose in stories and was decorated with divine apsaras in attendance on the central deities of the temple and fierce dvarapalas guarding the entrance to the abode of the gods.

Gopalakrishnan knew the temple was small, the gopuram modest, its statues crudely made. He had visited the immense Meenakshisundareswarar Temple in Madurai many times. How could this little village temple compare to that temple, with its hall of a thousand pillars, its innumerable finely made statues, and its many majestic, brilliantly colored gopurams thrusting high into the sky? This village temple was but a humble echo. Nevertheless, a simple pride stirred within Gopalakrishnan at the sight of the renovated gopuram, evidence that this village temple was not entirely without resources. The fields and gardens bestowed upon the temple centuries before by the Naicker chieftain to whom the village had once belonged were mostly intact. The annual revenue from these fields, supplemented by the donations of the rich landowners of the village, was enough for the day-to-day needs of the temple, its priest, and his assistant. In addition, the children and grandchildren of the village had in more recent years scattered to the many corners of the world — not only to cities like Madras, Bombay and Delhi, but to New York and London and Singapore. From the more prosperous of these scattered progeny a steady stream of donations and endowments accrued to the temple. It was because of one such donation, from a devout businessman who had settled in Dubai, that the gopuram was renovated.

A white Ambassador car came up the narrow street leading to the temple, forcing Gopalakrishnan to stand aside. In the backseat of the car were a man, a woman, and two children. The car went slowly past him and halted in front of Narayan's house. Probably Narayan's son and family, Gopalakrishnan thought to himself, home for a few days for Diwali, which was only a week away. Too bad Suresh was not coming for the holidays. How could the grand festival be the same without Suresh there to light the many lamps with which the thinnai would be adorned? Who would eat the mountains of sweets and savories Parvati would cook? So thinking he climbed the steps to the thinnai of Sarala's house. The plan of the house was roughly similar to Gopalakrishnan's — a courtyard around which rooms were scattered, and at the back two yards, one with a well and the other with cow stalls. But these stalls, unlike Gopalakrishnan's, still had cows in them. The house too was more splendid than his. Sarala's father, Mani, was one of the biggest landlowners in Paavalampatti. He was among those few Brahmin landowners of Meenakshisundareswarar Temple Street who had not sold all their lands in the years after independence. Those who had had done so for a variety of reasons ranging from children who had left for the cities to opposition to upper caste landownership. Mani had remained resolute against all such challenges.

Gopalakrishnan pushed open the front door of Mani's house and saw at once that Mani was entertaining friends. On the floor of the front veranda between the thinnai and the house proper had been placed a brightly colored jamakaalam of alternating purple, red, and green bands. On this thick cloth sat Mani and his friends, under the benign influence of a table fan on a stool. Vasu was there, and Neelakantan, and also — to Gopalakrishnan's surprise — Sundaram, the man who lived by himself in the last house by the trail to the river.

Sundaram was an anomalous character in the village. As far as Gopalakrishnan could remember, he had been in the village most of his life, but he was not married and had no children. Few people, and then only the very eldest, could remember his parents. He owned no land and how he subsisted was not entirely clear to Gopalakrishnan. Many an evening he was to be found in the temple, where he would sit silently, leaning against one of the pillars in the portico, in front of the sanctums in which the Shiva lingam and the idol of Meenakshi were housed. His bony hands clasped in his lap, he would watch with great sad eyes as the village girls came in groups, giggling, and the boys came after, shy and awkward, and as the men and women gossiped. He would watch as the devotees prayed and genuflected and circumambulated the deities, or as they waited for the bare-bodied priest in his white veshti to bring the sacred flame to them so they could touch it and then lift their fingers to their eyes to let the flame's power pass into them. Never had Gopalakrishnan seen Sundaram make obeisance to the deities himself. A quiet air of melancholy hung always around him as he sat in the portico of the temple. He was so quiet and uncommunicative he was something of a mystery to Gopalakrishnan. He made him uneasy.

Sundaram was, by ten or fifteen years, the oldest of the four men gathered in Mani's house. The others were all roughly of Gopalakrishnan's age. Mani, Vasu, and Neelakantan were playing cards. Sundaram was sitting quietly by them. Over this little party, the metal fan turned its head from side to side. With Diwali only a week away daily routines were suspended; it was a time for relaxation and celebration, for playing cards and gossiping late into the night with friends, for shopping for bright new clothes and visiting relatives.

"Come in, come in," Mani called out, when he saw Gopalakrishnan hesitating at the door. He was a well-built man with a broad, handsome face. "Come join us." He patted a vacant spot on the jamakaalam. "Shall we deal you in?"

Reluctantly, Gopalakrishnan stepped across the threshold. He had intended only to deliver the newspaper. He wanted to get to his study of the Ramayana as quickly as he could. Ramdas, the harikatha man, had been engaged to read from the Ramayana of Kamban on the day before Diwali. That was only six days away. Ramdas, who had taken that name because of his great devotion to Rama, was famous throughout the district of Thirunelveli because of the skill and passion with which he recited the Ramayana and commented on it extemporaraneously. Any old harikatha man could recount the story of the Ramayana; after all, that was his job. But Ramdas was special. Such was the widely held opinion. Gopalakrishnan, however, did not agree with the consensus. That was why there was much to prepare before Ramdas came. Gopalakrishnan wanted to show Ramdas up, to reveal that his erudition was not really erudition and his skill at recitation only empty verbal gimmickry.

"I came to give you the newspaper," Gopalakrishnan said, holding it out to Mani.

Mani looked surprised. "There was no need," he replied. "I have my copy here." And sure enough, next to Mani on the jamakaalam lay the exact same newspaper Gopalakrishnan held in his hand. Well!

Mani saw the expression on Gopalakrishnan's face and said, "I should have sent Sarala to you to let you know I got my own copy. Let it be. You are here now. It is good you came. You must join us in our game." He tilted his head back and shouted at the top of his voice, as if to some personage up in the sky, "Sarala! Sarala! Bring tea for Gopu Uncle!" Gopalakrishnan noted the four steel tumblers of tea and the little tray of muruku and maladoo by the men on the jamakaalam.

Vasu added his exhortation to Mani's. "Come, come," he said, his sagging cheeks stretching in a smile of encouragement. "Come join us in a game." He patted the vacant spot on the jamakaalam with one plump hand while with the other he delicately lifted a maladoo from the tray and deftly put it whole into his mouth.

Gopalakrishnan could not refuse. Parvati had already complained to him many times that the neighbors in Meenakshisundareswarar Temple Street viewed him as aloof and superior — just because he had gone away to Delhi and did not show the nosy interest in the lives of his neighbors that they did in his! Nevertheless, if he refused the invitation now, it would be like pouring oil on the fire of their resentment. He seated himself on the vacant spot on the jamakaalam and asked without much enthusiasm, "Are you playing rummy?"

Vasu quickly explained the rules they were following and dealt the cards, each of which had on the back a picture of a beautiful woman dressed in a sarong. Gopalakrishnan knew how to play rummy but was otherwise not much of a card player. He picked up his thirteen cards and looked at them without interest. He shifted the cards, arranging and rearranging them. He had to have what was known as a natural sequence. That was one of the rules. He frowned at his cards and rearranged them again. He felt confused. He took a card from the pack, then couldn't decide whether he needed it. He discarded it hurriedly when he saw that Mani, Vasu and Neelakantan were waiting impatiently for him to play. Mani, whose turn was next, picked up the card immediately. And when Mani pounced again on the very next card Gopalakrishnan discarded, Vasu demanded, "What is this, Gopu? You are feeding Mani cards? You have decided you want to make him win?"

Gopalakrishnan was preparing an appropriate retort when Mani threw down a card upside down to close the game. "I think I have won," he said. He showed the other players the cards in his hand, arranged neatly in the patterns specified in the rules. Gopalakrishnan, Vasu, and Neelakantan counted up their negative points.

"We are playing for money, you know," Vasu said with a sly smile meant for Gopalakrishnan. He produced a pencil and a notepad to make a note of who had won and lost how much in this round. Gopalakrishnan had lost the most — he had not been able to produce even one sequence out of his cards. "I didn't know we were playing for money," he protested.

"By the time we are done playing, Mani will have your bank account, your house, and the shirt on your back," Vasu said.

Mani laughed at the dismay on Gopalakrishnan's face. "He is playing the fool," he said to Gopalakrishnan. "We are not playing for money."

Mani's hair was gray, but the skin of his face had a smoothness that belied his sixty-five years. He had aged well. He was a man of some power in the village, and indeed in the district as a whole.

With regard to Mani, Gopalakrishnan often remembered what Ganapathy had once told him when Gopalakrishnan had commended him on his particularly good portrayal of a powerful village landlord in a play. Power, Ganapathy had said, coarsens the features of some people. These are the people for whom power is an intoxication. For other people, power is a means to an end. In the faces of such people there is intelligence and also conviction. For still others, power is a burdensome inheritance; you recognize their faces by the listlessness and petulance in them. And then there are those others who, while powerful and competent, have no ambition. Such people are able to make the exercise of power seem ordinary, benign. As an actor, Ganapathy had said, he had first asked himself to which category the character he was playing belonged. After that, assuming the facial expressions and mental habits of such a person was no longer difficult. The rest quickly fell into place.

Gopalakrishnan had teased Ganapathy for the turgid response to his simple compliment, but the impressive words had stuck in his mind (how insightful Ganapathy could be!). He found himself recalling them often when he encountered men of power. Mani, Gopalakrishnan felt, was of the last kind. He was one of the wealthiest men in the village, had always been one of the wealthiest. Paavalampatti was not large and in the grand scheme of things, perhaps, Mani's wealth was not extraordinary. But the authority that his wealth gave him in the village was as concrete and real as the black umbrella that he always carried with him on his tours through his fields and gardens. Ostensibly the umbrella was there to protect him from the sun and the rain. Really it was a symbol of his omnipotence, well recognized as such by the men, women, and children who toiled for him. All his life he had dealt with the lives of countless such workers. It was true he had a reputation for being calculating and strict, but then again Gopalakrishnan had never heard any stories of his unreasonable cruelty. No doubt the times had changed. It was no longer easy for wealthy landowners to behave in the kind of tyrannical ways they often had when the British were still in the country and needed the help of upper-caste landowners to govern. On the other hand, oppressive landowners had certainly not disappeared. Every second week Gopalakrishnan seemed to read a story about exploited bonded laborers in some part of the country or the other. It seemed to Gopalakrishnan at least a little to Mani's credit that he had kept up with the times so well. Of course he had never consulted the people who worked for Mani in arriving at this opinion. Would they credit Mani the way he did? It had never occurred to him to ask them.

Mani's wealth had been inherited from his father, and though he had done little to augment it he had not allowed it to erode either. Like his father before him, he sat on Meenakshisundareswarar Temple's governing board, which was comprised of the richest and most influential men of the village. He was also one of the most important patrons of the Paavalampatti Bhajan Society, which was separate from the temple but had a close association with it. One of the rooms in the temple had been given over to the society's use. At various times of the year the society organized religious discourses, dances, and performances of bhajans and other kinds of devotional songs. It was this society that had organized a festival of events on the three days before Diwali. The first day of the festival was given over to bhajans. On the second day the young men of the village had been persuaded to do some dances. On the third day, as a grand climax to the festival, Ramdas would speak.

Sarala appeared with the tea her father had called for. When she bent to place the tumbler of tea on the jamakaalam next to him, Gopalakrishnan saw that she had been painting her toenails when her father had interrupted her with his shout. Below the hem of her green sari, half her toenails were polished a bright pink. When Sarala was gone, Vasu said, "Gopu, is Suresh coming home for Diwali?"

"No," Gopalakrishnan replied. "He is drowning in work. When you have a successful business that's the way it is. You are working all the time. His partner is useless, lazy, doesn't contribute anything. I have tried explaining this to Parvati many times. She is upset that Suresh isn't coming home for Diwali."

"What business does he do?" Neelakantan wanted to know.

Neelakantan was a relative of Gopalakrishnan, a distant cousin on his father's side. Though Neelakantan's ancestral house was in the village, his father had worked as a health inspector first in the British colonial administration and then under the independent Indian government. The family had gone with the father to various postings all over South India. Neelakantan was a civil engineer by training, and for most of his life had worked in that capacity in Calcutta and then Bombay for a large company owned by Marwaris. He had come back to Paavalampatti after retiring from service. Until his own return to Paavalampatti a few months before, Gopalakrishnan's encounters with Neelakantan had been restricted to such communal occasions as weddings.

"Suresh is in the construction business," Gopalakrishnan told Neelakantan. "His business is doing really well now. At any one time he might be building three or four big apartment buildings. He writes to me in detail about his business, but who can keep track of all that he is involved in?"

"Is he a civil engineer then?" Neelakantan wanted to know. Neelakantan's front teeth protruded a little, giving his face a permanent expression of naiveté. Now he was tapping his protruding teeth with a fingernail as he studied the cards in his hand and waited for an answer.

Why was Neelakantan asking all these questions? Gopalakrishnan felt hot. He was sitting close to the fan but it did not seem to help. He checked to see if the fan had been set to its highest speed. It had. The black knob on the base of the fan was turned to 3; the blades were a blur. Still the air around Gopalakrishnan seemed to be hardly moving. What was behind this interrogation? At first Gopalakrishnan could not figure it out, and then it occurred to him that the questions might be motivated by the idea of hitching Suresh up with Sarala — everyone seemed to be intent on marrying Suresh off to Sarala! Of course, Gopalakrishnan decided, that was the reason. It had to be.

"Who needs a civil engineering degree to run a construction business these days?" Gopalakrishnan said to Neelakantan. "You need business acumen. You need connections. Civil engineers you can always hire." He felt pleased with his answer, with the subtlety with which he had woven into it an admonition of Neelakantan.

A new round of cards was dealt. The players returned their attention to the game. Sundaram sat quietly through the rounds of rummy with his head bowed and his long legs stretched out along the floor. Mani, Vasu, and Neelakantan did not seem bothered by him, but Gopalakrishnan found his presence discomfiting and did his best to ignore him.

Meenakshisundareswarar Temple Street was a close-knit community — a variety of intimate and not so intimate connections bound Gopalakrishnan to his Brahmin neighbors. Mani was not a relative like Neelakantan, but Gopalakrishnan had gone to school with him and in the decades after his departure from Paavalampatti had seen him every time he had returned on a visit. Gopalakrishnan knew Mani well, yet he did not consider him a friend. Friendship for Gopalakrishnan meant a heft, a substance, he did not feel in his relationship with Mani. Gopalakrishnan had once felt that heft — a deep and thoughtless familiarity — in his friendship with Ganapathy and felt it still when it came to Murthy, but it was his frank opinion that he and Mani, whom he had known longer than virtually anyone else in his life, had grown into very different people over the years. Mani had stayed in the village, and he had gone far away to Delhi. He had had so many more experiences than Mani could ever have had. How could they not grow into different people?

With Vasu, there was not even that shared memory of childhood. Vasu had not grown up in Paavalampatti. He and his family had come to Paavalampatti from a neighboring village a few years after Gopalakrishnan had left for college in Madras. He too owned land, though nowhere near as much as Mani. He had a degree in law and for a few years, during a period in his life long ago when he had not had much money, he had reluctantly practiced in a modest way, maintaining a poor little office in Thirunelveli Town. Then his three sons had grown up and gone away to work in lucrative jobs in different cities. The meager income from his land and his savings, supplemented by the support of his sons, was more than adequate for the life he led with his wife in the village. He decided he did not need to maintain his wretched practice as a lawyer anymore. His difficult years were over. Gopalakrishnan felt Vasu's improved station in life had made him brazen. He was not one to begrudge anyone his good fortune but he did not like the familiarity with which Vasu spoke to him.

After the fifth or sixth round of rummy, Gopalakrishnan decided he had wasted enough time playing cards. He cleared his throat meaningfully, looked at his watch, and said, "Is that what the time is? Have to get back home."

Vasu was gathering up the cards to deal them again. He looked across at Gopalakrishnan as he shuffled the cards, the sly smile Gopalakrishnan found so obnoxious stretching his drooping cheeks, and asked, "Off to study the Ramayana?"

It was the same question Vasu had asked that morning, when he had hailed Gopalakrishnan on his return from his walk. On hearing it now, Neelakantan made a strangled sound — the sound of a chortle being swallowed. Mani looked away with a studied expression. Sundaram lifted his bowed head and gazed straight at Gopalakrishnan, his eyes like searchlights, as if waiting intently for his answer. Gopalakrishnan had no intention of responding. He got up hurriedly from his place on the jamakaalam, mumbled an excuse about Parvati, and left. Walking back down the street to his house, he felt annoyed. The whole village seemed to have found out that he was engaged in a deep study of the Ramayana. How ever had the news got out?

The secret — now erstwhile secret — study of the Ramayana that Gopalakrishnan had embarked upon was because of Ramdas, who had come to Paavalampatti earlier in the year for a performance of harikatha. He had been brought by the Bhajan Society on the occasion of Ramanavmi to contribute to the festivities celebrating the birth of Rama with his recitations and commentary. This year, Ramanavami had fallen on a blistering hot day in March.

Gopalakrishnan had been there when Ramdas had spoken that day in the room of the Bhajan Society in the temple. He had been very displeased with what he had seen and heard on numerous counts.

Ramdas's long hair, neatly combed behind his ears, had a touch of white in it. Behind the severe black frame of his glasses, folds of tired flesh engulfed his eyes. Despite the white hair and the sagging flesh, however, Ramdas's manner was decidedly youthful. He was dressed in shirt and trousers of a fashionable cut. He read from the Ramayana of Kamban in an ostentatious and mannered voice. He peppered his commentary with English words and sentences and made what many members in the audience seemed to consider amusing and apposite references to contemporary events and issues. He was not at all conventional. Gopalakrishnan was not in the least impressed.

Ramdas had chosen for his address the passage from the Ramayana of Kamban describing the test by fire of Sita. Perhaps the fiery sun had put him in mind of the episode in which Sita proves her chastity after the great war that concludes the epic. Rama, the divine king in exile, defeats Ravana the Enemy and releases his beloved wife, Sita, from Ravana's clutches. But has his wife been chaste during the time she was held captive by Ravana? She proves her loyalty by jumping into fire and coming out unscathed. Ramdas's commentary on this passage did not stick solely to the account in Kamban. He noted that other poets had given alternative endings in which Sita is tested not immediately after the war, but only after Rama and Sita return home to Ayodhya. A time of peace and justice should have followed their return. Instead, incited by rumors circulating among the subjects of his kingdom, Rama demands, in one of these alternative endings, that Sita prove her chastity — prove that she had not had an "affair" (Ramdas had used the English word!) with Ravana during all the years she had been the enemy's captive. Just as in Kamban, she was to do this by jumping into fire. If she was pure, Fire, the great purifier, would leave her unharmed. If she was not . . . Well, the consequences were not described, Ramdas had observed with an exaggerated shudder, and then he had paused — Gopalakrishnan had found the pause quite unseemly — to let the imagination of his audience simmer a little with the thought of an impure Sita in the fire.

Ramdas continued with his discourse. What modern politician, he had asked with a sad expression on his face, was as eager to listen to the opinions of the people as Rama had been? Modern politicians made long speeches about democracy but all the time they were thinking only of deflowering young women. Which one of them was so attentive either to his "constituency" (again Ramdas used the English word here) or to the virtue of women? And so he went on and on, commenting on the passage from Kamban he had read, on the alternative accounts from other poets he had mentioned, weaving in references to not only politics but cricket and movies, intent on demonstrating to his audience the relevance of the supreme and divine Rama in contemporary times. His voice moved in and out of his ideas with practiced ease, rising swiftly for gravity or anger, falling abjectly when modest or in doubt. His voice made a shimmering dance of his devotion to Rama.

At the beginning of the harikatha meeting, Gopalakrishnan was bored. He had come more out of curiosity than religious feeling. He was not devout in the way that other of his neighbors at the meeting were. He did not expect to be illuminated about the Ramayana. He knew the stories of the Ramayana well, had grown up with them, breathing them in almost as if they were an element in the very air around him. He did not believe in the stories of Rama as religious scripture. How well he remembered the long discussions that Murthy, Ganapathy, and he would have on just such topics when they lived together in Delhi! He always found himself siding with Murthy against Ganapathy. No, stories like the Ramayana might very well be interesting, they might even be considered grand epic stories, but they could not be regarded as scripture. How absurd the very idea was. It was tantamount to regarding the *Iliad* or the *Odyssey* as religious scripture! Of course Ganapathy had disagreed with these arguments Murthy and he had made. But he too, Gopalakrishnan felt confident, would have been aghast at Ramdas and his interpretations. Had he not made fun of religious zealots of just the kind that Ramdas clearly was? Ganapathy was religious, but he was no zealot.

The day was drawing toward evening and soon the sun would be setting. Even so the heat was enervating. The two ceiling fans in the room futilely stirred the air over the gathered crowd, mostly the people of Meenakshisundareswarar Temple Street. It was rare for people in other parts of the village to come to the events organized by the Bhajan Society. Looking around at the people sitting on the spread-out jamakaalams beneath the pictures of gods and goddesses on the walls (the Rama illustrations had been removed from their usual locations and placed more prominently at the head of the room), Gopalakrishnan realized how old the population of the street had become. The younger people had left to work in the cities. Many came back on visits but few lived in Paavalampatti any longer. He knew Suresh would never live in Paavalampatti. In twenty or thirty years there would be no Brahmins left in Meenakshisundareswarar Temple Street. He was turning this novel thought over in his mind when his attention was drawn back to something ridiculous Ramdas had just said. He thought irritably to himself: And what does it matter if none are left? Look at these people gathered to hear Ramdas. Look at how they are listening to his presentation of the Ramayana as scripture!

Gopalakrishnan was not so naïve as to expect the Ramayana to be presented as anything other than devotional text. Religious interpretations were what one got at such a meeting. How ever could he be surprised by that? But to have Ramdas — with his fashionable shirt and modish glasses no less! — burst frequently into English and misrepresent the Ramayana, that was something else altogether. Gopalakrishnan couldn't speak to the different versions of the Ramayana Ramdas had mentioned, but Sita's test by fire was one of the most famous episodes of the Ramayana of Kamban. Gopalakrishnan knew it well. He had heard the story many times from his mother and his grandmother. He had always been taught to understand the episode in the exact opposite way to Ramdas. Surely everybody knew — Ganapathy certainly did, Gopalakrishnan reminded himself — that the episode showed Rama's frailty, his human limitation. It was evidence of the fallibility of Rama and the flaws that came with his human garb. Even if Rama was to be regarded as an avatar of the Supreme Being, in his human and mortal condition on earth he too was susceptible to the vagaries and prejudices that came with being human. Rama was not to be commended for making the innocent Sita jump into the fire. He was to be criticized and recognized as human. Everybody, even those who regarded Rama's story as scripture, knew that. Or so Gopalakrishnan had always thought; for if that was indeed the case then why was his frail, white-haired, usually hard-of-hearing mother, sitting next to him at the meeting, nodding her head so vigorously at Ramdas's strange interpretations? How uproariously she was laughing at Ramdas's limp witticisms! Gopalakrishnan was astonished at her behavior and the behavior of the others in the room. He had begun the meeting bored. By the time Ramdas's discourse had ended, he was casting disbelieving and irate looks at his neighbors. Look how they sat listening raptly to this charlatan fluff up with his wrong words what was after all only a story!

After Ramdas had finished, Vasu, who was the secretary of Paavalampatti Bhajan Society, stood up and said, "All of us will agree no one has ever come to Paavalampatti and read the Ramayana and told us about the greatness of Rama like Ramdas-Sir. His every word is gold. When he agreed to come I was so happy I did not know what to do. And now that he has come and given us his golden words, I feel so rich. Now I know why he is so famous. Ramdas-Sir, I want to thank you. Tell me, do you have some time? Can we speak about your wonderful words a little bit?" — Ramdas inclined his head magnanimously — "Yes, Ramdas-Sir has agreed to stay a little longer. If people have anything to say about the marvelous things we have heard, let them say it."

Gopalakrishnan lowered his head and tried not to listen. The questions and admiring comments that followed only encouraged Ramdas to expand upon the interpretations Gopalakrishnan had found so ridiculous. Ramdas gently swayed back and forth as he sat cross-legged on the mat specially spread out for him on the floor and steadily expounded on his earlier remarks. Gopalakrishnan lowered his head some more. Soon his head was in his hands. Once or twice, as he listened to the glowing praise of Ramdas, a challenging remark almost escaped his lips. He fought heroically to restrain himself. Vasu was preparing to bring the meeting to a close when he finally found himself yielding. Goaded by an especially gratuitous comment, Gopalakrishnan lifted his head and demanded of Ramdas in a quiet but clear voice, "Tell me. If someone asked you to jump into fire, how would you like it?"

The question was so preposterous the room grew immediately quiet. Parvati, who was sitting next to Gopalakrishnan on the other side from his mother, turned a horrified face toward him. Ramdas searched through the room to identify the person who had asked such an impertinent question. Gopalakrishnan and Ramdas were not far from each other and Gopalakrishnan could see very clearly the speculative look in Ramdas's eyes as they finally settled upon him. Who is this man? Ramdas seemed to be asking himself. The moment hung taut between the two of them. The room waited to see how it would break, to which side it would fall. Slowly Ramdas raised his right hand above his head, paused theatrically, and declared, his eyes behind his glasses fixed on Gopalakrishnan, "Whoever has faith in Rama is Sita. I too am Sita." There was brief applause from one or two people in the room. A shadow of triumph passed over Ramdas's face before he looked away from Gopalakrishnan. As if in relief, the room broke out once again into noise and motion. There was no need for Vasu to conclude the meeting. People began dispersing on their own.

Gopalakrishnan felt mortified. He stood up. Mani, who was across the room talking to one of his neighbors, caught his eye and nodded to him. One or two others also smiled and nodded. Were they pitying him? Were they saying it's all right, we forgive you? he wondered. Gopalakrishnan noted that Parvati was making a point of talking to people as they left. He felt uncomfortable waiting for her. He wished he had not made his remark. Outside, the sun had almost set. The gray of dusk was rapidly deepening into the black of night. Lights had already been switched on in one or two houses.

He, his mother, and Parvati walked silently back to their house. As soon as they were back at home, Parvati turned furiously to reprimand Gopalakrishnan for his question.

"But he knew nothing about the Ramayana," Gopalakrishnan responded peevishly. "He was talking so much rubbish."

"Let him say what he wants to say. If you don't agree with him, you can take it in through one ear and let it out the other. If there are ten people in the world, they will look at the same thing in ten different ways."

"You agreed with him," Gopalakrishnan accused her, a hurt expression in his eyes. "And Amma, when it is convenient to her, can't hear anything, but at the meeting she was nodding her head so much I was afraid it would fall off."

If Gopalakrishnan's mother had heard, she did not indicate that she had.

Parvati groaned and said, "How do you know I agreed with him? How do you know everyone else did? One or two people make remarks praising Ramdas and you think everybody agrees with him. That is the difficulty with you. You think no one understands anything except you."

The matter of Ramdas did not end there. More because of Parvati than from conviction, Gopalakrishnan had signed up as a member of the Paavalampatti Bhajan Society by paying the requisite amount of money. Sometimes, when he had nothing else to do, he attended the meetings of the society, which were held in its room in the temple. Few members came to these gatherings. It was at one such ill-attended meeting only a few weeks before, when a festival of activities to celebrate Diwali was being planned, that Vasu had suggested Ramdas be invited back. Gopalakrishnan's was the lone voice at the meeting to protest the idea. All his arguments were overruled one by one. Finally Gopalakrishnan had noted with exasperation, "But Diwali does not even have anything to do with Rama. It is when Krishna killed Narakasuran with the help of Satyabama, who drove his chariot for him. Ramanavami is the birthday of Rama. You invited Ramdas for that. Fine. That makes sense. Why would you call Ramdas to read from the Ramayana for Diwali?"

"Some people say Diwali is when Rama and Sita returned to Ayodhya after their exile," Vasu countered.

"Some people in the North say that. You know as well as I do that when we were growing up we were always told Diwali is about Krishna, Satyabama, and Narakasuran." He appealed to Mani, whose authority in the matters of the Bhajan Society tended to be final.

Mani said, "People should do what they want to do. I don't want to say anything about this. I don't even know if I will be able to come to the harikatha this time."

Vasu, who had never even lived in the North, then declared, "North, South, it is all the same. All the stories are our stories."

Despite Gopalakrishnan's protestations, it was decided Ramdas would be invited back to Paavalampatti for the grand climax of the festival on the day before Diwali. Gopalakrishnan resolved the same day that he would undertake a close study of the Ramayana of Kamban. Gopalakrishnan's dislike of Ramdas had been immediate and visceral; the gloating look on Ramdas's face at the end of his confrontation with him was imprinted indelibly in his mind. He would be ready for Ramdas when he returned. He would know the text of the Ramayana better than Ramdas. He would beat on the cracked drum of Ramdas's knowledge with such probing and well-informed questions that Ramadas's true nature would be quickly sounded out to all present. Of course, Gopalakrishnan would have preferred it if the whole village had not become privy to his plans. But that was the problem with a village. You never could keep anything to yourself.

The moment Gopalakrishnan came back from his visit to Mani's with the newspaper, Parvati said, "Look at what your mother is doing! Just go and see what she is doing." Her tone suggested she had been waiting impatiently for him to return. Parvati was standing in the dim light sifting down through the grill over the courtyard. Her hair was pulled back and tied into a bun, making her long face appear even longer in the half-light settling on her from above. Her arms were full of wet clothes. She was bringing them from the clotheslines in the backyard and transferring them to the aluminum rack that stood in one part of the veranda opening onto the courtyard. She did not want the clothes to get wet should it start to rain.

"Why? Where is she?" asked Gopalakrishnan, shutting the front door behind him. He felt weary just asking the question.

Parvati shook her head and continued on to the clothes rack with the burden in her arms. She had already relieved herself of the burden on her mind and had no intention of saying anything more on the topic. "Go and see for yourself," she said. "She is in the cow stalls."

Gopalakrishnan went reluctantly out to the back of the house, past the yard in which the bathroom and the well were located, to the little outermost enclosure, which had on one side the cow stalls and on the other the flush toilet his father had had built some twenty years before. When his father was getting ready to build the toilet, Gopalakrishnan had suggested that, for convenience, it should be inside the house. Paavalampatti Krishnaswamy Iyer's response to this suggestion was a stare that said, Look what you have become. A toilet inside the house? The very idea was filthy. So it had been built in the outermost enclosure. If it rained, they had to take an umbrella to go to the toilet. And if they wanted to use the toilet at night they had to open two doors — the door leading from the house into the yard with the well and the bathroom, and the door between this yard and the outermost enclosure. Safety was an issue. In the old days they had used chamber pots at night because of the very real threat of brigands. The times had grown more secure, at least in this village, and there were no chamber pots in the house anymore. Nevertheless, Gopalakrishnan did not like it if anyone wanted to use the toilet at night. He let it be known in no uncertain terms that once he had locked and barred the back door he did not intend to unbar it until the morning, just before he set out on his walk. If anyone complained, he pointed out that the man to be blamed was his father, whose willfulness had given rise to the inconveniently located toilet.

Of course, even the toilet's present location represented a compromise on the part of Paavalampatti Krishnaswamy Iyer. The outhouse that had preceded the toilet — it still existed though it was no longer in use — stood completely independent of the house, beyond even the little enclosure at the back, halfway between the back wall of the house and the trees. At least Paavalampatti Krishnaswamy Iyer had not demolished this outhouse and built the toilet there, at an even greater distance from the house. In the old days, when the outhouse was still in use, a sour smell had taken up permanent residence in it. Even twenty years later Gopalakrishnan could remember the smell well. It was a living thing, an invisible beast of great potency. Every morning the sweeper would come to collect the refuse and wash out the outhouse. After he was gone, strangely enough, the stench would be strongest, as if the sweeper, full of resentment at the job the world had thrust upon him, had deliberately roused the beast that had made the outhouse its lair.

The outhouse was a simple affair — four brick walls, no roof, no door, though the entrance had been veiled by extending one of the walls around it. Inside, a trough ran along one side; the residents of the house squatted over it to do their business. Once, as a boy, Gopalakrishnan had surprised his elder sister, Gauri. In a hurry, he rushed through the entrance to find Gauri perched over the trough with her long skirt lifted high over her hips. Both he and his sister had been at that awkward age of puberty. They looked at each other in surprise for a moment. Gauri's thick eyebrows drew together in shock. Gopalakrishnan turned quickly on his heels and hurried back out. The encounter was brief, it was nothing — he remembered only a flash of bare thighs and upturned face. Frankly, he had seen more on a number of other occasions. How could it be otherwise when he was still sharing a room with Gauri? There had even been an unsettling moment when he had glimpsed his sister in their shared room as she examined her emerging prepubescent breasts. The door had not been fully shut. Gauri was turning this way and that way in front of the mirror and stroking and feeling the breasts with an amused fascination. He had hurried away from the door only when he noticed his mother observing him with suspicion from a distance.

If Gopalakrishnan could be said to be at fault on that occasion, in the outhouse incident it was Gauri. Since the outhouse did not have a door, there were well-established rules governing its use. The metal pot of water and the soapdish that every patron carried were to be placed on top of the wall as a signal to others that the outhouse was in use. The rule was strict. The presence of the chombu and the soap tray was the only signal to the rest of the world that the outhouse was occupied. Gauri had neglected to put the chombu and soap dish on the wall. Her only explanation, when their mother heard them arguing about it later and quizzed them, was that she was in such a hurry she could not stop. She was unapologetic, which was not surprising for Gauri. What was surprising was Gopalakrishnan's mother's response. What use was mild scolding with a girl as incorrigible as Gauri? On the other hand, with Gopalakrishnan — her favorite, on whom she doted — she was severe, even furious.

Gopalakrishnan could not understand it. It was rare for his mother to reprimand him. Now she called him into the kitchen, gripped an ear between finger and thumb, and talked at him in an angry whisper, because she did not want his father to hear of the episode. "Have you no shame?" she hissed at him. "Is this how you behave with your sister? You are not children anymore. How many times have I told you to be more careful? How many times?" Her eyes, usually so soft, were as hard and black as sapota seeds. Her grip on his ear felt like the metal clamp she used to lower hot pots from the kerosene stove to the floor. He looked at her speechless.

Soon after that, Gopalakrishnan's mother made him move his bedding out to the interior veranda of the house. Henceforth he was to sleep there at night, and Gauri and his mother would sleep in the room that had formerly been his and Gauri's. The ejection had a bewildering effect on Gopalakrishnan. It confused him. He brooded about it for days. Why had Amma done this? How was it that he had fallen foul of her when he had not been at fault at all? He could not understand it. Amma usually favored him over Gauri, but now it was Gauri who was favored. What had changed? He felt himself unfairly treated, even abandoned. A part of him hoped he would be returned to his room when his mother's inexplicable anger cooled. His mother's anger did cool. How could she remain angry at her favorite? Nevertheless, Gopalakrishnan remained exiled. There was no redeeming return for him to the old arrangement. The room that had once been his became the "girls' room" now. At night, his mother disappeared into this room with Gauri. Gopalakrishnan's father too had his own room. Gopalakrishnan was left on the veranda feeling woefully alone.

Now, according to Parvati, Gopalakrishnan's mother was in the cow stalls. Gopalakrishnan did not need to be told what his mother was doing there. He could guess quite easily. Like the outhouse, the cow stalls were no longer in use. In the time of Gopalakrishnan's grandfather they had housed two prize cows that produced the creamiest milk in the village. They had stood white and tall, with brown eyes and wet, black lips, sometimes swaying from side to side as if they were tired and wanted to lie down. The scent of hay and milk and manure emanated from them. Before he became so grievously ill that he was confined to bed, his grandfather would milk the cows himself, his huge body hunched over as he squatted next to each cow in turn. As a boy, Gopalakrishnan had been transfixed by the way his grandfather moved his practiced hands rapidly under the cows. Sometimes his grandfather would beckon him closer and squirt a little of the warm, sweet milk into the cup of his hand. Gopalakrishnan would then quickly lower the tip of his tongue to lick up the milk before it all drained away to the ground.

Paavalampatti Krishnaswamy Iyer had sold the cows many decades before, when Gopalakrishnan's grandfather was sick and confined to his bed and too feeble to protest. Since then the stalls had become the repositories of odds and ends — a broken stool, a torn suitcase, a scratched and dented cricket bat (where had that come from?), a holdall from the old days of train travel. All the objects that had passed through the house and no longer had a proper place in it, all the forlorn objects that Paavalampatti Krishnaswamy Iyer wanted neither to keep nor discard outright, had migrated slowly into the stalls over the course of his long life.

Gopalakrishnan's father and his mother had fought many battles over the cow stalls. Gopalakrishnan's mother was one to throw things away, his father to hoard — not any and every thing but things that had once belonged to him, and that he had considered his. Paavalampatti Krishnaswamy Iyer may have been dead for nearly a year, but Gopalakrishnan's mother was still not finished fighting him over the cow stalls. Now that he was gone and could no longer overrule her she was determined to score a final victory. This was the reason she had been nagging Gopalakrishnan, ever since his return to the village, to clear out the stalls. To Gopalakrishnan the job seemed enormous and futile. Where would these objects be sent? To what use might the emptied stalls be put? Gopalakrishnan's mother had no answer to his reasonable if inconvenient questions, but that did not stop her from nagging him.

When Gopalakrishnan arrived at the back of the house, he saw that his mother had already moved things around in the stalls. Now she was trying to drag out planks of wood. Gopalakrishnan remembered that his father had bought these planks when the bathroom was being built. The planks had lain in the cow stalls for so long now, the pile had sunk so deep into the dirt, that the bottom-most plank was barely visible. Gopalakrishnan's mother was eighty-two years old and frail. Long gone was the strong but finely made, pretty woman who, when he was still a child, had lain with him on a mat on the floor on hot, drowsy afternoons and told him stories from the Panchatantra or of King Vikramaditya and the vampire. Why, then, was she here exerting herself so strenuously?

"Amma, what are you doing?" demanded Gopalakrishnan.

Gopalakrishnan's mother was dressed in a faded blue nine-yard sari. She had managed to drag one plank off the pile and out of the stall. The plank, green-black from its years in a dark and dank corner of the stall, looked quite disgusting in the sun.

"You don't need to be involved in this. Who called you? I can take care of all this myself," Gopalakrishnan's mother said, without turning around. She was lifting up another plank from the pile. Her thin arms shook from the effort.

Gopalakrishnan made her stop. "I told you I was going to do it," he said to her. "Why can't you be patient?"

"You have been saying you will do it for months. Are you waiting for me to die before you do it? How patient do you want me to be?"

This was his mother's new way of talking. Since her husband's death, she seemed to have suddenly discovered an interest in her own mortality. She liked to mention it every chance she got.

At first, Gopalakrishnan had been remonstrative. "Don't talk like that, Amma," he had said. "You will live a long time. People live longer and longer now. I don't want you to talk like that anymore. I don't like it."

To this his mother would say, "I will die soon. I know I will. Who wants to live a long time? Can I just live and live and live because you want me to?"

"Don't say that, Amma," Gopalakrishnan would implore. "I told you I don't like you talking like this."

"All right," she would say. "I won't do it." But in a few moments she would add, "Who can understand what old people go through?

Old people live in a country of their own. I won't live long. I know it. . . ." And so she would go on.

Gopalakrishnan saw that the more he expressed concern the more he encouraged her. Once or twice he even thought he could discern in her voice relish at his apparent distress. His suspicions made him wonder. So, more recently, he had begun to ignore his mother when she made these shocking references to her own death. Ignoring her was not easy for Gopalakrishnan. It was only a compromise between his desire to rebuke her for her suspected manipulation and his remorse at his base suspicions. Generally, Gopalakrishnan's mother took his silence as an invitation to provide a coda to her original comment.

This time, she said almost inaudibly, ruminatively, as if talking to herself, "I am at death's doorstep. Why should anyone listen to me? Parvati only has to ask you once to move something for her and you will go running to do it."

So that was what it was.

Standing by his mother, amid the detritus of his father's life, Gopalakrishnan made no comment. He understood now why his mother had come out to the cow stalls this afternoon. He silently lifted a plank off the pile and carried it out of the stall. It was heavy. How had his mother managed to move the one plank that she had? He placed the second plank on top of the first. He did not know why he was moving the pile out of the stall to a location just outside where it was sure to get in everybody's way even more. A line in English suggested itself to him, an echo of something half remembered, probably from all the reading and memorizing his father had made him do when he was still living at home in Paavalampatti. *It was not for him to reason why; it was for him to do or die*. How fitting. He was dredging up his father's beloved passages in his mind even as he was clearing out his things. He smiled grimly. His mother noticed his smile and said in a voice full of self-pity, "I'm a big joke to you. I know it."

It was too much.

Gopalakrishnan could not speak.

He moved another heavy plank, and another. His arms ached and he was sweating. His mother watched silently, squinting up at him from behind her thick glasses, which veiled her eyes. For some time now she had not been able to see properly. She had always been small, but age had shrunk her even more. Looking down on her as he moved the planks, Gopalakrishnan could see the patches of brown on her head where her scalp showed through her sparse white hair. He could not tell what she thought of his exertions on her behalf. He hoped she was happy. He would have been happier to leave the cow stalls alone, to let these dismal remainders from his father's life lie in their dark corner till this cycle of time had come to an end and Kalki came riding on his white horse. Did this old woman even care that he was going to so much trouble for her? He lifted another blackened plank and found that he was short of breath. His heart sounded in his ears like a loud drum. He let the plank fall back onto the pile and turned and spoke sharply to his mother, "You go inside. I might hit you with one of the planks by mistake." He felt so angry with his mother. To his surprise, she turned obediently and hobbled slowly back to the house. Gopalakrishnan lifted the plank again and carried it out to the growing pile outside. What was the point of all this? He shook his head at his foolishness. He counted the number of planks left. Two more. He would finish moving the pile and then stop. That should satisfy his mother.

The last plank was well and truly embedded in the mud. Gopalakrishnan had to strain to lift it up. He exerted himself on the small portion of the plank available to his fingertips. Finally the plank rose from the bed it had made for itself over the years. He thought he had found a secure grip on the plank's slimy underside when it suddenly slipped from his fingertips and fell with a clatter to the ground. He saw the underside of the plank was covered with a green and white ooze that had black flecks in it. Insects crawling around in the slime? Disgusting! His fury mounted moment by moment. That was it! No more meddling with the things in the stall. If his mother really wanted to clean out the stalls she would have to make some other arrangements. He could not do it, would not do it. He strode back to the house. When he entered, his mother was sitting on the floor outside the kitchen drinking her afternoon tea.

"Amma, I have done whatever I can with the cow stalls. I don't want to have anything to do with clearing them out anymore," Gopalakrishnan said to her.

His mother looked up at the sound of his voice and said, "What?"

Here we go, Gopalakrishnan thought to himself. Amazing how fickle Amma's hearing had become. One moment she heard everything perfectly and the next nothing at all.

Gopalakrishnan began to repeat sharply what he had said, and then he looked down at the shrunken figure seated on the floor, at the face small and shriveled because too many teeth had fallen out, at the bony hands nursing the tumbler of tea, and his anger ebbed. He looked away and said, speaking more loudly so she could hear, "I said I have done what I can for today."

"Yes, of course. What you have done is enough," his mother reassured him. "You can do some more tomorrow. Little by little you can finish it. Parvati has made you too tea. Go and get it from her."

Gopalakrishnan hurried into the kitchen to wash his hands and get his tea. Living with his mother was not easy. She had changed a lot after his father's death.

Death had been sudden. Paavalampatti Krishnaswamy Iyer had complained of dizziness and shortness of breath one day and the next morning he was dead. Even in death he had chosen a different path from his own father. Gopalakrishnan's grandfather had lingered, fighting his cancer year by declining year. Gopalakrishnan's father, who prized neatness and punctuality, met his death as if he had made an agreement with it, as if he had an appointment with it he could not dishonor. The cause of death was not clear. The doctor could best surmise that he had had some kind of heart attack in his sleep. What did the exact cause matter when the man was dead? As soon as Gopalakrishnan got the news in Delhi, he took a flight to Madurai and hired a car there to take him to Paavalampatti. He was in the village within a day, before even Gauri — coming only from Madras — had arrived. Parvati was to come later by train.

In Paavalampatti, Mani had already made all the arrangements for the cremation. It was summer and not advisable to delay. As soon as death was confirmed, the body had been removed from the bed and placed on the floor with the head facing toward the south, as custom required. It had been washed and dressed in a new veshti. Slabs of ice in buckets had been placed around it to preserve it in the heat. Gopalakrishnan could not tell whether it was the effect of death, the chill of the ice, or his own innate nature that had forced his father's familiar features into a permanent grimace. The lips were stretched thinly beneath the small, snub nose. The forehead seemed stiffened into a frown. At the appointed time, Mani and a few other men who were relatives lifted onto their shoulders the bed of bamboo sticks and stiff coconut fronds to which the body had been transferred. Slowly, they carried it out from the house in which Paavalampatti Krishnaswamy Iyer had lived virtually all his life — in which he had loved and hated, had known pettiness and worry, happiness and anger. The men and women who had gathered were quiet, as if quietness was the appropriate respect for a man of such few words. Gopalakrishnan's mother sat dry-eyed in the puja room. She had let it be known that she felt no need to look one last time at the husband with whom she had spent virtually her entire life. She had not emerged from the puja room even when it was time to put uncooked rice in the mouth of the body. The rice was an offering the living made to the dead. It was both a gift of farewell and an acknowledgement of continuing debt. But who among those gathered had the heart to compel the bereaved widow to do that which tradition demanded?

Slowly the men walked with the body to the cremation ground. If anything of Paavalampatti Krishnaswamy Iyer endured in the world, whether good or bad, it would endure with the people and things he left behind. It would endure with the wife who stayed in the house and with the son who accompanied the body on its final journey, carrying fire to light the pyre in a clay pot hanging from a rope. What was the body but that part of Paavalampatti Krishnaswamy Iyer that no longer had a place in the world? At the threshold to the house, where his wife and the other women remained by custom, the body began parting from the world in which it had done things and felt things. Now only the son with some of the male relatives, neighbors, and friends would escort the body to its final threshold in the cremation ground. There the son would light the pyre and a final door would open. Across this fiery threshold no son, no matter how loyal and loving, could go. Every body made its journey into death alone, leaving behind in the world only that part of its life that could be left with others. Everything else it took with it forever into that final silence.

Gopalakrishnan's mother was profoundly transformed by the death of her husband. Was the startling metamorphosis because of something Paavalampatti Krishnaswamy Iyer had taken with him into the fire of the funeral pyre? Or because of something he had left behind with his wife of more than half a century? Gopalakrishnan's mother herself would not have been able to say. She did not talk much about her husband's death. She did not wallow in her grief. She did not make an exhibition of it. Nevertheless, a subtle change began to manifest itself in her almost immediately and grew more and more pronounced as the days went by. When she wanted something (no matter how trivial; a trip to the temple in Thirunelveli, for example), she would brook no denial. If Gopalakrishnan hesitated, she would say, "Here I am, an old woman on the verge of death. You can't even do this small thing for me?" Certainly, Gopalakrishnan's mother had always had her own methods of getting her way, but the nakedness with which she pursued her own interest now was something new altogether.

Age had introduced numerous painful conditions into her body. She complained about them incessantly. If it was not her arthritic joints, then it was her ulcerous stomach; if not her ulcerous stomach, then the inflammation of her urinary tract. All day she spoke about her infirmities and ailments. She had had them before the death of Gopalakrishnan's father; now she found them so intolerable, they seemed to have taken over her life. It was as if with the death of his father, she too had stepped across a mysterious threshold of her own. Gopalakrishnan did not know what to make of the changes in her. In a matter of weeks it was hard to believe she had once been in charge of the whole house, that what became Parvati's kitchen when she arrived from Delhi had been hers.

It became evident to Gopalakrishnan in the weeks he stayed back after the cremation that his mother could not be left alone in the house. Gopalakrishnan went through his father's papers and found that his mother had the house and enough income to maintain herself in the village. Paavalampatti Krishnaswamy Iyer, ever a man of duty and order, had made sure that his wife would not lack for anything after his death. Under these circumstances Gopalakrishnan decided to find someone — someone like his cousin Lalitha, the indigent widowed daughter of his mother's sister — to live with her in the house. As it was, Lalitha was tossed unceremoniously from relative to reluctant relative; the arrangement would be mutually beneficial. Yes, that was the thing to be done, Gopalakrishnan decided. Lalitha would be brought to Paavalampatti.

Gopalakrishnan's mother was in the puja room, resting for a while, when he sought her out to present his idea to her. She had just finished praying. A faint smell of vibhuti and burned oil from the extinguished lamps hung in the air. She sat up on her mat to hear what her son had to say. She heard him patiently and then was forthright in telling him she detested his idea. She did not like Lalitha and would not countenance any arrangement that brought her to Paavalampatti.

"Then you have to come to Delhi," Gopalakrishnan replied, frowning. He was annoyed by her quick dismissal of his idea. From the shelves, the gods watched as Gopalakrishnan stood towering over his mother on her mat on the floor. It was afternoon. The village was quiet, so quiet Gopalakrishnan himself felt the loud weight of his every word bearing down on his frail mother. He paused and said, "There is no other way."

Gopalakrishnan's mother peered up at him from behind her thick glasses and said, "Why should I come to Delhi? You want to transport an old woman like me, already halfway to the cremation ground, all the way to Delhi. But you don't talk about coming back here. You have been retired for so many years now. Why don't you come here? What if I die on the trip to Delhi? Is that what you would like to happen to me? . . ."

Gopalakrishnan groaned inside. He stopped listening. By the time he made himself pay attention again, his mother was saying, "Listen to me, Gopu. If you don't want to come back here to be with your dying mother, I won't force you. Leave me here and go to Delhi. I will manage by myself. Just don't come to me with all this talk of my going to Delhi or Lalitha coming here. I may be old and dying, but I am not afraid to live by myself. After all the things that Lalitha has said about me behind my back, you want me to let her into this house? You don't know what she is like. She will treat me like her servant. That will never happen. If you can't come back home even for your dying mother, that is all right. I can manage."

And so, reluctantly, Gopalakrishnan was forced to consider the notion that he would have to move back to Paavalampatti. He did not like the idea, but what other option was there? It was true, he began telling himself, that life in Delhi after retirement was not easy. It was now more than five years since he had retired from service and every year his pension went less far than the year before. Alas, he had never been very good with money, knowing neither how to invest wisely nor how to accumulate wealth through frugality; and then there had been various amounts spent on Suresh over the years. He had not, like many of his more prudent colleagues in the civil service, bought a house in Delhi when it was still possible to do so. No longer in subsidized government housing, he was finding rents in Delhi had become exorbitant. Indeed, the very cost of living there had become outrageous. Paavalampatti was a village. His pension and his meager income from his savings would be a small fortune here. He would be able to live much more comfortably. Paavalampatti was changing he reminded himself. It was not like the old days. There was cable television now and he would have a telephone installed. Also, Parvati did not like Delhi. She would certainly be happy to leave and come to Paavalampatti.

Gopalakrishnan reasoned in this fashion until he had reached a conclusion. He then went to Parvati to share with her his idea of moving back to Paavalampatti. It was morning and she was by the bathroom in the backyard, getting ready for her bath. She had a towel in her hands and her gray hair was loose on her shoulders, making her look older than she was. "I don't think it's a good idea," she said after listening to him.

"Why?" Gopalakrishnan asked, surprised. "You are always complaining about Delhi, how you don't like it there. I thought you would like the idea of moving back to Paavalampatti."

"I don't care about Delhi. But what about Suresh?"

"What about him?"

"You want to leave him alone in Delhi?"

"Alone? He is twenty-seven years old, Parvati! You talk as if he is still a baby in your arms."

"So what if he is twenty-seven years old? You know how he is. Have you forgotten all the things he has done? All the trouble he has given us? You talk as if he is the most reliable of people. I don't think it is a good idea to leave him alone in Delhi. I am afraid of what he will end up doing."

"Suresh is the owner of his own business now. He and Aloke have made such a success of it. Suresh is not the way he was before. He is responsible. He knows how to take care of himself." Aloke Mishra was Suresh's partner in the construction business.

"Why can't Amma come to Delhi?"

"She is too old. She won't be able to adjust to Delhi. You know how it is there."

"Then let Lalitha come here to be with her. That way you can solve two problems in one go. Lalitha needs a place to stay and Amma needs someone to look after her. It is the obvious thing to do. That is a good plan." She looked pleased at having thought of it.

"Lalitha?" Gopalakrishnan said. "She can hardly look after herself. How will she look after Amma?"

"Lalitha is a very capable and good woman."

"I don't want to say anything about her as a person. All I know is she won't be able to stay here and take care of Amma." He threw up a hand to emphasize that he didn't want to talk about Lalitha anymore.

"I see you have already made up your mind," Parvati observed. "I will leave Delhi happily. I have no love for that place. All I know is this — it is not such a good idea to leave Suresh by himself in Delhi right now. His business is still new. What if he messes it up just as he has messed up so many things before? If he were married it would be different."

"Am I against his marriage? I would be happy to see him married. Don't mix up different issues here. The problem is you keep treating

Suresh like a child. That's what the problem is. It will be good for him if we are not there. He will become more independent."

To this Parvati made no reply.

"I am the one who should be unhappy," Gopalakrishnan said, annoyed at her silence. "I am not like you. I like Delhi. Who wants to live in a village?"

"I have told you what I think. You can do what you want now." With that Parvati went into the bathroom and shut the door.

"What do you want me to do, Parvati?" Gopalakrishnan asked her through the shut door. "You want me to leave Amma here alone, by herself?"

And so, a few months after Paavalampatti Krishnaswamy Iyer's death, Gopalakrishnan and Parvati wrought a cataclysmic change in their lives. They moved to Paavalampatti from Delhi.

Gopalakrishnan took his tumbler of tea — his second tumbler of the afternoon — from Parvati in the kitchen and went to his room. He set the tumbler down carefully on his desk amid the books with which the desk was burdened. The three red clothbound volumes were the original Tamil text of the Ramayana of Kamban edited by T. K. Chidambaranatha Mudaliar. Each volume contained two of the six books of the twelfth-century epic. He had found the volumes on his father's bookshelves, the pages yellowed and eaten by bookworms. His father had acquired them as a gift in 1953, soon after they were printed. On the title page of the first volume was an inscription to his father: "For Teacher Krishnaswamy Iyer — T. Shanmugam/Courtallam/1953." The first line was in Tamil, the second in English. Courtallam was a town not more than ten miles from Paavalampatti. The title page also indicated that the publisher was based in Courtallam. Gopalakrishnan found this interesting. Was T. Shanmugam connected to the publisher? Had his father then had some kind of association with this publisher in Courtallam?

Gopalakrishnan did not know the answer to these questions. What Gopalakrishnan knew was that Courtallam had a waterfall famous for its medicinal properties. Gopalakrishnan had been there many times. The town was not big: a little conglomeration of shops and houses under leafy trees and looming hills surrounded the waterfall, which fell in two tremendous torrents from a high cliff onto a rocky platform guarded by metal rails. Onto this platform crowded the people who journeyed to Courtallam for its healing waters, the men to one side under one torrent and the women on the opposite under the other. It had never even occurred to Gopalakrishnan that this little town was home to a Tamil-language publisher who had prepared a major edition of the original Ramayana of Kamban and with whom his father might have had a connection. What else did he not know about his father? Surely there were other such bits and pieces that would remain, forever, beyond his ken.

Ostensibly it was this edition of the Kamba Ramayana given to his father that Gopalakrishnan was now studying in preparation for the return of Ramdas. The language of the ancient epic was demanding and T. K. C., the editor, had helpfully annotated difficult words and interjected commentary of his own. Nevertheless, Gopalakrishnan had quickly discovered that after the many years of relative neglect in Delhi, when he had used it for little more than writing letters to his father, his formal Tamil was not adequate for the archaisms of the epic. It was fortunate for him then that the bounty of his father's bookshelves included an English translation of the Ramayana of

Kamban. The seven black hardbound volumes of this English translation — the last book of Kamban's epic, the Book of War, was in two parts — were also on the desk, rising in a neat pile by T. K. C.'s edition of the original Tamil. In addition, Gopalakrishnan had found on his father's bookshelves two English retellings of the Ramayana — one by C. Rajagopalachari, the other by R. K. Narayan. They too lay on the desk, next to the notebook he had bought in Ramu's store when he had embarked on this project of study.

The notebook — its cover, already peeling, depicted a smiling boy in shiny black shoes striding off to school with his canvas bag on his shoulders — was full of Gopalakrishnan's writing. Gopalakrishnan had begun by laboring through the original Ramayana in Tamil, but then he had quickly shifted to the shortened English retellings by Narayan (the easiest version of the Ramayana) and Rajagopalachari. Then he had read the English translation. It was only now that he was returning to the original. In the notebook he had copied passages, both in English and in Tamil, that he considered relevant. He had made notes to himself of thoughts that had occurred to him in his research.

Surveying the books on his desk, Gopalakrishnan felt discouraged. It was already late afternoon and he had not done even a moment's worth of work — not one single moment's worth! — on the Ramayana. All day it had been one thing after another. How could it be otherwise with two women like Parvati and his mother in the house? Only six days were left to the harikatha and so much remained to be done. The whole village knew of his elaborate preparations by now. He had no choice but to go through with his scheme. If he did not, Vasu and his friends would think he was afraid of Ramdas. No doubt Vasu had already informed Ramdas of Gopalakrishnan's preparations. A vision of Ramdas's gloating face congealed in Gopalakrishnan's mind. How bright Ramdas's eyes would grow behind the black-framed glasses when he saw Gopalakrishnan had not come to the meeting! How triumphant would be the glance Ramdas exchanged with Vasu!

The very thought of Ramdas and Vasu exulting in this fashion was galling. He was not afraid of Ramdas. Why should he be? Why should he ever fear a village charlatan like Ramdas? If he felt a certain anxiety about the approaching showdown, it was only because he had not been able to prepare properly. When he had embarked upon this plan of confronting Ramdas he had felt confident of himself. He would study the Ramayana of Kamban carefully and no doubt find all kinds of ways to tear Ramdas and his silly ideas to shreds. He had no doubt he was capable of doing this. But the lack of time was worrisome. Would he even be able to finish reading the Tamil original in the days left him? But then again maybe it was enough that he knew the essential story of Kamban's Ramayana in detail. He had known the story well before, and now, after reading through the various versions in English, he knew it even better. Perhaps there was no need to read Kamban all the way through in the original Tamil. Perhaps what he had done was sufficient.

An encouraging thought. No sooner had it suggested itself to Gopalakrishnan, however, than a memory of Ramdas reading passages out from Kamban's original text in his high-pitched voice arrived on its heels. Ramdas liked to read a passage — such an unctuous reading manner he had too — and then drop his attention heavily on a word or a line from which his commentary would proceed to spread outward like ripples from a stone thrown into a pond. When Gopalakrishnan remembered how smoothly Ramdas did this, he felt discouraged. There was no escaping it; a diligent study of Kamban in the original was required. But with Parvati and his mother in the house, where was the time? What foolishness had led him to think he would be ready for Ramdas? What had possessed him to think he could study anything, let alone Kamban, with two women in the house?

Gopalakrishnan's desk was under the window that opened onto the veranda on the street side of the house. Sitting at his desk, Gopalakrishnan could see into the street. A man went by on a bicycle, his white shirt gray with sweat. The chain of the bicycle made a harsh scraping sound that could be heard for a time after the bicycle itself had disappeared from view. Prakash, the son of a neighbor, went racing down the street in the opposite direction, shouting to someone to wait for him. Prakash was rowdy, mischievous, an eight-year-old boy with huge, intelligent eyes fringed by long curly hair that cascaded down his forehead. He reminded Gopalakrishnan of Suresh at that age. Gopalakrishnan could not see Prakash from his desk, but he could hear the unmistakable voice. A smile came to his lips when he recognized it. Agitated by Prakash's shrill passage through the street, a crow rose from its perch on the roof of the house opposite, hung in the air with its black wings outstretched for a long undecided moment, and then settled once again on its previous spot. Once again it cocked its head alertly, one eye looking down the street in the direction of the temple.

Gopalakrishnan tore himself away from these mundane happenings and returned his attention to the desk. He drew the notebook to himself. He had begun by laboriously copying passages he considered important into the notebook. He had quickly become bored with this and graduated to writing down questions and comments that occurred to him as he read. Pages and pages were filled with his ruminations on Rama's rigorous education by the sage Vishwamitra, renowned for his sternness. More pages concerned the character of Hanuman and other monkey allies of Rama, and other such commentary filled other pages. Gopalakrishnan went through the notebook to find the last thing he had written in it — "Rama is the perfect, obedient son. But what would he be like as a father? Would you want him as a father?" This was an interesting question; Gopalakrishnan was pleased with himself for having thought of it. He was not sure what, exactly, it — anymore than the other comments he had made to himself in his notebook — had to do with preparing for his confrontation with Ramdas, but it seemed to him a novel and intriguing question. In the epic, Rama was the eternal son, and also of course the eternal husband, but of him as father there was nothing. Gopalakrishnan was aware of the story of Lava and Kusa, the sons of Rama, but Kamban made no mention of this story in his epic.

Kamban began his epic with the adventurous boyhood of Rama in Ayodhya, his attachment to his younger brother Lakshmana, his training by the sage Vishwamitra, his winning of the lovely Sita by the tremendous feat of stringing the great bow of Shiva. He sang — even Gopalakrishnan, with his modest ability to read archaic Tamil, could recognize the music of his language — of how Dasaratha, his doting father, resolves to retire from the throne and leave Rama, his eldest son, king; how this news is greeted with rejoicing throughout Ayodhya. He described how there is gloom at this news in the palace of Queen Kaikeyi, for she is provoked by her maid Kooni, "the crooked," to view this turn of events as dire. Rama is the son of the queen Kausalya. Will he look to Kaikeyi's well-being when he is king? Thus sowing the seeds of familial discord, Kooni instigates Kaikeyi to remind King Dasaratha of his ancient promise of any two wishes she might have. Kamban suggests Kooni devises this stratagem because Rama as a child had once pelted her with mud balls. The drama, as the writers Gopalakrishnan had read pointed out, is human. With one wish Kaikeyi demands the exile of Rama to the jungle for fourteen years, and with the other the throne for her own son, Bharatha. Dasaratha, the doting father, is aghast. Rama, the ever-devoted son, renounces the throne and departs into exile with Sita and Lakshmana so that his father might be able to honor his word. Unable to bear this unexpected and tragic denouement, Dasaratha dies. And then Kamban told how Bharatha refuses the throne but Rama will still not return from exile, because he will not permit his father's word to be proven false; how Rama, Sita, and Lakshmana live in the jungle until Sita is abducted by Ravana the Enemy; how Rama, with the help of Hanuman the monkey and his monkey army, defeats and kills Ravana, frees Sita, and returns home to Ayodhya at the end of the fourteen years of exile, to rule as the perfect and most just king.

Kamban had portrayed Rama the prince, the brother, the husband, the warrior and (above all) the obedient son — but where in all this was Rama the father?

What kind of father, then, would Rama have made? Was there a clue to the answer in Rama the son? Rama was rather strict in his interpretation of his duties as a son. Could it not be said that he had put the honor of his father and the sanctity of his obligation as a son above his duties as a ruler? If he was the perfect king, did he not owe it to his subjects to ennoble their lives by his rule? Could the perfect son be the perfect king? What manner of father would such a son have made? Surely he would have demanded the same obedience of his children that he himself had so unthinkingly given his own father. But would he, in his turn, have been eager to involve himself in their lives? Or would he have been distant and duty-bound, coming home in the evenings to shut himself up with his books —

or rather, probably, leaf parchments in those days — in his library that grew shelf by shelf through the years? What demands would he, a man of such iron principles, have made of his children? What burdens would he have placed on their heads for the rest of their lives?

Questions, questions, questions. They might not have much to do with his preparations for the impending encounter with Ramdas, but they were good questions nonetheless. He felt them to be so. Gopalakrishnan added them now to his notebook, writing them on a fresh page with his Parker fountain pen (a gift from Murthy on the occasion of a promotion more than twenty years before). He was reading over with pleasure what he had written when the long hoot of a train sounded in the distance. The afternoon train from Thirunelveli Town. That meant it was past five. And so much work still to do! But he felt encouraged by his musings. He took up the first volume of T. K. C.'s edition of the Kamba Ramayana in the original Tamil to press on with his reading. He had already read almost to the end of the second book of the epic — the Book of Ayodhya — but when he opened the volume it fell open on a page from the first book — the Book of Boyhood. It was the early portion of the epic in which the poet describes the marvels of Ayodhya:

None were generous in that land as none was needy;
None seemed brave as none defied;
Truth was unnoticed as there were no liars;
No learning stood out as all were learned.

Perhaps Ayodhya long ago but not, certainly, Paavalampatti today, Gopalakrishnan thought. Especially the part about learning. With frauds like Ramdas about, learning in Paavalampatti stood out like the Taj Mahal next to a slum dweller's jhopadpati, like an elephant next to an ant. He flipped forward, trying to find his place in the volume. He had neglected to place a bookmark. He was eager to begin reading and felt impatient as he searched for his spot. The pages fell open on another passage from the description of Ayodhya, one he had marked with bold arrows in the margin when he had read it a few days before because he had been amused by it:

Some women in that bright city
Spent their time in flower gardens,
Sported fawn-like with young men,
Went out to bathe, drank toddy —
Their red lips pallid with the drink.

Fawn-like! How did one sport fawn-like with young men? He meant if one were a woman of course. How did one do that? He certainly had never been with a woman who had sported fawn-like with him.

Though . . . though there had been that one time in Delhi before his marriage to Parvati — fawns did not come to mind when he thought about it, really — when he had gone with Murthy and Ganapathy to a place . . .

It had happened on the first day of a monsoon season. A day when the rains had fallen from the sky with a thunderous, torrential clamor into a dry and desperate Delhi, the pelting rain like a fervent benediction over the aching city. In the cozy intimacy of the barsaati, a shirtless Ganapathy at the kerosene stove. The friendly crackle of frying pakoras. The smell of wet earth entering like a thief through the open window to mingle with the smell of frying oil and kerosene. Tea, boiled to that perfect state of pungency. Murthy and Gopalakrishnan lounging on the mattress on the floor.

The aimless talk. The comfortable silences. A bottle of whiskey that Ganapathy has magically produced. Three glasses. And in the corner Murthy's radio playing Hindi film songs with a rainy association—*Jiyaa bekaraar hai, chhaayee bahaar hain. Aajaa morey baalamaa, teraa intajaar hai*. Ganapathy in the center of the room now, twirling round and round and round, a ladle in his hand, singing along with the radio — "O come, O come, O come, my love. I am waiting for you, waiting for you, waiting for you" — *Tujh ko nazare dhoondh rahee hain, mukhadaa to dikhalaa jaa. Raste par hoo aas lagaaye, aanewaale aa jaa*. Ganapathy's paunch bounces up and down, his breasts flap from side to side. His yearning voice tries to keep pace with the radio — "My eyes are searching for you, show me your face before you go. I stand in the street full of desire; O come, you who are to come." Murthy's narrowed eyes. The thunder outside. The pouring rain. The darkening room as the rain draws its mantle of water closer and closer around the city. As the song ends, Ganapathy stretches a hand out in the direction of Murthy, his pliant flesh taut for the moment with longing.

Murthy laughs harshly, throws a pillow at Ganapathy. "What's the use of you?" he cries. "What's the use?"

Ganapathy smiles enigmatically and replies, "There are places I can take you." Silence. Murthy — and it is Murthy who must speak — says nothing. "Very discreet. Do you want to go?"

The sound of the rain. The smell of earth and pakoras. The radio. The gathering gloom. The bitter taste of whiskey in the mouth.

Suddenly, Murthy flings himself up from the mattress. "All right. Let's go. Let's do it."

The three of them hurry through the dark, wet streets under two umbrellas, Ganapathy under one and Murthy and Gopalakrishnan under the other. It is night now. In the light of the occasional streetlamp, the rain is white and ghostly. A taxi. They need a taxi. And they find one parked under one of the streetlamps, the rain undulating in the wind over the black and yellow car. They pour laughing into the back seat of the car, shaking their wet umbrellas on the floor. The dozing driver, reeking of beedis, comes awake. Ganapathy leans forward to tell him where to go. In the rearview mirror, the driver's bloodshot eyes are knowing. His thin lips spread in a smile. He ignites the engine and the taxi lurches forward eagerly. The tenebrous city speeds by. They pass the occasional hunched figure under an umbrella. They pass slum children dancing in the rain in the distance. They pass men gathered under the canvas awning of a shack in the yellow light of a hurricane lamp. The taxi passes through the broad avenues of New Delhi, the monumental buildings like shadowy etchings in the rain. They are heading into Old Delhi.

The taxi turns into a narrow lane, and into another narrow lane, and another, and another. Gopalakrishnan does not know this part of the city. Now Ganapathy is directing the driver. The car draws up in front of a darkened gate. A house set discreetly back behind bushes. A solid, respectable-looking house with curtained windows from whose edges light seeps out into the gloom of the wet night. The sound of laughing voices muted by the rain. Also, in the distance, a woman's voice singing, climbing octave by tantalizing octave to a place Gopalakrishnan has never been. Not the kind of house in which loud women stand at barred windows like animals in a cage. Gopalakrishnan has read about such houses full of loose women. He has been afraid they would go to such a house. Ganapathy motions with his hand that they are to wait in the car. He disappears through the gate. Murthy and Gopalakrishnan do not look at each other as they wait. The rain drums on the taxi incessantly. The driver takes out a beedi and lights it, filling the taxi with its acrid smell. With his bloodshot eyes he watches his two passengers steadily in the rearview mirror.

Ganapathy comes back. Everything is arranged. Everything is taken care of. Now the moment is upon Gopalakrishnan, the moment of decision. He doesn't want to go in, and for a moment he thinks Murthy doesn't want to either, but then Murthy suddenly gets out of the car and runs through the rain without an umbrella or a backward glance. Gopalakrishnan waits for a long moment and then follows with a dry mouth. He runs through the gate, past the fat guard in a kurta he has not noticed before because of the gloom, and up the path. The front room he enters is large and full of old bulky furniture. He and Murthy wait awkwardly inside the door. In the center of the room, a man sits on a faded green sofa with a woman. A faded carpet lies on the floor. On a table in front of the sofa stands a vase of pink plastic flowers. There is perfume in the air. The man is older with tired eyes, slicked-back hair, and a thin moustache very like Murthy's. The woman is older too and is wearing a lot of makeup. Her hair is done up in a fancy, film-y style. She holds a cigarette between two fingers, the smoke from it coiling and uncoiling in the air. Is this the woman? Gopalakrishnan feels frightened. He looks at Murthy but Murthy does not return his glance. Neither the man nor the woman on the sofa, lost in a whispered conversation, pays Murthy and him the least mind. Where is Ganapathy?

Then Gopalakrishnan sees the other women, the two young women — girls really, surely they can't be much older than girls? — standing in another part of the room. One of them steps forward now, gestures to him, and leads him down a corridor to a dimly lit room with a cot, a rickety wooden table, and incense sticks burning their heavy scent into the air. A crude painting of a lovelorn woman in a suggestive pose hangs on the wall over the cot. A ceiling fan turns above. The young woman who has led him to the room seats herself on the cot and looks at him, measuring him, assessing him. She looks as if she is from the Himalayan area, her eyes just a little slanted, her skin just a little paler. Her loose hair is parted in the middle. Two clips above the ears hold the hair back so that it falls neatly past the shoulders long and black and straight. She is dressed in a yellow sari of some thin, gauzy material. She is not pretty, but she is not at all what he had expected. She looks so fresh and young. He feels desire stir within him. She speaks to him invitingly. He is frightened. He has never been with a woman before.

She reaches out a hand and touches him on the back of his hand. She takes his hand in her fingers slightly damp with sweat and pulls him gently forward onto the cot, which is covered with a sheet of a design familiar to him. He has seen it in the textile shop near the clamorous vegetable market frequented by the housewives of the neighborhood in which he lives with his friends Murthy and Ganapathy. The woman has pushed off her clothing except her blouse. Her pale nakedness — her stomach, her arms, her thighs leading to the secret place he cannot bear to look at — shines in the dimly lit room like a beacon. She unbuttons his shirt, coaxes him out of his trousers with experienced fingers.

He is on top of her. He is frightened. He is inside her. It hurts. What is this that is gathering itself inside him to leap into the abyss? An involuntary moan escapes his lips. He wants and does not want to keep moving forward in the darkness. But then the edge is under his feet and he is falling, falling, falling. When it is over, he feels as if he has and has not done it, as if it is and is not he who has had unspeakable sex with an unnameable girl. He does not like how he feels, He lies for a long time on top of the girl, really no older than him and possibly much younger, and she is kind — or perhaps only well paid — and lets him lie there. His face is in her oiled hair. Now he can smell her in a way he could not before. She smells of coconut oil and fresh sweat and something else he cannot name. He feels her smell inside him, and though the feeling of that smell inside is unsettling, not to his liking, he stays on top of her. What is he waiting for? She stirs under him. He raises himself on one elbow, ashamed and dissatisfied, and looks at her face and she looks back at him, expressionless. He sees he is wrong. She is pretty, perhaps even beautiful. She has finely shaped cheekbones and flawless skin.

This is the moment he notices she is still in her blouse. Why is she still wearing it?

Now he does something. In future years, he will remember the evening with the woman with embarrassment and he will never again engage in such an unthinkable, scandalous practice. But this thing he does — this deliberate thing he does to the woman — will fix the evening forever in his mind. It is the only act from that evening that will sometimes make him feel — not without shame — like going back to a room in a house in a narrow lane in an unknown part of a city. He reaches out and clumsily unbuttons the woman's blouse. He pushes the blouse aside and uncovers the breasts, small and vulnerable. What are these faint black marks on them, fading into the skin? He does not know but he will not let them stop him. He will have the breasts in his hands. He has never felt a woman's breasts before and the desire to feel them is irresistible. He will touch them. He touches them. He touches them again, more curiously, more probingly. The woman lets out a low gasp and jerks her face away. He does not look at her face as he feels for her breasts so he can squeeze them again.

Loudly a voice woke Gopalakrishnan, startling him back from that house in Delhi. He looked around him, at the desk, at the books, at his notebook, at the undrunk tea grown cold in the tumbler, at Meenakshisundareswarar Temple Street, at the dim light growing dimmer outside the window as the end of the day approached. And he remembered where he was.

The voice called out to him again. It was Parvati, talking to him excitedly, crying, "Are you listening? Look! Look who is here. You will be surprised. Come and see who has arrived!"

PART TWO

GOPALAKRISHNAN EMERGED from his room to find Suresh sitting at the dining table, or rather flung untidily across it next to his black travel bag. Suresh did not sit up or turn his head at his father's approach. His arms were stretched out any which way on the table and his eyes were closed, as if he were ready for sleep. His long hair fell over his eyes. The stubble of a beard shadowed the outline of his angular face, deepening its brooding expression. His arms were long, his legs were long, his face was long — like Parvati's. Everything about Suresh was long and taut. Even flung as carelessly as a rag doll across the top of the table his body could not disguise its athleticism.

Over Suresh, Parvati and Gopalakrishnan's mother were standing, their faces stretched from end to end by grins of pleasure.

"Suresh?" Gopalakrishnan exclaimed when he saw his son. "You said you couldn't come for Diwali this year. Everything all right? Why here so unexpectedly?"

Suresh neither stirred nor made a sound in response. Gopalakrishnan's mother said: "What kind of ill-omened talk is this? Is this the way to welcome a child who has come all the way from Delhi by train to be with his family for Diwali?"

"That's not it, Amma," Gopalakrishnan said, frowning. He did not like the tone his mother was taking in front of Suresh. How difficult she had become! He continued to Suresh, "Why did you come by train? You should have taken the flight. What is the use of wasting so many days in the train?"

When still Suresh did not reply, Parvati said, "He did the right thing taking the train. No need to waste money on flights." She turned to Suresh and said: "But you should have called to say you were coming."

Gopalakrishnan persisted: "How much does it cost to fly these days? He could have easily taken the flight. Three days to come from Delhi by train and three days to go back. How many days will he have with us now?" Ever since Gopalakrishnan had taken the flight after his father's death (the only time he had flown for a personal reason), he talked as if flying were the most obvious of transportation choices.

So it went around Suresh, the words of his parents and his grandmother ringing over his head like bells in a busy temple at the time of evening worship. In the midst of it all, he himself remained as imperturbable as an idol, making not the slightest move to break his stony silence. He did not raise his head, nor did he speak a word. Finally Gopalakrishnan noticed and said to him, "You are tired. Go. Go have your bath. And then eat something. You look as if you will fall asleep any minute."

Gopalakrishnan's mother added, waving her bony hands at Suresh to get him moving, "Yes, child, go and wash off the train grime. I'll make you dosas. Thin and crisp, just the way you like them." Showing surprising energy, she hobbled away to the kitchen and started banging around. Gopalakrishnan could hear her muttering to herself, complaining about the way Parvati had organized the kitchen. Shortly, Parvati would follow her and she it was who would make the dosas promised to Suresh. In the meantime Gopalakrishnan's mother shuffled briskly about the kitchen, looking into this box and that one, trying to find this ingredient or that one.

Suresh heaved his long body off the table and stood up. He was dressed in blue jeans and a loose T-shirt. He towered over his mother and his father. He said, without looking at either of them, "I wanted to surprise all of you. That's why I didn't call. We decided to take a few days off. What is the point in working, working, all the time?" He pushed his disheveled hair out of his eyes with his long fingers.

Suresh was tall and lean by nature and his athletic inclinations — he had been a track star in school and in college and was a marvelous cricket player — had amplified what nature had provided. He lifted his bag from the table and carried it into the room Parvati shared with Gopalakrishnan's mother. When Suresh visited, he slept on his grandmother's bed and she slept on her mat in the puja room. The arrangement was well established.

Gopalakrishnan felt a swell of pleasure inside him. "Suresh is here," he said to Parvati. "Now we will have a good, proper Diwali. If I had known he was going to come home I would have bought his Diwali clothes when I bought ours last week. Fortunately I have a nice new shirt that I don't need and a brand new veshti. He can wear those on Diwali day. And then we can give him some money for new clothes. It will be better that way. He will be able to buy himself whatever he wants when he gets back to Delhi."

"How suddenly he has come," Parvati said, musingly. "How unexpected it is." She looked as if she wanted to say something more.

"So what if it's sudden? He is here. That is what is important. We can have a proper Diwali now." Gopalakrishnan's pleasure made him forget his own initial surprise at seeing his son.

After his bath, Suresh sat silently at the table by himself and ate his dosas. His manner said "Don't disturb me" and Gopalakrishnan thought to himself again that he should not have taken the train for such a short visit. No wonder he was so tired. Gopalakrishnan knew how his son could be when he was fatigued and left him alone. Parvati, on the other hand, tried to make conversation with Suresh from the kitchen: "How is everything in Delhi?"

Suresh did not reply. After he had eaten he flung himself on his grandmother's bed and promptly fell asleep. The rest of the family ate dinner two hours later, at eight o'clock, without Suresh. After dinner, Gopalakrishan went into the room in which his son was still sleeping. The bed Suresh had thrown himself on was across from Parvati's. The Godrej almirah Gopalakrishnan had moved in the afternoon stood between the two beds, looming in the darkness. In a corner, the red light of the electric mosquito repellent burned like a malevolent eye. The room's only source of illumination came from the overhead fluorescent tube out on the veranda, where Parvati and Gopalakrishnan's mother were seated before the television, watching a popular Tamil weekly show in which a man in a huge truck hunted down and killed members of a large and wealthy family. Both windows in the room were open and the ceiling fan was churning away madly; nevertheless, the air in the room felt stifling.

Suresh had removed his kurta and thrown it on the floor by the bed, where the ceiling fan was making its sleeves noiselessly rise and fall, rise and fall. For a moment, when he had first entered the room, Gopalakrishnan had had the alarming sensation of someone stealthily crawling out from under the bed. Instinct, powerful and primordial, made his shoulders stiffen; a moment later he saw that it was only Suresh's kurta and the feeling ebbed slowly away, leaving behind a surplus of tenderness. He stood looking down at Suresh, who was flat on his back and had his face turned away to one side. His two arms were stretched out, palms turned upward. His mouth was open. His chest was bare and offered up to the world. Gopalakrishnan observed all this and felt fond and fatherly: such an unexpected pleasure to have Suresh home for Diwali, such pleasure indeed. The gratifying thought in his mind, he went back to his room to continue his reading of the Ramayana.

Hours later, Gopalakrishnan awoke in the middle of the night, as he often did, to drink some water. He kept a stainless steel tumbler of water in his room, on a wooden stool by his bed, for this very purpose. He sat up and was reaching for the tumbler when he noticed the flickering light in the veranda outside his room. The luminous hands of the clock on his desk said three-thirty. Had Parvati forgotten to switch off the television? He stood up to check and saw, through the doorway of his room, Suresh before the television. Other than the television's bright glow, the veranda was dark, and also quiet. Suresh had muted the television. Eerie in their soundlessness, the images flashed forth into the hushed cavern of the veranda. Iridescent colors danced across the shiny Formica top of the dining table. At the other end of the table, Suresh sat slouched in his chair like a man in a trance, bathed in the lurid glare. He was still without his kurta, his chin resting on his chest, the palpitating glow from the television spreading a changeable film of brilliant light across his face. Only his eyes — perhaps the effect of the angle from which Gopalakrishnan was observing him — were wells of darkness. The remote lay on the table in front of Suresh, who was sitting perfectly still. Thinking he had fallen asleep in front of the television, Gopalakrishnan was about to call out when Suresh reached out and pressed a button on the remote. An advertisement for a car jumped instantly to the bright green of grass and the blue and yellow of uniforms — a cricket match.

A tall man in yellow pounded silently across the green grass, swung his arm round, and released the white ball down the track. At the other end a man in blue raised his bat high above his head and watched the ball swing past him to the wicket keeper, also in yellow. The ball was tossed back to the bowler, who returned to the top of his run. This time the ball cut sharply into the batsman, who was forced into a defensive stroke. But the white ball beat his proffered bat and soundlessly rapped him on the knee roll of a blue pad. The bowler jumped into the air and turned in a loud appeal to the umpire — his mouth an enormous O of excitement, his index finger pointing straight up at the sky. The camera hurried back to show the crowd in the stadium on its feet, roaring. Soundlessly. The umpire took a while to think, then shook his head. The bowler turned to glare at the batsman, who was walking around, looking up at the sky, talking to himself, perhaps praying to his gods. Perhaps the prayer helped, for the next ball from the bowler swept past the waiting fielders to the boundary. Four runs. And the ball after that raced to the boundary again. Another four runs. The bowler turned to glare at the batsman a second time. But it was too late. The bowler had no more balls to bowl. An ad for a soft drink flashed onto the screen. The bottles were wickets. A bottle top was the ball. The colors turned orange and red and pink. . . .

Suresh stirred once more to touch the remote. The picture on the television jumped to a musical scene from a popular Hindi film.

The setting for the song was a clean and modern European city at night. (Gopalakrishnan did not know what city, though there seemed to be some kind of a landmark prominently positioned in the background. He thought it was European. He could be wrong. Maybe it was Australian. Or American. He would not know, having never traveled out of India, unlike many of his colleagues. There was a story about favoritism to be told here.) The streets, the people, the shops — they were all modern. The black and red and white sports cars in the street were all in perfect condition. Under the properly working streetlamps, the perfectly groomed European men and women were all busily rushing about with briefcases and shopping bags. The shops that lined the street were all brightly lit and glamorous. A woman, an alluring Indian woman with long hair and knee-high boots and tight leather pants, was strutting down this perfect and modern street singing soundlessly, occasionally swinging around the post of a streetlamp, while European men and women passed her without paying her any heed. Soon it became evident that she was desperately wooing a sulking, round-faced man in a tight red shirt. Every time the woman strutted up to him, the man turned his face and walked away with his arms folded across his chest. The woman remained in pursuit. The two came to stores with mannequins in fashionable clothes in the windows. The woman posed against one of the windows and slowly, as the camera refocused, it became evident she was posing just like one of the mannequins in the window. Or perhaps the mannequin was posing like her, for it was dressed like her, with the same top and the same leather pants and the same boots as her. The mannequin had the same green eyes as her. It had the same brownish-blondish hair. . . .

Suresh touched the remote again and the picture returned to the cricket match. Gopalakrishnan recognized the batsman who had scored the eight runs. Sachin Tendulkar. World's greatest batsman. Gopalakrishnan remembered that a triangular series involving India, South Africa, and Australia was in progress. Suresh was a tremendous fan of cricket. No wonder he was awake. He was watching a replay of the match he had missed because he had been on the train. No doubt he had woken up and hadn't been able to fall back asleep. Gopalakrishnan suddenly felt himself an intruder. He had stood watching Suresh from the darkness of his room for so long without his knowledge, as if he were spying on him, while

Suresh was intent upon what he was watching, lost in the ghost world of the television. He felt guilty. Silently he returned to his bed, leaving Suresh as he had found him, slumped in his chair, his chin resting on his chest.

How fine a cricket player Suresh had been! Cricket had been one of his passions from an early age. Even when he was only eight, he could be found with his friends playing cricket in the dusty maidan behind the block of R. K. Puram government flats in which they had lived at the time. An old bat, tennis balls, bricks for wickets. Even with such elementary supplies he had shone as a player. No other boy had come close to him in talent! Sometimes, if he was home, Gopalakrishnan would walk down to the maidan to watch Suresh. With what eagerness he had played, flinging his thin body at the ball without fear. He would come home covered with dust, his school uniform filthy. Parvati would yell at him, "Look at you. I have told you so many times not to rush out to play in your uniform. Look at what you have done to it. I will have to wash it now. What if it doesn't dry by tomorrow? How will you go to school? How many uniforms are we to buy for you?" Innumerable were the times Gopalakrishnan had protected Suresh from his mother's anger. "Let him be, Parvati," Gopalakrishnan would say soothingly, using the tried and tested tone that he knew worked with her. "He's a child. He was having a little bit of fun. His uniform got a little dirty? Let it be now. I'll wash it after dinner." Of course Parvati would never let him wash the school uniform.

So what if school had never been Suresh's strong point? At cricket he had excelled. When he was twelve, over Parvati's objections ("Let it be, Parvati, let it be"), Gopalakrishnan had bought him a full kit of cricketing essentials — bat, pads, balls, gloves, shoes — and enrolled him in a weekend coaching camp, which was held on the grounds of one of the Delhi colleges. Every weekend Gopalakrishnan willingly took him on his scooter to the camp, waited there, and then brought him back. At the camp Suresh was like a peacock unfolding its radiant feathers. His talent spread itself, resplendent, in the shadow of the gray buildings of the college. A few weeks into the camp, the coach, a thickset man with a square jaw who had played for Delhi in national tournaments, called Gopalakrishnan aside.

"Your only son?" he asked as they stood by Gopalakrishnan's Lambretta scooter, watching the coach's assistant make the boys run laps around the maidan with its hard-packed dirt. Gopalakrishnan felt proud to see Suresh far in front of the other boys. He and the coach spoke in English.

"Yes," Gopalakrishnan replied.

"I thought so. Your good name?"

"Gopalakrishnan."

"South Indian."

"Yes."

"Government service?"

"Yes."

"Brahmin?"

"Yes."

The coach nodded. Gopalakrishnan knew the coach was Punjabi. He did not know what caste he was.

"I like your son's playing. He is very good. Big heart." The coach indicated with his hands how big. "If you like I can give your son special attention. You want me to?"

Cricket became the center of Suresh's life. He was an attacking batsman. In high school he was an indispensable member of the team. The team rose or fell on his performance. Soon he was traveling away to play with the team in regional and national tournaments. He was often mentioned in the newspapers. Gopalakrishnan began maintaining a folder of clippings. Until then, Gopalakrishnan's interest in cricket had been desultory; now cricket became the center of his life. Evenings and weekends father and son talked cricket. Gopalakrishnan learned the names of all the current players on the national team. He, too, turned to the sports pages first thing in the morning.

Parvati did not approve. "Cricket, cricket, cricket!" she would say. "All the time cricket! When will he study?" But it was cricket that got Suresh admitted into one of the better Delhi colleges on the sports quota. A poor student, he would not have found admission in this particular college were it not for his ability as a batsman. In college, his coaches thought him a natural. Gopalakrishnan remembered the headline from a profile of him in the weekend youth section of Murthy's newspaper — "A Young Natural Batsman: P. G. Suresh." Murthy had taken a personal interest in the profile, the opening of which went (Gopalakrishnan had memorized it by heart): "I want you to meet a young man you will probably get to know well in years to come. His name is P. G. Suresh. He is a natural attacking batsman." A dashing picture of Suresh with a bat against his shoulder accompanied the article.

A natural batsman. By the time Suresh was in college even Parvati had reconciled herself to the idea that cricket was his key to a better life. Not the way she would have wanted him to secure his future. She would have preferred the tried and tested way of becoming a doctor or an engineer. Nevertheless. What was past was past. Now that cricket had got him into college, it could get him a job after college — the kind of job that would otherwise be beyond him because of his poor performance as a student. If he kept up with his cricket he could get a good job on the sports quota, perhaps in a bank, perhaps even State Bank of India, where he would have a steady job with a steady monthly salary for the rest of his life. She wanted him to keep up his cricket at least until he had such a job. She did not care what happened to his cricket after that. This was how Parvati thought. Meanwhile Suresh thought of the national tournaments. He imagined himself playing in India's national side. He even fantasized himself a household name. *P. G. Suresh dances down the wicket and lofts the ball high over the head of Malcolm Marshall. It's a six! A six! The crowd is going wild, absolutely wild. What a way for this great batsman to score his maiden century on his debut for India's national side!* Gopalakrishnan and Suresh had often made up such commentary in jest.

Jest it had remained. None of it had come to pass. Forget the national side, Suresh had not even managed to land the kind of ordinary job that Parvati (and, yes, he Gopalakrishnan too sometimes) had dreamed of. One after the other all the doors that had opened for Suresh because of his prodigious cricketing talent had shut in his face when his cricketing career foundered. And then . . . But what did all of that matter now? Things had worked out fine for Suresh in the end. That was what was important. . . .

When Gopalakrishnan fell asleep the television was still silently flashing its images into the veranda. He awoke at his usual time the next morning but almost did not go for his morning walk. Despite the early hour, the air in his room felt trapped and stale. The ceiling fan did not help. The air lay heavy on him, as if he were lying under his mattress rather than on it, or as if someone had sneaked into his room in the middle of the night and placed a great sack of rice on his chest. He felt tired. He had to make himself roll out from under this feeling of lassitude. When finally he did, he saw that the television had been switched off. Suresh, it appeared, was back in bed. The house was dark and still. Gopalakrishnan went as quietly as he could to ready the house for the new day by removing the heavy iron bar from the wooden back door. Next he brushed his teeth, leaning against the white washbasin and vigorously scraping his brush up and down, back and forth, just as his father had taught him. Then he descended the five steps from the thinnai to the street. Even here the morning felt heavy. It had not rained during the night. The open air of the street felt as sodden as a wet mop cloth.

A scruffy white dog, one of its hind legs broken, came hobbling down the street from the direction of the temple. Gopalakrishnan knew the dog. He had often seen it recumbent on the steps of Paavalampatti Railway Station, its head on its paws, its rheumy eyes sullenly surveying the people passing up and down Station Road. The dog, head lowered, now came straight at Gopalakrishnan. He had no option but to step aside to let it pass. The dog's wheezy breathing was preternaturally loud in the heavy stillness. From somewhere in the village a radio blared momentarily and then was switched off. At this sound — scandalous intrusion on the morning's delicate repose — Gopalakrishnan nearly turned on his heels and hurried back into the house. The only reason he did not was because he could not imagine the day without his morning walk.

Gopalakrishnan was about to set out in his usual direction toward the temple when he remembered what had happened on the trail along the river the previous day. What about the snakes? He hesitated in front of his house, wondering what to do. He did not wish to make changes to his routine. But when he recalled how he had rushed and scrambled, how his heart had hammered away in his chest when he had reached the top of the embankment of the highway, his feet began reluctantly to move in the opposite, unaccustomed direction, away from the temple, toward Station Road. He felt deflated, as if he had been tested and found wanting, though by what he could not say. He was so disappointed with himself that his feet dragged on the road and he could not find his usual rhythm. He was unhappy but would not turn around. Disconsolate and divided, he went down Meenakshisundareswarar Temple Street to Station Road, turned right there at the corner past the house that had been converted into a post office, went past the modest entrance to Paavalampatti Railway Station (three steps leading up to the empty, dark platform beyond the barred ticket window), and turned left onto the highway. On the highway, he went past the still shuttered shops beyond the railway gate, past the banyan tree (no one here either), and came to the Kizhaku Vaasal Selvi Temple standing guard at one end of the village. At this point he turned left onto the path along the canal. By this time the morning had unfurled a cloud-filled sky over the village. The vegetable gardens beyond the canal were shadowy and mysterious in the dim light. The sun, hidden behind the clouds, was diffusing its light timidly into the air. He came to the village mosque where the Muslim men were just beginning to gather under the tamarind tree with their morning beverages. He had arrived at the mosque earlier than usual. The group under the tree was small. The young man with whom he customarily exchanged a wave of the hand was not yet there. The three or four men who had arrived were busy greeting one another and settling themselves comfortably on the bench. They did not see his approach. He felt unaccountably disappointed.

Soon thereafter Gopalakrishnan found himself back home. Parvati was brushing her teeth at the washbasin in the internal veranda. She looked up from the basin when he came in, surprised.

She rinsed the paste out from her mouth and asked, "Back so soon?"

"Looks like rain," he said by way of explanation. How could he tell her he had cut short his walk by almost half because he was afraid of snakes? She would be angry with him for having used the trail by the river all these months. He wondered how he could bring his walk back up to its usual length — something to think about before the next morning.

Gopalakrishnan had his bath under the shower because Parvati had remembered — for once! — to switch the motor on when she had woken up. Then he drank his coffee and ate some idlies for breakfast, sitting at the dining table with his mother. His mother loved idlies. She ate them silently, chewing them patiently with her dentures. When she was done, she said, "Suresh is not awake yet?"

From the kitchen Parvati — was there anything she did not hear? — said, "Is Suresh still sleeping? I'm going to wake him."

"Let him be, Parvati," Gopalakrishnan said. "He was awake half the night."

"Awake half the night?" Parvati asked from the kitchen. "Why was he awake?"

"I woke up in the middle of the night. He was watching a cricket match."

The moment he mentioned cricket Gopalakrishnan regretted it. There was a pregnant pause in the kitchen. He waited for Parvati to say something. Before she could, Gopalakrishnan's mother, who had not followed the exchange between Gopalakrishnan and Parvati, said, "What is for lunch today?"

"Roti, subzee, and dhal," Parvati said.

North Indian: in honor of Suresh's visit no doubt. Gopalakrishnan's mother did not like North Indian food. She preferred her sambhar and rasam and rice accompanied by vegetables cooked with lots of grated coconut; she much prefered this to the garam masala she seemed to find in every North Indian dish. She got painfully up from the table. "Why this kind of food?" she said and shuffled into the kitchen to see what she could do to remedy the situation. Gopalakrishnan could hear Parvati and his mother arguing in the kitchen. He used the opportunity to escape to his room with the newspaper.

Time evaporated slowly into the damp, gray morning. Still Suresh did not emerge from the bedroom.

Gopalakrishnan had a second tumbler of coffee while sitting out on the thinnai. A man went past in the street wheeling a bicycle with a cardboard box tied to its carrier. He stopped in front of Narayan's house and called out loudly, "Is anybody there? It's Kumar," at which Narayan's wife came out to the thinnai of her house accompanied by her grandson, whom Gopalakrishnan had watched arrive in the white Ambassador car the previous day. Narayan's wife made the man take the box down from the bicycle so her grandson could see what he had brought. The box was filled with firecrackers for Diwali — sparklers and flowerpots and atom bombs and many other kinds of firecrackers for which Gopalakrishnan did not even know the names. Gopalakrishnan watched as each thrilling surprise emerged from the magical cardboard box. He was amused at the excitement with which the boy went through the box, exclaiming at every new kind of cracker he found. Gopalakrishnan finished his coffee and went back into the house to see if Suresh was awake. Suresh might have been up most of the night; even so, it was late. It would be time for lunch soon.

Suresh was still in bed, but he was not sleeping. He lay on his back, supporting the back of his head on his interlocked fingers, staring up at the ceiling. A dark line of hair emerged from under the cord of his pajamas and snaked up the center of his stomach to spread itself over his chest. Black smudges had formed under his eyes. When his father appeared in the doorway to the room, he looked at him steadily but did not say anything. "Any plans to get up any time soon, Kumbhakarna?" Gopalakrishnan asked, pretending to frown. "Or are you planning to spend your whole Diwali vacation in here on the bed?" Only the previous evening, Gopalakrishnan had been reading in the Ramayana about Ravana's brother Kumbhakarna, who loved to sleep.

Suresh looked away from his father and got out of bed. He went silently past his father to the washbasin to brush his teeth. When Parvati heard him at the basin, she shouted from the kitchen, "I have your coffee here. Come and get it."

But Suresh did not go to the kitchen. He went out to the back of the house, where the toilet and the bathroom were. He was gone a long time. Gopalakrishnan did not mean to be nosy but he followed Suresh out there after a while. Lunch was waiting. Suresh was neither in the bathroom nor in the toilet, but by the outhouse at the back, leaning against a wall, his back to the house. A towel was slung over one shoulder. He was smoking a cigarette. Gopalakrishnan was touched that Suresh took so much care to hide his smoking. He retreated quietly to the yard, near the well, so as not to embarrass him. From there he called out, "Suresh, where are you? Hurry up! Time for lunch." Down at the bottom of the well a silvery patch of sky floated on the black water. Gopalakrishnan's black silhouette was down there too, cut out of the silvery patch. If he leaned forward, the silhouette lengthened. If he leaned back, it grew shorter. Otherwise there was very little to mark the silhouette as his. It was just the head and shoulders of an indeterminate, human shape. Gopalakrishnan went back to his room, to his newspaper.

By the time Suresh had had his shower, it was so late the other three were already sitting at the dining table waiting for him. The food was on the table — the rotis soft and brown on a plate; and in three stainless steel bowls the yogurt, the yellow masoor dhal with onions and garam masala, and the potato-tomato-cauliflower subzee. Another bowl had white rice, for what meal could ever be complete without rice? Parvati had also made some lemon rice especially for Gopalakrishnan's mother. Two large plastic Coca-Cola bottles filled with water had been brought straight from the fridge. The weather was oppressive. Gopalakrishnan poured himself a tall tumbler.

"How will you eat your food if you fill your stomach with water?" his mother said to him. He ignored her and drank anyway.

Suresh entered the house through the back door and sat in the only free chair at the table, next to Gopalakrishnan. His lanky hair was wet from his shower. He was wearing the same T-shirt and jeans he had been wearing when he arrived.

Sitting across from him, Parvati said, without preamble, "What's the need to stay up all night to watch a cricket match? What is there in this cricket-vricket that you have to be up all night? All India does is lose anyway."

Gopalakrishnan said, "It's not true that India only loses. We have Tendulkar." He understood what Parvati was really saying. He wanted Suresh to know he did not think like Parvati.

"What did you say?" Gopalakrishnan's mother said. "Okra? Yes, okra would have been so much nicer." She had heard Tendulkar as the Tamil word for okra. She was pushing the roti and the subzee from one side of the plate to the other, not at all happy with the food.

"Not okra," Gopalakrishnan said speaking loudly. "Tendulkar. Tendulkar! Cricket player. World's greatest batsman." He was going to say more, but seeing the blank expression on his mother's face he gave up.

"How many days have you come for?" Parvati said to Suresh.

Suresh shrugged. "A few days. I can go back whenever I want."

Parvati frowned. "You can go back whenever you want? What does that mean?" she wanted to know.

"I work for myself. Who can tell me what to do? I can take as much leave for Diwali as I want," Suresh said. He reached across his father's plate to help himself to more dhal.

"What kind of talk is that?" Parvati said. "So what if you work for yourself? You will get back only what you put in. You put in nothing, you get back nothing."

Suresh looked directly at his companions at the table for the first time since he had sat down and laughed mirthlessly. "If I put in nothing I will get back nothing?" he asked. "You should see how we work. Night and day."

"You must have a ticket to go back," Parvati said to Suresh. "When is it for?"

"I don't remember," Suresh said. "Sometime next week. Maybe two or three days after Diwali. But I can change it if I want to."

"You don't remember?" Parvati asked.

"I had one of my men go get the ticket. He told me when the return ticket is for. I have forgotten."

Gopalakrishnan saw Parvati was not happy with the answer. But she did not say anything. She too turned to the food on her plate. It was a while before she said: "How is Aloke?"

"Fit," Suresh said in reply to Parvati, using the English word as Hindi slang. He spoke in Hindi because he knew it irritated Parvati. "What worries does he have? His father has two big houses in Delhi. He is completely fit. No need to worry about him."

"You said you had had some difficulties with him," Parvati reminded him.

"Difficulties?" Suresh said. He kept his head lowered over his plate.

"You said something when you called last month."

"O that! Those kinds of things keep happening. That's nothing."

Parvati frowned. "Have you fought with him?"

"I told you," Suresh said. "There is no trouble between me and Aloke. Why would there be? He is my business partner. He is my best friend. What kind of trouble could there be?" He continued eating with his head lowered.

"I don't know what I would do if you have fought with him," Parvati repeated, as if she hadn't heard him.

Suresh threw the piece of roti he was putting into his mouth back onto his plate. "Look, Amma," he said, lifting his head to look at her. He had switched back to Tamil. The dark smudges under his eyes seemed to have grown darker. "If you keep asking me questions like this I will leave the table." He made a small gesture with the hand that had held the roti to signify departure.

"Let him eat," Gopalakrishnan's mother said, intervening. "He is here for Diwali. That is enough. You can ask him your questions later."

"Paati," Suresh said to his grandmother, as he returned to his food. "You are the only one happy to see me."

Gopalakrishnan felt betrayed that he had been included in Suresh's admonition.

"I am enough, child," Gopalakrishnan's mother said. "You eat your lunch."

After lunch Suresh went out. He did not say where he was going and Gopalakrishnan and Parvati did not ask. Gopalakrishnan, back at his desk with the Ramayana book in front of him, felt annoyed with Parvati. Instead of being happy to see Suresh, she had subjected him to all this questioning. She knew how moody Suresh could be. There had been no need to question him as if he were a child. Certainly, he had turned up unexpectedly, but he had explained why and how. Clearly he was still tired from the train journey. What need was there to nag at him in that way when he was still so fatigued? Parvati was always worrying Suresh was still the irresponsible child he had been many years ago. But he was twenty-seven years old now. He had been running his business responsibly for three years. How long did she mean to treat him like a baby not yet weaned off milk?

While Gopalakrishnan was at his desk thinking in this fashion, Parvati was resting on her bed as she often did after lunch. It was her time to herself when most of the chores of the day were finished and she was able to retire to her bed. She liked to prop her pillow against the wall and spread out on the bed, half-lying half-leaning, with the latest issue of *Kalki* or *Mangayar Malar*. In *Kalki*, she liked to read the fiction — domestic melodramas of husbands and wives and children. The other she liked for the lucid, accessible articles it carried on contemporary issues. Of late she had been following a series introducing and explaining computers and the Internet. What ever would she, who had never worked in an office or earned any money, have to do with such things in the remainder of her life? Nevertheless she liked to keep herself informed about such matters.

Today, however, the *Mangayar Malar* lay in Parvati's hands unread. She leaned back against the pillow with her eyes closed. The pillow had a faintly musty smell because of the damp in the air. When had she last changed the pillowcase? She would change it when she got up. The ceiling fan futilely pushed the heavy air from one side of the room to the other. She felt more tired than usual. She had a terrible headache; she had had it since lunch. Her fault. She should not have nagged at Suresh like that. Suresh's father had not approved of her questions during lunch, she could tell. But what could she do? The questions were popping in her head like black mustard seeds in hot oil. She could put a lid on them, but would that stop them from sputtering away in her head? When Suresh had called the previous month, she had asked and he had said he would not be able to come home for Diwali, that he was too busy. And now, suddenly, here he was, without any kind of forewarning. What was she to think? There had been enough trouble with him in the past.

There had been the time, not even four years ago, when Suresh was supposed to be in Bombay with a cricket club. By chance, she and Suresh's father — sometimes she wished that he could be Gopalakrishnan, or better still Gopu, to her too, but he could never be that, no, never, she had not been brought up that way — had found out he was not. A friend had come looking for Suresh and revealed inadvertently that he had not gone to Bombay, that he was no longer in the club's first eleven. How frightened Suresh's father had grown! After many frantic phone calls they had been able to find out that Suresh was in Kulu Manali with friends. Suresh's father had gone immediately to the hill station by bus to find him. Father and son had returned to Delhi grim faced. In Manali, Suresh's father had found him in a rented house with three other boys and two girls. As he had described it, the house was at the end of a secluded lane. It was small. There were only two sparsely furnished bedrooms, a kitchen, a bathroom. Suresh's father had found Suresh asleep in one of the bedrooms, stretched out on a sheet thrown on the floor, his arm around one of the girls curled up next to him. From the window of the room, the valley stretched away below green and tranquil. Hearing Suresh's father describe what he had found in Manali, Parvati had felt the world was upside down in that house. The boys all had long hair, the girls short. Drink and drugs and God only knew what else lay scattered everywhere. When Parvati had heard Suresh's father's account, she had gone into Suresh's room to confront him. Suresh's father had stayed in the living room, his face like crumpled paper.

"What were you doing in Manali?" Parvati had demanded of Suresh.

Suresh was sitting on his bed. He had looked up at her, frightened. "Nothing. I just went with some friends to relax."

"You were supposed to be in Bombay."

Suresh had looked away. "I am no longer in the first eleven."

"You lied to us."

"I knew you would be disappointed, Amma. I didn't want to disappoint you. That's why I lied." Suresh had returned his eyes to her, pleading.

"You didn't want to disappoint me? What does that mean?"

"I know how you feel about my cricket. I knew you would feel bad if you found out I was no longer in the first eleven."

"Why are you not in the first eleven? What happened?"

"It's all politics. The coach wants to push Arun to the front. He has given him my spot on the team."

"Maybe that's because Arun listens to the coach and takes his cricket more seriously than you do. Why can't you listen to what the coach tells you? How many times have you missed practice?"

Suresh had not said anything in reply.

"Your father says he found drink and drugs everywhere in that house in Manali." She had used the English words for drink and drugs. She had spoken them as if they were dirty, filthy words.

"I had nothing to do with those things."

"There were also girls there."

"It's not like how you think it is."

"How can I believe you? How can I believe you, Suresh? You lie to us all the time. You have given up on your studies long ago. Cricket is the one thing you know how to do and that too you will spoil now. I can see that. I can see that so well!"

To that outburst Suresh had had no reply. Parvati and Suresh had looked at each other silently. Her son was a man now, but how easy it was to see still in his face the boy he had once been. The boy-man's room was filled with all the things he had collected through the years. In a corner was his guitar with the strings broken. On the wall was a poster of Bruce Lee. His clothes lay scattered everywhere. On his desk were cassettes and sports magazines. On a shelf his father had specially put into the wall were his trophies, gathering dust. She had searched through the boy-man's room many times when he was not there. She had found cigarettes, but never had she found drugs and drinks.

Lying in her bed thinking of all this, her head pounding, Parvati felt like crying. She could not understand why she felt such foreboding regarding Suresh's abrupt arrival in Paavalampatti. Suresh's father did not seem worried. Why did she? Suresh was twenty-seven years old and it was true he had been working hard at growing his construction business — it was really Aloke's business, strictly speaking — for the last three years. Hooking up with Aloke was the best thing Suresh had done. He and Aloke were old friends, going back to college. Parvati suspected Aloke looked up to Suresh, who had always been very popular with his friends. Aloke's father was himself a businessman. The start-up money had mostly been Aloke's father's and Aloke was the senior partner, for how could Suresh's father invest as much as a businessman like Aloke's father could? Even so they had given as much as they were able. Under Aloke's father's guidance, Aloke and Suresh had made a go of the business, she could not deny it. They had begun with small contracts for residential houses obtained through Aloke's father, who had a furniture factory now but had once dabbled in construction. She herself had seen how hard Suresh worked before she had left Delhi to come to Paavalampatti. Day and night he was at some construction site or the other. This kind of work seemed to appeal to him. He could not bear to sit in a room with his nose in a book, but he liked talking to people and organizing things. Because of the hours he kept, she worried about his health, but mostly she felt relief, relief that he had found a place for himself in the world.

And yet she had not shared all this with Suresh during lunch. She had nagged at him but not told him she knew how hard he worked, how happy she was at his success.

It was fear — that old, well-known fear — that had made her talk the way she had. She was afraid that if she said anything approving to Suresh his run of good luck would come to a precipitate end.

Parvati got up from her bed and crossed the courtyard of the house to Gopalakrishnan's room. Gopalakrishnan was at his desk, his head bent low over his notebook, in which he was writing. Another book was open on the desk in front of him. The hair on the back of his neck was thick and unruly — time for a visit to Super Haircutters; she saw he was stroking his chin with the fingers of his left hand as he wrote, a well-known gesture she recognized as a sign of concentration. Parvati felt a rush of anger when she saw him in front of his desk in this fashion. What was the great need to study the Ramayana like this to confront Ramdas? What would he prove by doing so? People would only be amused. They would laugh at him behind his back. Her anger did not dissipate as he stopped his writing and his stroking and looked up.

"Has Suresh said anything?" Parvati asked, seating herself on the bed.

"About?"

"His business. What else? What else would I be asking about?"

"I have not had the chance to talk to him. What could have happened? Why are you so concerned?"

"It would be nice if you too were a little concerned. He is here so suddenly."

"You don't understand your own son. He probably didn't even think of calling. He is trying to make himself look good by saying he wanted to surprise us. You should not believe him when he says that."

"He seems as though his mind is somewhere else."

"Not sure I understand what you mean."

"Haven't you noticed how quiet he is?"

"O, Parvati, there is no end to the things you worry about! He is tired from his trip. He will be himself when he's recovered from the journey. Just watch."

"I was very nagging during lunch."

At this, Gopalakrishnan remained silent.

"I know he is making an effort in this business he is doing with Aloke," Parvati continued. "I worry this too will go wrong."

"He needs luck," Gopalakrishnan observed.

Parvati thought to herself: How little he knows Suresh! Needs luck? How many times has Suresh sent away good fortune knocking on his door with all the arrogance of a Kubera in his palace? Aloud she said, "If he gets married to a good sensible girl, he will have someone he can talk to, someone who will be a companion to him in his life. She will make him sensible too."

"If he puts his mind to his business and works hard at it, that will be enough," Gopalakrishnan replied. He did not want Parvati to bring up Sarala.

Gopalakrishnan and Parvati heard the front door open and shut. Suresh appeared in the internal veranda. He picked up the newspaper lying on the dining table and glanced at his parents through the door of Gopalakrishnan's room, speaking not a word to them. Gopalakrishnan and Parvati too said nothing to him. Suresh disappeared to his grandmother's bed. Soon the rustle of the newspaper could be heard.

"Will you go to Ramu's store?" Parvati asked her husband. "I sent a message to him days ago about things we need. We need many things for Diwali. He has not sent them."

"Tomorrow," Gopalakrishnan replied. "I don't have any time today."

They continued to speak for a while, but now their conversation was changed, pulled into a new shape by the silent, invisible gravitational force emanating from Suresh in the other room.

Lying on his grandmother's bed, across from the one his mother had just vacated, Suresh listened to the voices in the other room. Appa and Amma were talking about him. He felt certain about that. Their voices were only a murmur, but even this murmur was enough for him. It was the kind of murmur that it was. He had heard it so many times in his life. Quiet but urgent. Anxious.

Pregnant with foreboding. He did not need to hear the words. The murmur said one thing only — Suresh is letting us down again. If only they knew how bad things really were, he thought to himself. But what was the point in saying anything to them? It would all be just like every other time in the past. He would try to share something. They would criticize him. He would say something more. They too would add to what they had already said. And then Amma would get angry. And Appa would begin to look sad and hurt. And after that what was there that anyone could possibly do? Better Amma's anger even.

That is how every real conversation with Appa and Amma always turned out. Every real one. For instance, the one just before he had started his business with Aloke.

Without asking him, or Amma for that matter, Appa had gone to Murthy Uncle. To see if Murthy Uncle might not give him, prodigal Suresh that he was, "advice" in his time of "trouble." About careers, about options, about "attitude." About how important this time in his life was — this time when he was becoming a man of the world. Things like that. Murthy Uncle was alone in Delhi at that time — Lakshmi Aunty had gone to Madras for a long holiday; their son, Varun, was already working in Qatar as a journalist. Suddenly one evening, with no forewarning whatsoever, Appa had turned up at home with Murthy Uncle. "Murthy Uncle is here to talk to you," he had said.

An announcement. Not a request. Nor an invitation. On hearing it, Murthy Uncle looked uncomfortable. He said quickly, "Your father wanted me to come and see how everyone is doing. How could I say no? Suddenly I have been turned into a bachelor. What will I do sitting at home by myself? That's all it is." But then, switching to English, he proceeded to do exactly what Appa had brought him over to do. How he had spoken, his voice steadily growing louder and slower and more solemn. He had begun by sitting up straight on the sofa; soon he was sunk deep into it, as if the weighty words he was speaking — these important words emanating from his mouth and flying around in the room — were all settling down on him. Murthy Uncle had begun by talking about how hard young men had to work to make anything of themselves, make no mistake, the world gave them nothing, but soon he was talking about himself as a young man. How hard he had worked, how the world had given him nothing. How he had done this, that, and the other. How cleverly he had managed this man, that man, or someone else to get where he wanted to go. It was always this way with Murthy Uncle. Appa alone could never see it.

Through all this, Amma was in the kitchen augmenting, because of the sudden and unexpected appearance of Murthy Uncle, the dinner she had already cooked. Now as Murthy Uncle went on speaking and speaking and spinning out his words, it grew louder and louder — dishes clattering, noisy pouring of the contents of one vessel into another — in the kitchen. At last, Murthy Uncle ended by saying to him, "And that is what I have tried to teach Varun too, Suresh. This is the advice I have for all young men today." Murthy Uncle leaned back expectantly in his sofa, looking quite pleased with himself. Appa, sitting next to Murthy Uncle on the sofa, looked encouragingly at him as if he should say something in reply. But what was there for him to say to such a lecture? So he refused to say anything at all — anything whatsoever. He sat and glared silently at his father until Murthy Uncle started shifting around, not knowing what to do, made uncomfortable all over again. Rude. Very rude he had been to Appa and Murthy Uncle no doubt. And then, adding to his rudeness, he stood up and disappeared into his room, reemerging only when Murthy Uncle was gone, to say to Appa in a voice as calm as he could make it, "Why did you do that? Why did you embarrass me like that? Bringing Murthy Uncle here to talk to me as if I were some kind of a problem child. How could you do that?" It had been important to him that he say properly what he wanted to say, really express what he was feeling, so he had tried very hard to keep his voice calm.

Appa acted surprised and said, "I embarrassed you? I embarrassed you?! You are the one who embarrassed me, Suresh. Murthy Uncle is like family. He spent all this time talking to you because he cares for you like family. He puts articles about you in his newspaper. He has always wanted you to do well. And what do you do? You don't even thank him. Not one word of gratitude you speak to him. I felt so ashamed."

And then the words kept tumbling out. More and more words. He had spoken, his voice rising. Appa had spoken. He kept shouting — yes, he admitted it — and Appa kept saying, all hurt and sad, "I try to do something helpful and what do I get in return?"

Soon Amma got angry too and said, "What need is there to shout?" She was shouting too, but who could ever point that out to her? He had not even bothered to try. He had posed just one question to her, "How do you think I felt? Appa asks Murthy Uncle to come over and give me a lecture without even consulting me. How do you think I felt?" At this Amma looked over his shoulder at the wall behind him and said, "Maybe there was no need to bring other people into our affairs. But is that a reason for you to be shouting like this?" After that she would not say one word more. At least his question had stopped her shouting. Appa kept saying to her, "What did I do wrong? I asked my good friend to speak to my only child. Is that wrong?" Even then she would not say anything.

If ever he tried to bring anything important up with Appa and Amma, this was the way his conversations went. When ever had it been different?

Gopalakrishnan came to the lane that would take him back across the railway tracks to Meenakshisundareshwarar Temple Street but did not turn into it. He had determined the previous evening that this was how he would extend his morning walk so it could return to its usual length — rather than turning back toward his own street he would continue on along the path by the canal that formed the southern boundary of Paavalampatti. The shallow canal, usually a dry and pebbly channel along which dogs and pigs rooted, had been filled with water by the rains that had fallen days earlier — where was the rain that should have fallen since then? Its sodden slope fell sharply away from the path on which Gopalakrishnan walked. In the pearly light of the overcast morning he could see, across the canal, a shadowy figure moving through a field of spinach, bent over a basket. Gopalakrishnan passed the Muslim houses to his left and came to an open expanse of land across which he could see the railway tracks cleanly dividing Paavalampatti into two halves.

Gopalakrishnan had never ventured this way before, but he knew the Paraiyar houses lay in this direction. He strode briskly along thinking of his conversation with Parvati the previous day. Suresh had remained glum and incommunicative. He had lain on his bed reading and dozing, dozing and reading. When it was time for dinner, he had announced from his bed that he was not hungry, and then had emerged abruptly when they were done eating to wolf down some food standing in the kitchen over the sink. What was going on? Parvati had shot a look fraught with meaning toward Gopalakrishnan but declined to utter a word — not one single word — remotely connected to Suresh's behavior. And so Gopalakrishnan had thought to say something to Suresh. He was searching for the right moment when he realized that Suresh had already gone back to sleep. What ever could be the matter with Suresh?

Reluctant to disturb him, Gopalakrishnan had gone into the kitchen where Parvati was washing the dinner dishes, her back turned to him. "Perhaps Suresh is not well," he had said to her. "Let him rest. I will talk to him in the morning." He had addressed the bent back of her head where the gray knot of her hair stuck out — so it certainly seemed to him — like an accusing finger. Parvati had continued to wash the dirty dishes, her vigorous scrubbing under the open tap splashing water onto the adjoining black topped kitchen counter. She had neither spoken nor made a gesture. "How much water you are wasting!" Gopalakrishnan had exclaimed before striding back to his room and the Ramayana.

Beyond the maidan the canal along which Gopalakrishnan was walking turned away into the fields. All of a sudden — as if springing out to ambush him — the Paraiyar huts of the village appeared. Gopalakrishnan had not noticed the Paraiyar cheri earlier because it was hidden behind a line of low scrub trees. The moment the path had rounded the trees he was at the very edge of the cheri. Here he hesitated for a moment because he saw the path would take him straight through its very heart. But there was no other way. Go forward through the cheri, go back the way he had come — these were the only choices. He went forward.

The path now became the main street of the cheri, opening into a rough and unkempt stretch of dirt that ran haphazardly through the collection of Paraiyar huts and houses. Gopalakrishnan passed one or two houses of a better sort with tiled roofs and walls of plaster. Outside one of them a battered green TVS-50 moped stood on its stand, its sputtering engine sending spurts of odorous smoke into the waterlogged air. The owner of the moped was nowhere to be seen. And then Gopalakrishnan was among the main huts of the cheri. These huts, with clay walls and roofs of thatch hanging low, almost to the ground, lined the street in a disorderly manner. Some were set back from the street; others were so close Gopalakrishnan could hear the sounds of people inside waking up to the new day — the loud bang of a metal utensil here, a voice calling out impatiently there. Some huts were mean, little more than hovels. Others were substantial, with walls painted white and doorways leading into gloomy interiors. The doorways opened straight onto the dirt path, so that the interior of each hut was at street level.

Outside one such doorway a little boy played barefoot in the clean sand with a red plastic ball. As Gopalakrishnan approached, he picked himself up to watch the strange man in his white veshti walking through the cheri so early in the day. The boy's ripped khaki shorts dangled awkwardly below his bulging belly; he clutched at them with a hand to keep them from slipping down his legs. Flies buzzed insistently around his enormous eyes, which were bright and intelligent in his pinched face, beneath a mop of dull brown hair. Gopalakrishnan hurried past the boy, head lowered. There was a time when it would have been unthinkable for someone like him to enter the cheri. The contamination! The pollution! The number of rituals he would have had to perform to cleanse himself because he had placed himself in proximity to this little boy, to these so-called untouchable huts!

Laughable. Absolute madness.

Gopalakrishnan advanced farther into the cheri. He heard a commotion of raised voices around a communal water pump. A line of women stood with red and green and brown plastic containers at their feet. At the head of the line was a big woman, with enormous breasts and thick arms, working the handle of the pump even as she exchanged fiery words with the equally enormous woman standing next in line to her. The water burst from the pump intermittently with every firm downward stroke of the handle, falling into an orange plastic bucket. From the mouths of the two women words poured without pause.

"What will you do?"

"You just watch what I do."

"I am not afraid of you. Do whatever you like."

"Are we not human beings? We have to stand in line to get our turn at the pump and this woman thinks she can come like Indira Gandhi and do whatever she wants." The appeal was to the other women in the line.

"Speak to me, woman. Why are you speaking to them? Are you afraid to speak to me?"

"Just because her man works in the district office she thinks she is Indira Gandhi!"

"Indira Gandhi has been dead for a long while. I am still here."

"Woman, at least my man doesn't drink all day like your man. Who wants a man like that even if he works in the district office?"

"Don't make me start talking about your man. The things I could say about him!"

"All of you women are standing in line here with me. You tell me. Is it fair that this woman jumps to the head of the line? Is it fair?"

A murmur of discontent began to ripple through the line of women.

"Woman, why do you lie? You know I was here before you and marked my place with my bucket. Why do you want to lie?"

Other voices began to join in the quarrel, some on this side and some on the other. The commotion grew louder. From one of the huts a man's voice rang out: "Quiet! What is all this fussing early in the morning?"

Gopalakrishnan was hurrying past, head lowered to his chest, when the two quarreling women noticed him. They stopped their heated exchange to look at him. The commotion subsided a little as other women too paused in their quarrel to stare at Gopalakrishnan. He could hear them discussing him.

"Who is that?"

"I have seen him around the village. His house is by the big temple."

"What does a big man like him" — the tone was sarcastic — "want here at this time of the day?"

"Who knows?"

"Maybe he wants to get water from the pump like us cheri women."

The women laughed uproariously at the notion. Gopalakrishnan scurried on, his embarrassment a dry lump in his throat, chin to his chest. He raised his head only when he had come to the end of the cheri. What he saw then was a huge mound of garbage. Discarded toys and shoes and bottles, torn paper and plastic bags and cloth, half-eaten fruit and vegetables and meat — Gopalakrishnan could see all these jumbled together in a mound of rubbish that had surely taken years to burgeon to such an enormous size. Two pigs and a dog — the same white one with a lame leg he customarily saw around the village — were burrowing into the mound with great intent. In front of the pile someone had placed a rude sign in Tamil painted in black on a wooden plank nailed to a stick — WHOSE RUBBISH IS THIS? WHY IS IT HERE? WHY HAS IT NOT BEEN REMOVED? And below was the signature of the sign maker — A HUMAN BEING. Who had placed the sign there? What did the cryptic message mean? The stench grew more and more unbearable as Gopalakrishnan approached. His steps faltered at the repugnant sight and were it not for his reluctance to run that gauntlet of women again — no, he could not do that — he would have turned back.

Gopalakrishnan hastened past the noisome mound and found a way to cross from the path to the railway tracks so he could walk back along them to his part of the village. This was not what he had envisioned. This business of going farther along the path that ran by the canal would not do. It would not do at all. How then was he going to get his walk back to its desired length? How was he to find a route through the village? Snakes on one side, a great mountain of rubbish on the other. This matter of the walk was turning into an impossible riddle.

As Gopalakrishnan arrived back at his house, weighing these questions in his mind, he was surprised to see Suresh and Sarala sitting on the thinnai. Suresh had already had his bath. His long hair, combed back straight from his forehead to fall on his nape, was still wet. His face, freed from the shadow cast by his usual overhang of hair, was fresh and shining. The dark patches under his eyes had disappeared. He had finally discarded the jeans and T-shirt in which he had arrived in the village and changed into a clean white shirt and a veshti. Gopalakrishnan was surprised to see his son in this garb — Suresh was not one to wear such clothes. He looked a new man in the veshti, which Parvati had no doubt searched out for him. Gopalakrishnan could not help thinking how handsome Suresh was. How clearly these clothes brought out his resemblance to Parvati's uncle, who was renowned for his good looks. Suresh had the same expressive eyes and full lips. The likeness was unmistakable now that Suresh had combed his hair back in the exact same way that Parvati's uncle used to do. Next to Suresh, Sarala seemed a little wisp of a thing. Because the two were sitting so close to each other Gopalakrishnan could see how much smaller she was than Suresh — he could see how physically mismatched they were. How could Parvati even think that Suresh and Sarala would make a good couple?

Suresh and Sarala sat facing each other, the one towering over the other. Suresh sat cross-legged, his back to the wall of the thinnai. Sarala sat opposite him with her back to the street. A respectable distance remained between them and yet there was something intimate in the way Suresh was bending toward Sarala, whispering something to her that made her giggle uncontrollably. Gopalakrishnan quickly looked up and down the street. It was empty.

"What now, Sarala," Gopalakrishnan said loudly. "What did you need to grind today?"

Suresh remained as he had been, leaning forward, but Sarala jerked abruptly away from him. She looked embarrassed. "Grind . . .?" she asked. "Grind? I didn't bring anything to grind, Uncle. I heard brother Suresh had come. I thought I would come and say hello. That's all." She was wearing a pink bindi on her forehead to match her pink sari. A strand of hair had come loose to fall over her face. She quickly tucked it back behind her ear.

Suresh, still leaning forward, turned his newly glowing face toward his father and said, "You went for your morning walk?"

"Yes."

Suresh said to Sarala, "Every day my father walks. Without fail."

"I know," Sarala said. "I see him sometimes."

Suresh kept looking at his father and repeated, "Without fail."

"Yes," Gopalakrishnan agreed, proudly. "Without fail." He entered his house and looked for Parvati.

Parvati was in the kitchen. Gopalakrishnan could hear her chopping vegetables. He went to her and said, "Did you see? Suresh is up. He has had his bath. He and Sarala are sitting on the thinnai chatting. You were worrying about him for nothing yesterday. Are you satisfied now?"

"I saw them. Why are they sitting on the thinnai? People might notice. They should come inside. People like to talk," Parvati said. She was cutting eggplants in long purple slices. Her knife sounded click-click-click on the wooden cutting board.

"Let people notice."

"This is a village. What if people start talking?"

"Let people talk! I don't care about such things."

"Fine. Let them talk. I too don't care," Parvati said. "Finish your coffee quickly and go and have your bath. You have to go to Ramu's shop later."

Though Parvati sounded peeved, Gopalakrishnan could see she was not really. "How fine Suresh looks," he said to encourage her good humor. "Just like your Sudhu Uncle. That's exactly who I thought of the moment I saw him in his veshti."

When Gopalakrishnan emerged from his bath Parvati was out on the veranda around the central courtyard, talking on the phone with Gauri. Gauri had called from Madras to ask about their preparations for the impending Diwali festivities. It was her custom to call at least once a month. Parvati had already told her that Suresh had arrived unexpectedly from Delhi. Gopalakrishnan could hear

Suresh and Sarala still on the thinnai, laughing and talking in whispers. Didn't Sarala have any work at home? Wasn't she expected to help around the house? How indulgent her parents were!

Gopalakrishnan took the phone from Parvati to talk to his sister. Gauri still lived in the same house in Mylapore where Gopalakrishnan too had lived briefly, before moving to New Delhi. She did not have the facility to make long-distance calls from her home telephone and was calling from the phone booth at the corner of her street. As she spoke he could hear in the background car horns, bicycle bells, and the murmur of people thronging the street. Mylapore was one of the most congested parts of Madras. Gauri's husband, Prakash, had retired from Indian Bank many years before and Gauri and Prakash spoke often of moving to some other house in a less hectic part of the city. Gopalakrishnan did not think they ever would. Their four children lived in different parts of Madras and the central location of Mylapore was too convenient to abandon.

The moment Gopalakrishnan came on the phone, Gauri observed, "Parvati said Suresh has come from Delhi."

"Yes. He arrived day before yesterday."

"I thought you said he wouldn't be able to come."

"That's what we all thought."

"How is he?'

"Fine. Very fine. He was tired from his journey yesterday, but now he is fully recovered."

"He should have taken the flight."

Gopalakrishnan was pleased to hear this. "That's what I too said," he cried. "Exactly what I said!"

"Tell him to stop in Madras for one or two days on his way back. I haven't seen him in so long."

"I'll tell him," Gopalakrishnan said. "But I think he may not be able to. His business is doing so well now. He is so busy all the time because of it."

"Busy because of his business! Look at how you are talking. Has he become such a big shot now that he has no time for his aunt? What is the use of talking to you, Gopu? Is he there? Call him. I'll tell him myself. How can he say no to his aunt?"

Gopalakrishnan put the receiver down and called out, "Suresh! O Suresh! Your aunt is on the phone from Madras. She wants to talk to you."

Sarala would have to go home now.

Sure enough, Gopalakrishnan heard Sarala insisting over Suresh's protestations that she had to leave.

While Suresh was on the phone with his aunt, Gopalakrishnan read the newspaper in his room. He could hear Suresh asking after his cousins. Every now and then Suresh would burst out laughing. Even as she had grown older Gauri had not lost her mischievous sense of humor. Aunt and nephew were close. They were especially fond of each other. Gauri indulged Suresh, and Suresh for his part reveled in his aunt's attention. He could spend hours in her jolly company. With her, he could chat in the way that he liked — without seriousness, without inhibition, just to while the time away. He could never do the same with his own parents.

At the end of the phone call Suresh switched on the television and sat down at the dining table. Gopalakrishnan came out of his room to join him. From her room, Parvati asked, "When will you go to Ramu's shop?"

"Not now. After lunch," Gopalakrishnan replied. He made a face in Suresh's direction. Suresh looked at him for a moment, as if taken aback, and then smiled.

Suresh was watching cricket. India was batting and South Africa bowling. Gopalakrishnan sat across the table from his son and watched the match with him. They did not speak beyond brief questions from Gopalakrishnan's side to which Suresh gave brief answers.

"How is India doing?" Gopalakrishnan asked.

"Well," Suresh replied.

"Will we win?"

"Not sure yet."

"But what is your feeling, Suresh?"

"Can't say."

So it went between them. On the television, the Indian batsmen were playing defensively. Gopalakrishnan could see how engrossed Suresh was in the match.

"Why are they being so cautious?" Gopalakrishnan asked. "They should hit out a little."

"Can't afford to lose a wicket at this point."

"What's the use of that? Sometimes you have to take a few chances to win."

When Suresh did not reply to this observation, Gopalakrishnan turned his attention to the television screen.

Years before he and Suresh had spent time together in just this way. Gopalakrishnan felt himself transported to Delhi when Suresh was still a boy and they would watch cricket together and — despite Parvati's rebukes — Suresh would jump up and down in excitement on the rickety black sofa they had finally discarded when they had left for Paavalampatti. Very gratifying indeed to be sitting like this at the dining table watching cricket with Suresh.

In the afternoon, Gopalakrishnan wrote down Parvati's instructions on a scrap of paper and set out for Ramu's village shop. He did this immediately after lunch, before Parvati had time to nag him yet again about the matter. Many essential ingredients were needed for the savories and sweetmeats — thengozhul, laddoo, payasam, and many other such items (Parvati's ambition had grown since Suresh's arrival) — that Parvati intended to make for Diwali. At the shop Ramu's son sat on a stool under a table fan reading the day's edition of *Dina Thanthi.* He was perhaps eighteen. Because of the humid, oppressive weather he was not wearing a shirt. It was only recently, after he had finished with high school, that he had begun helping his father in the shop. The son looked exactly like the father, only younger. He had the same stocky build, the same bulging eyes, the same ears that stuck out from the sides of his head. When he saw Gopalakrishnan he put his newspaper to one side and jumped up off his stool. He began briskly rubbing a cloth back and forth over the polished wooden counter of the shop in just the way that Ramu liked to do as he waited for a patron to speak. Gopalakrishnan was pleased to see the son in the place of the father. He had not forgotten the incident of two days before when Ramu had called out to him and he had ignored Ramu.

"Gopalakrishnan-Sir, what can I get you?" Ramu's son asked with an eager smile.

Gopalakrishnan frowned and showed him the list Parvati had written out. "Three days ago this list was sent to your father. Still the things on the list have not been delivered. What's going on? What kind of shop is Ramu running here?"

Ramu's son ceased his polishing of the wooden counter and took the list from Gopalakrishnan. "List? Appa didn't tell me anything. What list is this?"

"It's the list my wife sent you three days ago. Where is Ramu? I want to talk to him."

"Appa is at home. I don't know what happened. He always takes care of these things immediately, as soon as he gets the list."

"Is that so? He didn't do it this time."

"Appa always takes care of these things at once," Ramu's son insisted. He lowered his eyes to the list and turned the scrap of paper round and round as if confused, as if searching for a clue within it. A car roared by on the highway towards Thirunelveli Town. Under the banyan tree beside the shops a silver bus with Video Coach written on its side stood, engine throbbing, while passengers embarked and disembarked.

Gopalakrishnan let a disdainful expression appear on his face. "Let it be now," he said. "When will you send these things? We need them immediately. Diwali is only four days away, you know."

"Wait, Gopalakrishnan-Sir," Ramu's son said. "I want to check something." He hurried away into the interior of the plain but well-stocked shop where a bewildering variety of household items were arrayed. Sacks of rice, cans of oil, and tins of lentils were neatly arranged on the floor in the center of the shop in such a fashion that two narrow passages were left open on the sides. On the wooden shelves along the walls were boxes of matches and soaps, bottles of hair oil and juice concentrate, packets of biscuits and chips. At the very back of the shop, where Ramu's son now squatted on the floor going through something hidden from Gopalakrishnan's view, two battered white refrigerators stood against the wall. On a table next to the counter fronting the shop were twine, sheets of old newspaper in which to wrap merchandise, a scale, and funnels and mugs to aid in pouring oil. Over all these floated a smell both musty and flavorful that seemed the very distillation of the village shop, its very ghostly essence. Out of this smell Ramu's son returned in a moment, a happy smile on his face.

"I knew it!" he said triumphantly, Gopalakrishnan's list still in his hand. "Appa has already put all the things together. I see them in bags at the back of the shop. The old list was not clear about one or two of the things. That is why he did not send the things home. This new list is very clear. You will have everything today. Go home without any anxiety. The things will be with you today. I knew my father would have taken care of this!"

Gopalakrishnan felt deflated by the discovery. No doubt this was the reason Ramu had called out to him on his walk two days before. Nevertheless, he said, "What is the use of putting all the things in bags and leaving them there? He should have sent a message home if he wanted clarification. Or at least he could have said something to you. He left you in charge of the shop. He could have told you about the bags at the back of the shop. What if you hadn't thought to check? Is this the way to run a shop?"

"My father has been running this shop for more than thirty years," Ramu's son said obstinately. His voice had acquired a narrow edge of anger.

"All right. Let's not talk about this anymore. Just send everything home immediately."

Thus extracting a second promise about sending the items on the list through the delivery boy, Gopalakrishnan hurried home through Station Road. He should really return to the Ramayana, but he wanted to see how the cricket match had progressed in his absence. He had left Suresh in front of the television. The prospect of catching up on cricket with Suresh was pleasurable, even mildly exciting. The walk through Station Road was hardly anything; nevertheless Gopalakrishnan's face was damp with sweat by the time he arrived back at his home. The air was suffused with water. This was what happened during the rainy season: if it did not rain even for a few days the weather became impossible.

Suresh was not at the dining table. The television was not

switched on. Instead of the television commentary on the match, Gopalakrishnan heard the sound of the pages of a book being turned. Suresh was in his room, standing at his desk.

"What happened?" Gopalakrishnan asked. "Match is over?"

"Don't know. Didn't want to watch it anymore," Suresh said. He was a dark silhouette in the gray light entering through the window over Gopalakrishnan's desk. He held Gopalakrishnan's notebook in his hand and was leafing through it. Gopalakrishnan could see he had also looked through the other books on the desk. They had been moved about. When he had left for the shop all his books were on the desk neatly ordered. Now they lay tumbled about on the desk. One book lay open, its pages fluttering madly in the wind from the ceiling fan.

Gopalakrishnan came into the room and shut the open book so the pages no longer fluttered so desperately. "My notes on the Ramayana," he said, indicating the notebook Suresh held in his hand.

"Why are you reading the Ramayana?"

"Our bhajan society has arranged a harikatha the day before Diwali. There is a harikatha man named Ramdas. He knows nothing" — Gopalakrishnan flicked his fingers away from his thumb to indicate just how nonexistent Ramdas's knowledge was — "but he is famous in these parts. He is going to come for the harikatha. He came once before and spoke some nonsense about the Ramayana. No one except me said anything challenging to him. Not one person spoke up! How can we let him get away with his nonsense? I thought I would ask him a few hard questions so he knows not everyone in this village is a fool."

"You have written so much in your notebook."

"I have been studying the Ramayana carefully."

Suresh indicated the other books on the desk. “You have read all these books?”

“Yes,” Gopalakrishnan said proudly and then corrected himself, “except for one or two.”

Suresh went back to leafing through the notebook. “What kind of questions will you ask this . . . this Ramdas?”

“I can’t say exactly right now. I’ll have to see what he says.”

“What do you think he will say?”

“He will say one or two completely wrong things about Rama and Sita and then start talking about all kinds of things that have nothing to do with the Ramayana. Last time he was here he started to say all the wrong things that Rama had done were right and the right things were wrong. How can someone be quiet when that happens? That’s when I told him what I thought of his comments.”

“Silly.”

“Exactly what I thought. But your mother and grandmother were angry with me for confronting Ramdas. Let them be. You will see how I take care of Ramdas when he comes back. You will be here. We will go to the meeting together.”

“The whole thing is silly. Who cares about an old story like the Ramayana? What does it matter what it says?” Suresh was thinking to himself: Just like Appa to get worked up about someone of no consequence like Ramdas. All the important things in life he would slink away from; the unimportant he would confront valiantly.

Gopalakrishnan frowned and tried to understand what Suresh was saying: “What do you mean? Lots of people care about the Ramayana. Millions and millions of people do. Don’t you read the newspaper?” It was four years since the destruction of the mosque in Ayodhya by Hindus who thought the mosque stood on the very place where Rama was born. Ever since then the blue-skinned god was never long out of the newspapers. Why was Suresh talking like this?

"I know they do. But it is all very silly."

"There are some interesting things about the story."

"What is so interesting?"

Gopalakrishnan took so long to consider the question that Suresh continued, "All people do is fight and kill one another over this. What is so great about this story?"

"What you say is right," Gopalakrishnan said at last. "But you can't dismiss the whole thing. There are many interesting things about it. After all it is part of our culture. I mean . . ." He groped to make himself understood. "It is one of the great stories of the world. People read it and study it all over the world. Even in America and England and Japan. Why would they do that if there was nothing valuable in it?"

"You haven't told me one thing interesting about the story."

One interesting thing about the Ramayana. What was one interesting thing about it? Gopalakrishnan cast about in his mind for an answer. Where to begin? Suresh stood waiting, but Gopalakrishnan's mind wouldn't produce an answer. How unfair of Suresh to quiz him like this. Of course the Ramayana was a great work. Everybody knew it was. Ramdas was a fool but that didn't mean the Ramayana was not a great work. Gopalakrishnan felt flustered under Suresh's gaze. His mind was a morass of ideas about the Ramayana. For a moment he thought he had it — about how he didn't agree with what the Ramayana had to say about caste or women or a number of other matters, and yet there were things in there, things like . . . Things like . . . But the glimmering of an idea slipped away.

Suresh flung the notebook onto the desk and said, "All silliness." He went back to the dining table and switched on the television. The sounds of the cricket match started up again.

Gopalakrishnan did not follow Suresh. He sat down at the desk and began fussing at the books on the table, arranging them again as he wanted them. The schoolboy on the cover of the notebook smiled mysteriously at his fussing. When Gopalakrishnan was done bringing order back to the desk he opened the volume of the Ramayana he was reading at the right page and sat staring at the curling, snaking Tamil script. He read but could not take in what he was reading. His mind twisted and turned along the lines of Tamil without really following them. The exchange with Suresh was making him blind to the book in front of him. A slow anger grew within him. What had Suresh meant by talking in this manner to him? How rude he had been. Gopalakrishnan sat at the desk, his head bent over the book, not seeing what he was reading. It was as Parvati had said — Suresh had been in such a strange mood since his arrival. But was that a reason to be disrespectful to his own father?

Sitting at the dining table, Suresh too watched the television without really seeing it. He knew he had not behaved well — he had not been able to stop himself. The bowler ran up with the ball, the batsman swung his bat and sometimes hit the ball, the crowd yelled or groaned or remained silent in tense expectation — Suresh's eyes and ears took it all in, but his mind was not on the game. Instead he was thinking. Remembering — all that he seemed to do these days! — an incident involving him and his father and another cricket match.

It had happened many years before. He was still a boy. Not more than twelve or thirteen years old. But already an avid fan and player of cricket. Appa had promised to take him to a Test match at the Firoz Shah Kotla ground in Delhi. (The very ground at which the match on the television was now being played.) Australia was playing India. It was to be his first live match in a stadium that involved India's national side. He had convinced his father to let him take a day off from school so he could attend both Saturday and Sunday out of the five days of the match. His mother had been successfully circumvented. Tickets had been bought. For weeks he had crowed to all his envious friends at school about the thrilling experience that awaited him.

And then his grandfather, the great Paavalampatti Krishnaswamy Iyer, had arrived on a visit, his only visit to Delhi, which — wouldn't you know? — had coincided exactly with the eagerly awaited Test match. Thatha had been persuaded only with the greatest effort to make the long trip from Paavalampatti to Delhi. Thatha did not approve of Delhi, had no desire to visit it, had consented only because Paati had finally prevailed on him. He had arrived cantankerous and tired the day before the eagerly awaited event. Suresh, however, had paid Thatha little mind. What did he have to do with this aloof and stern stranger (so unlike his other grandfather)? He had never been close to Thatha. Never. Nothing at all like the way he had been and still was with Paati. His thoughts had all been of the impending trip to Firoz Shah Kotla the next day. He and Appa would leave in the morning on Appa's scooter, with a bag of food and water packed by Amma. What would the stadium be like from the inside? What would the seats be like? What would it be like to watch the match with thousands of other people? The match was poised at a critical juncture for India, which was fielding. Which meant Kapil Dev would bowl. What would it be like to watch Kapil bowl in person? In person. Not on the television.

He had hardly slept the night before. He had hurried out of bed at the crack of dawn. And then Appa had confronted him with the dreadful announcement: "We will not be able to go to the match today. You will have to go to school. Tomorrow is Sunday. We will go to the match tomorrow."

They were standing in the corridor of the R. K. Puram flat. The corridor, windowless and poorly lit, led from the bedrooms to the bathroom. Suresh could hear the voices of Amma and Paati in the kitchen. He had stood, stunned, still in his white pajamas. Had not even brushed his teeth yet. "Why?" he had croaked out finally. He had gone to bed early the night before so as to be as rested and refreshed as possible for the great adventure. He and Appa had been excitedly making plans for the trip only a short while before he had gone to bed. What could have happened since then? "Why, Appa?"

Thatha, standing like a phantom behind Appa in the dim light of the corridor, had spoken instead. Suresh had not noticed Thatha until that moment. Slowly shaking his narrow face from side to side, Thatha had said in his thin, steady voice: "Why would you miss school for a cricket match? Which is more important — cricket or your studies? Incredible the allowances made for children these days!" His voice had expressed fully how scandalous he found the idea. A portentous silence had descended on the apartment.

Suresh had ignored Thatha, a virtual stranger to him, and fixed his eyes on Appa. Urgently. Pleadingly. "Why, Appa?" he had asked again. "Why the change in plans? You promised. Today is Saturday. School is only half day. So what if I miss it? I have been working hard at my schoolwork as I promised. You know I have. I have told all my friends I will be going to the match today. How can I go to school now?"

"Tomorrow," Appa had replied, the expression on his face inscrutable because of the unrelenting gloom in the corridor. "Tomorrow is Sunday. We will go to the match tomorrow." Then Appa had crept away down the dark corridor toward his room without another word. Only Suresh and Thatha had been left in the corridor to glare at each other in the unnatural silence. Suddenly the sound of the transistor radio had burst out from his father's room.

And in that moment, for the first time in his life, Suresh had felt a pure and adult hate in his heart.

Borne aloft on scores of ardent voices, the song rose around Gopalakrishnan. He was in the room of the Paavalampatti Bhajan Society. It was the day set aside for bhajans, the first of the three days of cultural events organized by the society as part of the Diwali festivities. Restless and distracted, he listened to the voices of the singers and wished he had not come. He had not been planning to, but all day the house had felt stifling, comfortless. Until coming here, he had not gone out at all, had not even left the house for his customary morning walk! He had woken at the usual time but had been unable and unwilling to forsake his bed. Overnight the unsolved problem of an appropriate route for his walk had swollen to daunting proportions. What direction would he take now that his foray into the cheri had ended in such failure? So vexing had the question become it had kept him, disconsolate, in his bed. It was late, well past eight, before he had risen to meet the day. Parvati, already in the kitchen, had called out with loud concern: "Feeling all right? Why so late in getting up? Even Suresh is up and about." The words had clattered down on him like stones on a tin roof. He had passed wordlessly to the toilet in the backyard. And from that moment on the day had had a ragged, threadbare quality to it. All day annoyance had succeeded annoyance — Parvati's noisy banging in the kitchen, Amma's loud chanting in the puja room, the television's frivolous prattle just outside his room. Especially annoying was the television: Suresh stuck all day in front of it, glued to some nonsense or the other. How could he spend so much time watching it? How could he?

Then, late in the afternoon, as Gopalakrishnan sat at his desk trying to concentrate on his reading, his mother shuffled into his room to ask a question. She stood against his desk, looking down on him. The light from the window revealed the creases in her face, the hollow cheeks, the eyes grown so faded behind the glasses. She said, "Parvati says she is not going to the bhajan meeting because she has to make the Diwali sweetmeats and savories. Are you?" At first Gopalakrishnan felt only irritation at his mother's interruption. Then he thought about her question some more. His restlessness. His irritability. Could it be because he had been cooped up in the house all day? Thinking to himself that the bhajan meeting was perhaps just the diversion needed to darn the ragged day into wholeness again, he allowed himself to be persuaded by his mother.

Mistake. Here was Gopalakrishnan at the meeting and the day was only fraying even more. He was only getting more restless and annoyed as he listened to the hapless, tuneless voices of the singers around him — each no doubt hearing a Balamurali Krishna or an M. S. Subbalakshmi in own voice!

On this day the songs were all about Krishna, the devotional object of the singers. From the row of divine pictures that usually lined the brown painted walls of the room, the portraits of Krishna had been removed and arranged by Vasu's wife on a bench covered with a yellow silk cloth. The bench was placed prominently at the head of the room. On the floor in front of it oil lamps had been arrayed. In pride of place on the bench was a splendid picture of the blue-skinned god standing with one leg crossed in front of the other. The crossed leg rested lightly on its toes. A yellow flute pressed against his lips. Next to Krishna a peacock trailed the myriad brilliant eyes of its train along the ground and lifted up its head in adoration. In the far distance white cows grazed along the banks of a vivid blue river winding its way through green hills. With clear, untroubled eyes Krishna gazed out of these bucolic surroundings at his devotees sitting on jamakaalams in the village of Paavalampatti.

Around this large picture other, smaller, pictures of Krishna had been arranged. A striking one depicted Krishna with Radha. The ever-present flute at his red lips, peacock feathers in his hair, a garland of flowers around his neck — thus adorned, Krishna gazed away to one side while the radiant Radha, clad in a green skirt and holding a flower in her hand, stood beside him with eyes demurely cast down. Radha-Krishna. Radha's Krishna. The eternal lover with his beloved. And then of course there was the inevitable picture of child Krishna surprised in mischief, a pudgy hand smeared with incriminating butter at his mouth, the pot from which he had pilfered still in his lap. Yet another picture depicted Krishna guarding his cows — Krishna the cowherd, for whom Gopalakrishnan was named. The picture evoked for Gopalakrishnan the affectionate way Murthy used to tease him. "What, Gopu?" he would say. "Where is your flute? Where are your cows? Run away?" The memory made Gopalakrishnan cast a critical eye over the gathering in the room. Those were the days, those days in the barsaati in Delhi.

Look at the kind of people he was with now. Who among these could compare to Murthy, who knew so much, was interested in so much?

The bhajan audience comprised an assortment of his neighbors, mostly middle-aged or elderly. They sat in the pallid light entering grudgingly through the four windows of the room. Overhead three white ceiling fans churned the heavy and humid air. Some sat cross-legged, others with their legs stretched out and leaning against a wall. Resplendent saris made splashes of red and blue and green here and there. Gopalakrishnan observed that many of his neighbors had brought out their finest saris and veshtis and shirts for the occasion. Surely that pungence in his nose was mothballs? He was amused by their vanity. He noticed that very few of the younger residents of Meenakshisundareshwarar Temple Street were present. Suresh had not come. Nor had Sarala. No doubt Sarala would appear the next day, when the young men of the street were to present their dancing prowess. But Suresh . . . Of Suresh who could predict anything?

Closest to the many pictures of Krishna set out on the bench sat Narayan, who knew countless bhajans by memory and was the most adept of the singers. Him Gopalakrishnan liked. He was a small and modest man with sad eyes, a man with a habitually drooping demeanor. But his voice was rich and what he lacked in training he made up for with quiet and sincere fervor. He it was who always led during these sessions, enunciating with devotion — though still not, it was Gopalakrishnan's opinion, with the devotion of which Ganapathy had been capable — the first line that the others would then take up and repeat. If only, Gopalakrishnan thought to himself, looking around the room, the other singers were half as good. Here was Narayan's wife, basking in the glory of her husband, shamelessly raising her raspy voice higher than anyone else. And there, over on the other side of the room, sat Vasu in the midst of his cronies, his paunch hanging out from under his shirt. How loudly he was whispering to Sivaraman! Gopalakrishnan waited until Vasu caught his eye, gave Vasu a deliberate look, and then turned away to continue scanning the room, making note of who was talking without regard for the solemnity of the occasion and who singing with a flamboyance belied by actual ability.

Gopalakrishnan was still engaged in this indignant exercise when the bhajan came to a thundering conclusion. The singers followed Narayan's lead and rose and crested in a chant of "*Radhey-Radhey-Radhey-Radhey-RAADHEY-GOVINDA-Brindavan-Chandra.*" In the lull that followed Narayan conferred with the other bhajan adepts sitting around him. Gopalakrishnan saw they were encouraging Narayan to sing a song, not a bhajan, on his own. Narayan overcame his diffidence and reluctantly agreed. He announced the song — "Alaipaayuthey."

Immediately Gopalakrishnan began to listen attentively. The song was very popular. Gopalakrishnan knew it well because Ganapathy would sing it often. Stretched out on his mattress in the barsaati, splashing water on himself from the bucket in the bathroom, leaning aimlessly against the wall of the terrace — the mood could take Ganapathy at any moment and the song could burst from him whole or in fragments. Unlike Ganapathy, Gopalakrishnan did not consider himself a particular devotee of Krishna; yet he had learned through his friend to love the intimate ardor of this particular song. Even in his present mood he could not resist it. Sitting next to him, his mother too perked up. One bony hand came alive to keep imprecise time on her lap. Her lips moved soundlessly in unison with Narayan, who began low and gentle.

Restless as the waves of the ocean, Kanna,
is my mind.
Ebbing and flowing
in the joyous, melodious
song of your flute,
my mind is a restless ocean.

You stand still as an unmovable statue,
unmindful of the passing of time,
O marvelous player of the flute,
while my mind is a restless ocean.

How Ganapathy had loved this song. No one could sing it like he could. Not even Narayan, who sang it so well. With what subtle feeling Ganapathy had expressed its sentiments, his voice moving restlessly, searchingly, on the word *waves* and then pausing so steadily, so firmly, on *statue*. In his mind, Gopalakrishnan could hear Ganapathy as if he were singing right there in that room in Paavalampatti.

Moon without blemish
burns hot and bright as day.
My brow furrows
from looking toward you in hope.
Your sweet flute song
comes blowing on the wind. Eyes roll helplessly —
dizzy, faint, I am overcome.

Now Narayan's voice quickened, abandoned restraint. The cymbals in his hands rang more swiftly. Perspiration dripped from his face. He inclined his head backward to free his voice and his sad eyes grew small and distant with an emotion Gopalakrishnan could not name. His resonant voice overflowed the unlikely body to which it belonged and poured into the room with desperate longing. Around the room competing conversations and distractions faded away. Gopalakrishnan too felt his heart fill and stretch as if to bursting.

You rejoiced so in planting your foot
firmly on my restless mind!
You embraced me in a wild place,
woke my senses, made me bloom!
Like sunlight gleaming
on the resounding ocean waves
gleamed the anklets on your feet!

Is this your wish?
That I cry out like this to you —
wild, my mind liquid with longing —
while still you frolic with your other women?
Is this deserved? proper? just?

Narayan had not raised his voice. Yet his song seemed to have grown louder — more urgent, more yearning. Presently it sank back into a quiet sigh of resignation and release.

Like the earrings that swing
as you play your flute,
my mind swings, suffers,
restless as the waves of the ocean.
Kanna, my mind
is restless as the ocean
in the joyous, melodious
song of your flute.

Narayan concluded the song and a great murmur of approval stirred through the room. "Vah! Vah!" cried voices here and there. The man sitting next to Narayan clapped him loudly on his back. Through all the acclamation Narayan sat quietly, his body now a deflated bag of ordinariness. He wiped the sweat from his face with a hand towel and did not make any reply to the appreciative comments being put forward. He was surrounded, yet he was solitary.

Gopalakrishnan looked at Narayan and felt kinship. A realization, a startling revelation, seemed to come to him. Suresh's face appeared in his mind. Suresh, Parvati, his mother. How he was surrounded. And yet alone, very alone. He turned abruptly to his mother and said, "I am going home." He stood up and hurried his way through the seated people, his head hanging low. He wanted to get away from all of it. He picked his way without regard through the crowd of people seated on the floor. Many turned irritated faces up at him as he brushed past them. He stepped by mistake on the long sari palloo of a woman he did not know well but hurried on without even the merest of apologies. By the time he was outside in the street in front of the tall open doors of the temple, he felt truly overcome. Dizzy, faint, weak. Restless as the waves of the ocean. Yes, that was how he felt.

He sat hastily down on the rough stone steps leading into the temple and shut his eyes to make the world stop spinning around him. He had been sitting thus for barely a moment when he felt the flutter of a sour breath upon his face. He opened his eyes to see Sundaram just inches away, his tall figure bending low to look at him, his huge eyes, bulging and red veined, boring into him. The instant Gopalakrishnan's gaze met his, Sundaram turned away and entered the temple and found his usual place against one of the pillars of the portico. And into the spot vacated by him Gopalakrishnan's mother stepped. Gopalakrishnan felt his weariness keenly when he saw her standing small and fragile in front of him. "Why did you also leave?" he said to her. "You could have stayed if you wanted to." How he wished he could be by himself. Did he not deserve to be alone at least some of the time?

"I know when to stay and when to leave," his mother replied tartly. "What is wrong with you? Why are you sitting here? Are you feeling unwell?"

"Nothing like that," Gopalakrishnan lied. "I think I stood up too quickly. The blood rushed to my head. That's all."

"What did Sundaram want?"

"How do I know?" Gopalakrishnan said. "I shut my eyes for a moment. When I opened them he was standing over me. And then he just walked away without a word. He is a strange man."

"Don't you know his story?"

Gopalakrishnan did not reply. He did not wish to know Sundaram's story. Solitude was what he wanted.

"What happened to him when he was a young man, Gopu. Don't you know about it?"

"No," Gopalakrishnan said without interest and stood up. He slowly walked down the street toward his house, nursing the hurt he felt within. His mother followed, not to be denied the opportunity to tell her tale.

"It happened when I got married and first came to this village," she said. "A long time ago it was. Sundaram must have been seventeen or eighteen, only a little younger than me. He became involved with a low-caste girl from some other village. Said he was in love with her. Night and day he ran after her like a dog. His parents pleaded with him to come to his senses. Don't do this, don't behave like this, they begged him. Would he listen? No. He would steal away in the middle of the night to see this girl. So finally his parents locked him up in his room. They made a hole in the door. They would give him his food only through that hole. Two years he remained locked in his room. In the beginning he would stand at the window of the room and shout like a madman. I remember it very well. It was frightening to hear the shouts. But no one in the village did a thing about the shouting. How can you interfere in another family's affairs? After a few days there was only complete silence from that room. When they let him out after two years he was like this. I have never heard him speak even a single word."

Gopalakrishnan heard the story in shocked silence. Shaken, he stopped and said to his mother with disbelief, turning to look her in the face, "Two years? They kept him locked up for two whole years?" He looked back through the entrance of the temple at Sundaram seated against a pillar in the temple's gloomy portico. Dusk was approaching and birds had begun to twitter and flutter around the neem tree that stood in the courtyard of the temple. In a little while the priest would appear to conduct evening worship, but since most of the devout were at the bhajan meeting — their voices now loud with another bhajan — Sundaram was alone in the portico. He sat gazing fixedly at the black stone Shiva lingam, barely visible in its dimly lit sanctum.

Gopalakrishnan's mother nodded her head solemnly in reply to her son's question. Her white blouse hung loose and sacklike from her gaunt shoulders. She shook her hand in front of her son's face to emphasize what she was saying. "Two years! Sundaram's elder brother had gone away to study to be a doctor. One day he came home, saw what was going on. He was very angry. He made his father let Sundaram out. People say he is the one who supports Sundaram even now. Without him who knows what would have happened to Sundaram?" Her voice had grown important with the story she was telling. She was pleased by Gopalakrishnan's response, gratified that she had shocked him in this manner.

"He never married," Gopalakrishnan observed.

"Married? What kind of a question is that, Gopu? Haven't you seen what he is like? Who will marry him?"

"What happened to the girl?"

"Who knows? Probably married someone of her own caste. You know how low-caste people are. What do they care whether she had been with a man or not?"

"Two years! I did not know any of this about Sundaram." He resumed his walking.

"You were not even born when it happened. At first all people could do was talk about it. And then as time went on they didn't want to talk about it at all. Sundaram's brother took him away for many years. Yes, now I remember. All the years you were growing up here Sundaram was with his brother. Maybe that's why you don't know about it. All that was a long time ago. More than fifty years. Now who even cares? Maybe Mani and a few other people know. No one else. No one likes to talk about such a terrible thing. The quicker you forget something like this the better."

When they arrived home, Suresh was still at the dining table in front of the television, his hair falling over his face. Gopalakrishnan wanted to go up to Suresh and say, "Do you know the story of this old man Sundaram who lives in the village here? Do you know what his parents did to him? What have I ever done to you that you think you can be so rude, so hurtful to me?" Instead he avoided Suresh's glance in his direction and passed straight into his room and lay down on his bed. He felt exhausted and abandoned, as if he had been carrying a great weight and the weight was now gone but the weight's disappearance was no relief. It was unusual for him to lie down when it was not his bedtime. But his head and his arms and his legs felt so heavy he felt he could not carry them anymore.

Then he heard his mother tell Parvati in the kitchen how he had abruptly left the meeting and how she had found him sitting on the steps of the temple. He made himself get up from his bed then. He did not want Parvati interrogating him. Already that morning he had skipped his customary walk. There would be so many questions, so many concerned inquiries. That would never do. So he sat at his book-laden desk with his back to the rest of the house and looked out of the window at the evening gathering itself in the street outside.

The phone was ringing. Gopalakrishnan knew there was no one home to answer it except him. It was the day after the bhajan meeting. Suresh, Parvati, and his mother had gone to the temple to attend the dance performance organized by the young men of Meenakshisundareswarar Temple Street. He had made the excuse that he had not yet finished his reading of the Ramayana. Still it took him a while to raise himself from his bed and make his way into the internal veranda where the black phone sat on its stool, clamoring insistently for his attention. He picked up the receiver. It felt heavy in his hand. The plastic smell was familiar and irksome in his nostrils. He stared listlessly at the phone on the stool and spoke into the round mouthpiece of the receiver, "Hello?"

At first there was only breathing — labored, unwholesome — at the other end of the phone line. Then someone asked in Hindi: "Who is this?" The voice was thick and unhurried, as if it had clotted deep in the throat of the speaker and was oozing slowly out.

Gopalakrishnan was surprised to hear Hindi. Who was calling that spoke Hindi? Unusual. The sound of the alien language focused his mind a little. He replied, speaking in his heavily accented Hindi, "Gopalakrishnan. Who are you?"

From the earpiece of the receiver the labored breathing pressed loudly into Gopalakrishnan's ear, whistling in and out, like wind blowing through trees in the dead of night. Then the voice asked: "Is Suresh there?"

That explained the Hindi. The call was for Suresh. From Delhi probably. Gopalakrishnan replied, "He has gone out. He will be back in a little while. Who shall I say called?"

"Motherfucker."

Mother . . .?! The word fell like a sharp slap on Gopalakrishnan's ear. He could not believe he had heard right. He could not have. Why would someone use that word with him? — "What did you say?"

"You heard me right. I said motherfucker."

Gopalakrishnan frowned in confusion: "Why are you talking like this?"

"I know who you are. You are Suresh's father. Your son is a motherfucker. Tell that motherfucker we know where he is."

"You know where he is?" Gopalakrishnan's voice had grown small, anxious.

"We can get him."

"Get him?"

"Are you deaf, old man? Don't you hear me the first time I say something to you? I said we know how to find him. This is not a game. We'll break his legs. Tell your motherfucker son we'll do things to him he can't even imagine. There is time still."

"Time?"

"Just tell your motherfucker son what I said, old man. He'll understand."

And then once again the breathing came. Behind it someone chuckled. A horn blared. An auto-rickshaw *phut-phut-phut*-ed past and then faded into the distance. Long after the click at the other end of the line had released him from these distant sounds — how distant exactly? where exactly had the call come from? — Gopalakrishnan stood with the clammy receiver against his face. It was only when he could not ignore the complaining beep-beep-beep from the phone any longer that he returned the receiver to its cradle. When he did he found he was drenched with sweat, his face and his hands and his armpits dripping with it. He sat down on one of the chairs around the dining table and stared at the phone on its wooden stool, now so mute and innocent.

Who was it that had called? What did he want with Suresh?

We'll break his legs.

The phone call was a mistake.

Yes, that is what it was.

A mistake.

Relief. But only for a moment. Gopalakrishnan remembered. The voice had mentioned Suresh by name.

How then could it be a mistake?

Gopalakrishnan stood up abruptly to fetch Suresh from the Bhajan Society room in the temple and then just as abruptly sat back down. The sounds of the young men singing and dancing had been reaching him faintly from up the street for a while. Now there was only silence. The meeting was probably over. Suresh and

Parvati and Amma would be home any minute. He sat at the table and waited. Dusk had fallen by now, but he did not switch on the lights. He went over the conversation in his head, looking for reasons to counter his growing trepidation. He was still engaged in this desperate exercise when Suresh stepped in through the front door.

Gopalakrishnan looked at Suresh and said simply, "A man called for you." He could not say a word more.

Gopalakrishnan could not see Suresh's face in the darkness, but the voice that reached Gopalakrishnan was edged with worry: "For me?"

Parvati followed Suresh into the house. She said to her husband, "Why are you sitting in the darkness like this? If I am not home nothing gets done. Has someone died that the house is in such darkness at this time of the day?" Muttering to herself, she went up to the wall where the switches were located and flipped two of them. Two fluorescent tube lights flickered, struggled to come on, and then light flooded the internal veranda. Parvati was wearing a deep purple sari with rows of little yellow mangos — one of her finest and favorite silk saris. She went into her room to change into a more ordinary one. "You should have come," she said to Gopalakrishnan as she passed him. "You missed something wonderful. The boys were so good. They had practiced their dancing so well."

Gopalakrishnan blinked in the sudden light and said to Suresh, "Yes, for you. The caller spoke in Hindi."

Suresh had dressed in a veshti and shirt for the dance performance. Vibhuti made a white streak in the center of his forehead. Gopalakrishnan found the vibhuti incongruous, for Suresh was not religious and generally never used vibhuti. He must have followed some of his companions at the dance and daubed it on his forehead, Gopalakrishnan thought to himself.

On hearing his father's words of confirmation, Suresh came slowly up to the dining table, stood with his hands resting on the back of one of the chairs that surrounded it, and waited for more. The harsh white light directly above the dining table revealed the way his hair fell away from his temples. In years to come he would begin balding here, at his temples. The light made him look older than he really was.

Gopalakrishnan's mother, who had gone into the puja room, spoke from there, "Yes, Gopu. How can you be like this? Diwali is only two days away. Is it right for you to leave the house in darkness like this?" She switched on the light in that room too. Then she called Suresh to her because she wanted his help in lighting the little clay oil lamps in front of the pictures of the gods. Her arthritic hands were acting up. She did not want to struggle with the matches.

While Suresh helped his grandmother, Gopalakrishnan sat and waited. Suresh came back into the veranda slowly, reluctantly. Gopalakrishnan looked at Suresh and his fear was palpable inside him, but instead of speaking the question uppermost in his mind, he said, "I am ashamed to tell you how the man on the phone spoke. Such filthy language."

Clad in one of her ordinary cotton saris (she was still adjusting the palloo over her shoulder), Parvati emerged from her room and asked, "Did someone telephone for Suresh? Who was it? Was it Aloke?"

Suresh said, "What did the man want?" His face was turned away, as if he could only look at his father from the corners of his eyes, not directly. He spoke as if to the television next to which his father sat.

Gopalakrishnan recognized the manner. How often he had seen

it before, whenever Suresh was anxious or afraid! Gopalakrishnan's own dread regarding the telephone call flared higher, overcoming his inhibition. The inauspicious words came tumbling out, "The man who called said terrible things. He said he would break your legs. He did not give his name. He said you would understand what he is saying. What is he saying, Suresh? What does he want? He said there was still time. Time for what, Suresh?" There. He had spoken. Now, let what will be, be.

Parvati, who was on her way into the kitchen to get dinner ready, stopped, turned, came back to the dining table. Her gray hair was done in the usual knot at the top of her head. She looked from her son to her husband and back. "Break legs?" she asked. "What is this, Suresh?"

Gopalakrishnan looked at his son standing on one side of the table and his wife on the other. The white light from the overhead fluorescent tube — strange alchemy — added years to Suresh's face and he realized, once again, how much his wife and son resembled each other. He saw how the face of each was long, how the nose and the eyes and the curve of the lips of the one echoed the other. He saw how they were united, his wife and his son, and was reminded of his own unity with them. But in the same instant he felt too the terrific fragility of this unity he had taken for granted. Was it not because he had taken it for granted — because he had taken as a given something that had to be earned from moment to moment — that he had been angry and dejected after his disagreement with Suresh over the Ramayana? A phone call like wind in the trees. A voice out of another world. A message full of menace. And in a moment that which lay between him and his son and wife, that which had seemed so safe, was become violable. Gopalakrishnan felt a remorseful rush of love and tenderness for his wife and his son at the thought.

Suresh crumpled into a chair across the dining table from his father and said in a whisper, almost as if to himself, "What do you care? You are sitting here far from Delhi. What do you care what happens to me?" He did not look at either his father or his mother.

Parvati said, "I knew something was wrong. When you arrived so suddenly I knew something was the matter." Her tone was sad rather than accusing.

Still, Gopalakrishnan intervened, "Let Suresh speak. Who was this man who called, Suresh?" Within, he felt his love for his son like a dull swelling hurt.

"We owe him money," Suresh said in a low voice.

"Who do you mean we?" Parvati asked.

"Aloke and I. Who else could it be?"

"How much?" Gopalakrishnan wanted to know.

"A lot. Aloke knows exactly. But it is a lot more than we can pay."

"You must have some idea?" Parvati insisted.

Suresh hesitated. "Maybe forty lakhs, maybe fifty lakhs. Something like that."

Speaking at the same time, Gopalakrishnan said, "Fifty lakhs?" and Parvati, "Fifty lakhs!" Neither could fathom that much money. After a lifetime of working Gopalakrishnan had nowhere near that much.

Suresh saw the expression on their faces and said, "It is not as much as you think it is."

The remark made Parvati furious. "Suddenly all this money is nothing to you?" she asked, her voice rising unintentionally. "Suddenly you think fifty lakhs is nothing?"

"How did you come to owe so much?" Gopalakrishnan asked.

"It was the Shree Nivas Apartment Complex project in the Trans-Yamuna. We thought it would do well and borrowed heavily. But then it didn't."

"You borrowed from men who use language like that? From men who say they will break your legs?" Gopalakrishnan wanted to know.

"Aloke arranged the money. No one else would give us what we wanted. We were sitting on all this land and thought apartments there would be snapped up in no time. We had borrowed from banks against the land but needed more. Sometimes you have to do things like this in business. What would you know about that?"

Parvati was still thinking of how enormous the sum Suresh had mentioned was. "Why would anyone give you two so much money?" she asked.

"I told you. Aloke arranged all the money. He knows all kinds of people. I don't know what all he did to get the money. I told you. We thought the apartments would be snapped up in two minutes. Who could know we would lose so much money on it?"

"Where is Aloke?" Parvati asked.

"When we found out we didn't have the money, we talked about what to do. Aloke thought it would be best if we went away for a while. He is in Bombay with a friend."

Parvati said, "Aloke did this, Aloke did that. Aloke thought this was best, he thought that was best. That is all you say. What were you doing while he was doing all this? Can't you think for yourself?"

Gopalakrishnan said, "Why didn't you go to Aloke's father for help? He would have helped you with the money."

"How could we? His own business is not doing well. It is this downturn in the economy. Anyway, I did mention it, but Aloke didn't want to do it. He has already given us so much money. How could we ask him for more? He has helped us so much."

Gopalakrishnan slapped his right hand hard on the tabletop, surprising even himself. He snorted, "Helped you? What kind of a father lets his son go to goondas for money? Why didn't you come to me with your problem? I would never have let you do it!" He felt very angry at Aloke's father for not being more responsible.

Suresh lifted his head slowly, as if it were heavy as stone, and glared at his father. "Don't say a word to me about what you would have done. Don't speak a word to me!" he said. His manner was sullen, dangerous.

Still Gopalakrishnan rushed on, his love and fear goading him on, "Why not? What have I said that is so bad? Aloke's father should have found out what you two were doing in your business! He certainly should have done at least that."

"At least he was in Delhi," Suresh replied. "At least he was there with us."

Gopalakrishnan was taken aback. "What are you trying to say?" he blurted out.

"You know what I am saying. Aloke's father is the one who gave us money to set up the business. He helped us in so many different ways. There is no need to criticize him or Aloke. What did you do? How much money did you give us? It was nothing. Did you give us any help? You came running away here. What is the use of asking me all these questions now?"

Suresh was shouting. His voice was shaking. His face had metamorphosed, the features become swollen and distended. It had twisted itself into a grotesque mask Gopalakrishnan could not recognize. Bulging eyes, flaring nostrils, twisted lips. A kathakali mask of fear and fury. Gopalakrishnan looked at Suresh, speechless. It was Parvati who said sharply, "Don't speak to your father like that! Are we big business people like Aloke's father? Can we help in the way Aloke's father can help? Think about that before you start speaking any which way you like."

The lips of the mask had been moving soundlessly, as if struggling to articulate something more. At Parvati's reprimand, the mask collapsed back into Suresh's face. Suresh rose abruptly from the table, making a quick involuntary gesture of dismissal with his left hand in the direction of his father, and flung himself out the front door into the night outside. "Where are you going?" Parvati called after him, looking at Gopalakrishnan and willing him to do something, say something. But Gopalakrishnan neither rose from the table in pursuit of his son nor called out to him. He sat and looked at Parvati helplessly and asked in a woeful voice, "Why does Suresh hate me so much?"

Parvati looked back at him wearily for a moment and then turned and followed Suresh out. What could she say to the question? She did not know how she would even begin an answer to it. She wanted only to find Suresh, to figure out what to do about the terrifying predicament he was in.

The train came alive with a lurch. Sitting by the window on the yellow painted bench, Gopalakrishnan was flung forward and then abruptly back again against the hard wooden backrest. He hurriedly gripped one of the rods barring the window in a belated attempt to steady himself. With his other hand he reached across his lap and gripped his black zipper bag with the fading white TAYATA ELECTRICAL GOODES — INDIA'S OWN — PUMPS AND MOTORS legend on its side. The bag contained his valuables — bankbook, checkbook, wallet, pens (three in number), address book, and fresh handkerchief. He did not want it tumbling to the floor from where it was ensconced between his thigh and the wall of the coach. Instinctively, his hand felt the zipper of the bag to make sure it was securely fastened. It was. Nevertheless, Gopalakrishnan held the bag in a tight grip.

Outside the window of the train Paavalampatti gathered speed. As the train advanced, the low houses of the village, half-glimpsed from behind the coconut and banana trees and the scrub, fled in the opposite direction. The back wall of the school — gray and in considerable disrepair — appeared and disappeared. The railway crossing where the tracks met the highway came into view up ahead. The gates were closed, barring passage on both sides to the waiting pedestrians, cycles, two mopeds, two bullock carts, a red Maruti van (JESUS WILL SAVE YOU written in gold across the top portion of the windshield), and a mud-splattered green bus. To one side of the gates the banyan tree spread its profuse branches over the little food stall with its hissing blue-flamed kerosene stoves. A knot of men — agricultural laborers, shirtless, with white cotton towels wrapped above their sun-darkened faces and with hoes and spades and metal baskets in their hands — waited before the stoves for the woman in the stall to minister to their needs. Outside his store, Ramu stood watching the passage of the train, a glass of hot coffee in one hand. *Once upon a time he would pass carefree along this very stretch of the highway during his morning walk. A lifetime ago it seemed. Was it only three days since his last attempt at a morning walk, the one made disastrous by his detour through the cheri? And only yesterday that the phone call regarding Suresh had come? Yet such change had come crashing into his life. He felt like, like . . . What was the common saying? How did it go? A kite adrift. The binding twine of his life snapped, as if by some great wind. Flung unmoored into a frightening, measureless sky.*

Even as Gopalakrishnan watched, the little scene at the railway gate was snatched from him and the train was past Paavalampatti and swinging around to head toward Thirunelveli Town. When it was on the bridge crossing the Tamarabarani River, Gopalakrishnan could see in the distance the green bus that had been at the railway gate. It too was on a bridge crossing the river — the white bridge at which he used to leave the trail during his morning walks. Behind the bus and the bridge, determinedly thrusting themselves above the treetops, rose the temple spire and the satellite dish marking the rough location of Meenakshisundareswarar Temple Street.

Suresh had still been asleep when he had left. The plan Parvati and he had come up with — Suresh knew nothing of it.

Glumly Gopalakrishnan watched the train cross the bridge and rush on toward Thirunelveli, through paddy fields laid out in brilliant emerald patchwork amid the faded colors of scrubland. In the distance, under the lowering sky to the west, were the hills beyond which Kerala lay. Within minutes, a cluster of trees appeared amid the brown and green landscape and the train slowed. It was the neighboring village of Maaranpatti, a village much smaller than Paavalampatti. The train was a local. It would stop at every station no matter how insignificant and take an hour and a half to travel to Thirunelveli.

No temple spire rose high to mark Maaranpatti's location. The station was an unpaved gravelly strip on which stood a little building painted an official yellow. Next to the building a gulmohur tree had scattered a few of its hard brown pods on the ground. Only a few months before both tree and platform beneath had been ablaze with glowing red flowers. Now, in November, the flowers were all gone. The tree was utterly altered. Gopalakrishnan's coach groaned to a halt in front of it, precisely where the few passengers waiting to board the train were all gathered. All clambered into Gopalakrishnan's coach and hurried down the aisle looking for a place to sit as the train left the station.

In Gopalakrishnan's compartment, nine people were already sitting on the two benches meant for eight. Opposite him sat an elderly couple, squeezed like him against a window by three raucous male college students with slicked-back hair and vibhuti on their foreheads. The woman sat by the window and the man — dressed in trousers like Gopalakrishnan — between her and the college students. Both were a little faded and small and quite a contrast to the vivid college students, one of whom wore a stylish, multicolored T-shirt with VERMONT written on it. Next to Gopalakrishnan on his bench were three men, office-goers by the look of their shirts and trousers. One was buried in a newspaper, another stared blankly at nothing, and the third slept with his head jiggling on the second man's shoulder to the rhythm of the train gathering speed out of Maaranpatti. A young but burly man with a thick black moustache shiny with oil stopped in the aisle next to the men and insisted there was space for him on the bench. He was a little breathless from his exertions in the oppressive weather and was clearly in no mood to be denied. The sleeping man was awoken and reluctantly everyone moved up just a little so that the newcomer could perch himself at the very end of the bench with his knees sticking out into the aisle.

Gopalakrishnan found himself pressed even farther against the window. Indignantly he moved his zipper bag onto his lap; but the complaint that had begun to rise within him faltered in his throat and expired into a barely audible "*tch*" before it could pass his lips. *Who did he think he was? Who was he to complain? What did it matter if he was squeezed right against the window?* His tongue felt dead as a slab of stone. He made himself as small as he could and turned his face once again to the fields and villages passing outside the window. A little barefoot boy in a khaki school uniform raced the train for a distance. A man in a white veshti stood on the broken circular wall of a well and stared at the heavy clouds in the sky. Little stations with black-jacketed stationmasters carrying red and green flags under their arms came and went. *He was just an aging man. A man approaching the last stages of his life. A man who should be living out the rest of his life quietly with grandchildren playing at his feet, not rushing to Thirunelveli on a desperate errand on behalf of a son who despised him. Why should anyone listen to the complaint of a luckless fool like him?* Gopalakrishnan looked out the window of the train but saw nothing.

"What is the matter? Where are you going this early with your bag?" his mother had said as he was leaving to catch his train, her words a mumble because she was not wearing her dentures.

"To Thirunelveli," he had mumbled in reply.

"Thirunelveli?"

"To get train tickets. Suresh and I have to go to Delhi."

"To Delhi? So suddenly?"

"There was a phone call. Suresh has sudden work in Delhi. I am going to help him with the work."

"You have to go to Delhi right now during Diwali? On the very day of the harikatha for which you have been preparing so much you have to rush off for tickets? What kind of work is this?"

"Important work," he had said and hurried out the house.

"But will you be back for the harikatha, Gopu?" his mother had called after him. He had not replied.

What was the harikatha to him now? He had not told Amma that, in addition to train tickets, his trip to town was intended to scrape together virtually all that he owned so that he could take it with him to Delhi and offer it along with his monthly pension to Suresh's creditors. How could he tell Amma the truth? Better that she interrogate Parvati. Parvati would know how to handle her. How could he tell Amma that now they were all likely to be dependent on the money and pension his father had left her for all their daily expenses? And, worse, that goondas were after her grandson? How could he tell Amma about these goondas who were so dangerous they might cripple Suresh, perhaps even — could it really happen?! — kill him?

The thought entered his head — it was not the first time — even as the train arrived at Thirunelveli Station. Gopalakrishnan's fellow passengers hurried out of the coach but he found it difficult even to rise from his seat. He stared out his window at the platform filling with alighting passengers. All his fellow passengers had dismounted before he followed them — compelled himself to follow them — onto the platform swarming with people. The elderly couple — they were much older than him, really — had paused on the platform by the juice stand to let the crowd thin a little. The burly man with the moustache had already rushed ahead, elbowing others out of his way, pushing them into a stack of boxes wrapped in gunnysack standing high in the middle of the platform. In his wake went the three college students, laughing and bantering among themselves. Why were the young always in such a hurry? Gopalakrishnan sent a meaningful look toward the elderly man, but the look was not returned. Now that he was no longer by the window in the moving train the air closed still and hot and humid around him. Sweat broke out on his neck and on his face. He opened his bag and took out the handkerchief. When would this weather lift at least a little? He wiped himself carefully with the handkerchief, but even before he had returned it to his bag sweat was beginning to bead his neck and his face once again.

The crowd streamed down the platform past Gopalakrishnan: college students dressed in brightly colored shirts and saris, middle-aged men in pressed trousers heading to desk jobs, barefoot laborers in grimy clothes in search of work, women traders bent under their baskets of goods, men of substance, adorned with gold rings and necklaces, come from their villages to transact important business in town.

Was there any like him in this crowd? Who here could claim to be as miserable as him?

A silver-painted metal overpass led from the platform over the tracks to the station exit, but most in the crowd were headed for the end of the platform, where they could simply cross the tracks without having to use the overpass. Gopalakrishnan avoided the crowd and went up the overpass steps. The railway tracks stretched away in both directions beneath. In the yard adjacent to the station coaches were being shunted into a siding with a great echoing clamor. Over yard and station hung a stench of tired metal and unwashed latrines and uncleared refuse. Outside the station, Gopalakrishnan ignored the inquiring shouts emanating from the yellow-and-black auto rickshaws lined up by the roundabout and headed down T.M.B. Street. He did not have far to go to his first stop for the day, his bank. He much preferred walking to being jolted along in those shaky contraptions.

T.M.B. Street was lined with shops and restaurants. Many were already open for business. Good Luck Photo Studio was yet shuttered but next door the proprietor of Kumaran Novelty Store was arranging rows of plastic toys on wooden shelves in front of his shop. Opposite, Nalla Ruchi Bhavan, an eatery at which Gopalakrishnan customarily stopped when he came to town, was bustling. It had the most wonderful idlies Gopalakrishnan had ever eaten — the soft, white, fragrant discs were served with the most delicious coconut chutney. The strong aroma of coffee wafted invitingly from the cavernous inside of the restaurant. O, *to sit in that cool dark interior under the whirring ceiling fan with coffee and idlies and little bowls of chutney and sambhar in front and the familiar shouts of the yajaman and his employees sounding back and forth overhead.* Gopalakrishnan passed Nalla Ruchi without stopping. Perhaps for lunch he could return here. With his bag under his arm he picked his way carefully through the pedestrians and the cycles and the auto rickshaws, past Saraswathi Book Mart and Thirunelveli Halwah and Modern Suitings Shirtings. At the end of the street he turned left on Madurai Road and walked alongside yet more shops. Opposite was the town's main bus terminus full of snorting buses and hurrying commuters. Dust and fumes rose from the terminus and rolled in a brown cloud through the entrance into the street along which he was walking. *How different from Paavalampatti. The sounds. The smells. The people . . .* Gopalakrishnan had escaped it all when he had left Delhi. Only recently had he been reminded just how much by a column Murthy had written on the urgent crisis in Indian cities. Murthy had written of the pollution, the population explosion, the decaying infrastructure. Once, Gopalakrishnan too had lived unthinking in the midst of it all. *Murthy's son was in Qatar. Also a journalist. Worked for some sheik's newspaper there. Earned in dollars and dinars. How fortunate of Murthy to have a son like Varun.*

Gopalakrishnan arrived at his bank. From the public cacophony of the street he entered into a subdued hum, at once intimate and profound, ordered by the peculiar rituals of monetary transactions Gopalakrishnan had always found faintly alien. It was a busy time in the bank: the next day it would close for Diwali. Under fluorescent tube lights customers stood against a white Formica-topped counter that ran the length of the main hall, gesturing for the attention of clerks lost in green ledger pages. In importuning hands they held passbooks for updating, or checks for deposit, or pink challans for cash withdrawal. In a far corner two men in veshtis stood with their backs to the hall, leaning against each other like lovers. But their true love was between them; they were counting thick wads of money with great, silent concentration. A bell rang in the cashier's cage, prompting others waiting on benches in the little space before the counter to compare the metal tokens in their hands with the flashing display board overhead. The one chosen from among them — a Muslim woman in black head scarf and robes — timidly hurried forward to receive her reward for her patience. Usually Gopalakrishnan would have resigned himself to standing with those at the counter, passbook or withdrawal slip in hand. Today he went onward — *What did he have in common with people such as these? Normal people, with their normal little troubles and desires?* — and proceeded to a room on the far side of the hall identified by the plastic sign on its door: MANAGER.

Srinivasan was the manager's name and he was well known to Gopalakrishnan. Gopalakrishnan had had an account in the bank for decades. He had opened the account at the insistence of his father, who had also banked there. Ever foreseeing the unforeseeable, his father had felt that if both had accounts in the same bank it would facilitate the transfer of funds between them in the event of an emergency. However, no emergency had ever presented itself.

Srinivasan, who was much younger than Gopalakrishnan, had been with the bank as long as Gopalakrishnan could remember. Gopalakrishnan had known him as a young, stick-thin man newly posted to the bank from Madras. Now he was much thicker in the waist, wore glasses for reading, and had the grave manner of one who had risen in the world to become a manager of one of the busiest banks in Thirunelveli.

Luckily for Gopalakrishnan, Srinivasan was not with a customer, as was often the case. He noticed Gopalakrishnan hovering at the open door to his small office, removed his glasses from his face, and waved him forward. Gopalakrishnan seated himself in the indicated chair, wondering how to tell Srinivasan the reason for his visit. Younger though Srinivasan was, Gopalakrishnan found him slightly intimidating. Why, he could not tell. After all, despite all his success, Srinivasan was only the manager of a bank in a little town, nothing more than a district headquarters. Gopalakrishnan, on the other hand, had gone away and made a successful career for himself in the central government in far-off Delhi. Why then should Srinivasan make him feel wanting?

On the desk between Gopalakrishnan and Srinivasan, ledger pages and challans and letters secured by round glass paperweights fluttered in the breeze from the ceiling fan. Sitting across from Srinivasan, Gopalakrishnan recalled the considerate letter Srinivasan had written him on his father's death. He had forgotten how well they had known each other. Whenever Gopalakrishnan had come to the bank in the company of his father, a little time had always been spent in the manager's office so his father and Srinivasan could exchange notes on what they were reading — each was always caught up in some worthy tome or the other. They lent books to each other, even occasionally gave them as presents. *When was the last time he and Appa had given anything to each other?* He had forgotten this about Srinivasan and his father.

"How can I help you today, Gopalakrishnan-Sir?" Srinivasan was asking now, his expression friendly, even familiar, as if to say "You are your father's son, I remember your father, I have not forgotten him." He had picked up a superfluous paperweight from his desk and was toying with it.

Practically all of Gopalakrishnan's money was in Srinivasan's bank in fixed deposits. He had consolidated all his savings here when he had moved from Delhi, arranging them in different kinds of fixed deposit accounts under Srinivasan's advice. There was little else — a few shares left to him by his father, a paltry sum in Parvati's postal savings account that she liked to maintain herself.

What would Srinivasan think of his reason for coming to the bank today? Appa. Paavalampatti Krishnaswamy Iyer. Man of iron determination and judgment. Would he have found himself in such a predicament before his bank manager? Never.

Reluctantly Gopalakrishnan told Srinivasan that he wanted to cash all his fixed deposits and take most of the money from his savings account. *Once, just in passing, Srinivasan had told him Appa had spoken of him often. What was it Appa had said? What did Srinivasan know about him?*

Srinivasan stopped rolling the paperweight from one hand to the other and put it back on the desk, where the light from the window fell on it and showed up the red and yellow and green flecks suspended in the glass. "Why do you want to do this?" he asked, looking curiously at Gopalakrishnan.

Gopalakrishnan felt as if Srinivasan was appraising him, measuring him.

"Emergency. I need it."

"Family crisis?"

Gopalakrishnan mumbled, "Something like that. I need the money at once." *For my son. Who cannot abide me. At all.*

Srinivasan frowned. "At once? These things usually take time. I'll see what I can do. You should know there will be a penalty if you cash your fixed deposits like this. You will lose a lot of money."

Gopalakrishnan felt weary, weary, so weary. "Manager-Sir," he said. "Let it be. If there is a penalty, so be it. As long as I can get the money today."

Srinivasan kept frowning. "I understand. Sometimes you have to do these things. It's like your father would always say, isn't it? 'Sometimes to gain something, you have to lose something.' When it comes to losing, what is a little money? The only thing is to be sure that one is choosing to lose the right thing to gain the right thing. Isn't that so? Isn't that correct?"

Gopalakrishnan felt himself tested. He felt the great weight of Srinivasan's eyes upon him. Why was Srinivasan frowning at him, expecting him to answer his questions? It was his money. What explanation did he owe this bank manager? But Gopalakrishnan did not voice this resentment. Instead he looked down at his black Tayata bag and felt a conflicting desire to tell Srinivasan everything — the phone call; Suresh's desperate predicament; his own anger, confusion, fear. He felt a compulsion to hand over everything to Srinivasan, to let him handle all his affairs, which he would no doubt do with the great competence appreciated in him by Paavalampatti Krishnaswamy Iyer. No doubt.

How bitter he felt. What use such bitterness?

At last, Srinivasan said, "I'll see what I can do. Perhaps we can find a way to avoid some of the penalty." He reached out a hand to tap a bell on his desk and told the peon who arrived in answer to send in someone called Kulasekaran. When Kulasekaran appeared Srinivasan said, "This is Kulasekaran. He will take care of things for you. Please go with him. Kulasekaran, take care of what Gopalakrishnan-Sir wants today, immediately, so he does not have to come back. Gopalakrishnan-Sir needs this taken care of urgently. You understand?" Was there not a hint of censure directed toward him in Srinivasan's voice? Gopalakrishnan could not be certain. Nevertheless, he followed Kulasekaran out of Srinivasan's office feeling judged.

Much later — how long the various transactions had taken! — he was in the street outside with a bank draft in his bag. He clutched his bag even tighter now. *"If you want to gain something, you have to lose something. Who has ever gotten anything for free in this world?" It was true Appa would often say that. He had forgotten.* The sounds and smells of the street swirled around him. He felt disoriented, overwhelmed, disheartened. The bank draft represented almost everything he owned. Srinivasan had been true to his word and had bent a rule here and a rule there to waive some of the penalties. Yet the bank draft that had finally been put in his hands by Kulasekaran represented barely a fraction of the amount required to pay off Suresh's creditors. This was all his life had amounted to. Not even enough to save his son, his only child. The thought brought a sudden tightness to his chest. *No wonder his son didn't care for him.* Parvati had tried to tell him Suresh did, he really did. But what else could she say? He placed his palm against his chest and pushed to relieve the tightness. Passing pedestrians gave him concerned looks. Feeling breathless, he made himself start walking toward his next destination. For train tickets — there was no chance he could just buy them in the reservation office at such short notice — he had gone for help to Mani who knew influential people all over Thirunelveli District. Mani had directed him to someone called Railway Raghu, who lived at Number 23 Muthuswamy Mudaliar Street. This was where he had to go now. He felt lightheaded and disoriented as he walked, as if there were one part of him walking and another contemplating the walking man from some great height.

What had Appa said about him to Srinivasan? What did Srinivasan think of him?

How he was worrying about this silly thing when there was so much else to worry about.

Muthuswamy Mudaliar Street was lined with houses built in the traditional style with thinnais and pillars in the front. Everything in it was mean and faded, the houses shabby and jammed together. The thinnais were low platforms barely two steps above the open drain running along one side of the lane. The pillars were chipped and cracked and badly in need of paint. Number 23 was the least destitute of these houses, but Gopalakrishnan still surveyed it with dismay. From a television in the front room of this house issued an old Tamil film song. "*Atho untha paravai polla vaazha vaendum. Atho untha alaigal polla aadu vaendum . . .*" The song was loud enough to drown out every other sound in the street. Gopalakrishnan had to yell numerous times before he could break through the wall of sound and make his presence known. Live like those birds in the sky? Dance like those waves in the sea? Who wouldn't want to? But was that any reason to thrust the song on the whole world in this fashion? What kind of place had Mani sent him to?

Eventually an old man appeared on the thinnai and asked in a surly manner, "What do you want?" The man's sole garment was a dirty veshti around the waist, perched precariously on an enormous undulating stomach. The rest of him — his arms, his legs, his chest

— was thin and flabby. What little hair he had seemed gathered not on his head, but in his bushy eyebrows and flaring nostrils.

"Paavalampatti Mani sent me."

"What?"

"Paavalampatti Mani. He sent me. I am looking for Railway Raghu."

They were shouting at each other above the television.

"Mani-Sir? He sent you? Come in then. I am Mr. Raghu."

Discarding his sandals at the door, Gopalakrishnan followed the old man into the wall of sound. The front room of the house was bare except for the television on a stool, a wooden bench along a wall, and the kind of low-slung easy chair Gopalakrishnan had in his own room in Paavalampatti. Raghu eased himself into the easy chair, leaving the narrow bench for Gopalakrishnan. When Gopalakrishnan was seated, Raghu leaned forward and scrutinized him carefully as the television flashed over them images of MGR — that star so incandescent that initials sufficed for a name — in his well-groomed hair singing with one arm raised up to the birds in the sky.

"Mani-Sir told you about me," he observed. He looked younger close up. His eyes were sharp and alive. His chin was firm, determined. "Your name?"

"Gopalakrishnan. I need tickets to Delhi."

"You also live in Paavalampatti?"

"Yes. Can you help me?"

"I have never seen you before. You have never come to me. I never forget anyone who comes to me asking me for my help."

"I have come back to Paavalampatti only recently. I was living in Delhi before that." *Until last year, when he had left Suresh alone in Delhi and come back to be with his mother.*

"When?"

"I came back last year."

"No. When do you want to go to Delhi?"

"As early as possible. Tomorrow if possible."

"Tomorrow's Diwali."

"Even so. If you can get tickets for tomorrow we will go."

"Impossible."

They were sitting side by side but it was still necessary to yell because of the television.

"It is very urgent. We must be in Delhi as quickly as possible." Gopalakrishnan felt frantic. Mani had told him if anyone in Thirunelveli could get him train tickets at short notice it would be Railway Raghu. He had worked in the Thirunelveli ticket office for decades. He knew everyone there. He had ways to conjure up berths where no berths existed. For a consideration of course. Or so Mani had said when Gopalakrishnan had gone to him the previous evening, after Suresh had stalked out of the house and Parvati had come back with no Suresh. It was Parvati really who had planned this whole desperate trip to Delhi. She it was who had decided he would go to his bank to collect all his money to take with him to Delhi to offer along with his pension (to be used to make monthly payments, if the goondas would accept that). And it was she who had suggested Mani might be of help in this matter of the tickets. Gopalakrishnan had gone along, happy to be given direction, happy to be shown a course of action that he could take. But what if it turned out that this Railway Raghu — this little old man in a dirty veshti in a dirty lane — couldn't help? To fly to Delhi at the last minute like this would be outrageously expensive. Parvati had pointed out that they had to watch every paisa now so that Suresh's creditors could be paid off. The panic within Gopalakrishnan surged. His lightheadedness, which had gone away, returned. "Very important," he shouted urgently at Raghu above the new song that had begun on the television.

Raghu looked at him speculatively. He picked up the remote on the arm of his chair and muted the television. "How many?" he asked.

"Two."

"That makes it more difficult."

Gopalakrishnan's panic and frustration grew. What a predicament he was in. How shameful to find himself begging like this in front of this old man. Another thought, an encouraging one, occurred. Surely this Railway Raghu was simply negotiating with him? Of course! That was what it was. Exactly what a man like Railway Raghu would do — take advantage of his troubles to get as much out of him as he could. "Don't worry," he blurted out. "There will be something for you. I will take care of you" — he tried to make his tone reassuring — "I know what to do. You just want to make sure you get what's yours, isn't it? You don't have to worry. I will give you whatever you want. I will take care of you." He made sure he spoke the last sentence in a most understanding, most meaningful tone.

Abruptly Raghu's face changed. His eyes grew distant and stony. He leaned back in his armchair and let out a sigh of displeasure. "What is it you said?" he asked. "You will take care of me? Why do you want to talk to me like this? You come here" — he spread his calloused hands in the air between them indicating their surroundings — "and ask me to help you. On the day before Diwali you come here bothering me in my own home. Did I ask you to come? Anytime you want you can leave." He paused as if to see if Gopalakrishnan would take up his invitation. "Anytime." When Gopalakrishnan made no move, he laughed mirthlessly. "Perhaps Mani-Sir hasn't told you about me. I was not some chuprassi in the ticket office for you to talk to me like this. It is wrong to buy train tickets through bribery and corruption, you know. Isn't that what you are asking me to do? Illegal. You could go to jail for it. Yes, you could go to jail for it."

Gopalakrishnan looked at Raghu in fear and confusion. His words had made Railway Raghu angry. That had not been his intention. He did not want Railway Raghu angry at him. He needed him on his side. "Raghu-Sir, you have misunderstood me . . ." he began to placate Raghu, and faltered when Raghu thrust a dirt-encrusted fingernail into his face in warning.

"I have not misunderstood you, Mr. Gopalakrishnan Iyer," Raghu hissed. He was no longer using the respectful form of the pronoun when addressing him, Gopalakrishnan noticed. "What is there to misunderstand in your words? I know you very well. I have seen many like you. You think you are better than people like me. I can see the way you look at me and my house. You are not better. You are worse. At least I know exactly who I am. You have all kinds of ideas about yourself. You want to be better than people like me. But in the end you don't have the courage, do you? In the end you are just like me, aren't you? You need me. That is why you come holding your nose to look for me in my own house. Yes, I am everything you think I am, Mr. Gopalakrishnan Iyer. But who is it that you think you are?"

The bitter words slashed into Gopalakrishnan. He felt them with the sharpness of knives. Terrible words. He made no answer to them. He sat ashen and rigid on his bench, as if paralyzed, as if the words had cut him deep down to the very place where he lived. Raghu observed him for a moment, and then the anger went out of his face and his mocking manner returned. He said, reverting ostentatiously to a respectful form of address, "Let it be, Gopalakrishnan-Sir. Don't think about all this so much. What are train tickets after all? In Delhi where you are going the politicians are taking suitcases of fresh banknotes for all kinds of favors you and I cannot even imagine. Who was it that only last month bought a young girl for his pleasures as if she were a cow or a goat? You are not doing something like that, are you? Are you? All you want are train tickets to Delhi, isn't it? That is nothing. It will be done. Here, write down names and ages on this piece of paper. My number is here, on this card. Call me tomorrow. I will do the best I can. Mani-Sir has sent you. I will not be angry with you. I will tell you how much money to bring when you call. Now write down the information and go."

Gopalakrishnan's shaking hands did as the old man bid and then he stumbled down the broken steps and fled the house without a backward glance. At the head of Muthuswamy Mudaliar Street he fell into an auto rickshaw that could take him to the railway station. A couple of hours remained before the afternoon train to Paavalampatti, but where else could he go? He knew many people in town but how could he bear to see them, talk to them, be with them? The auto rickshaw passed Nalla Ruchi Bhavan. Lunch. He had not eaten anything since he had left Paavalampatti. He let the auto rickshaw rattle on to the train station, a pink building topped by domes. He took the overpass to the platform from which he knew his train would leave. He walked down the platform past the Vegetarian Light Refreshment stall until he came to a cement bench. He sat down on the bench to wait for the train, his bag with the bank draft inside held tightly in his lap. *That old man. Railway Raghu. How he had spoken to him! Asking him who he thought he was.*

Since no train was expected at this platform for quite a while he had it virtually all to himself. Behind the counter at the Vegetarian Light Refreshment stall a lone attendant kept watch over the vadas and the bondas and the biscuit packets. Lazily, the man swung a folded newspaper back and forth, fanning himself and the flies hovering greedily over the array of food. Beneath the edge of the platform the silvery metal tracks stretched in the direction of Paavalampatti. Suddenly a series of sharp explosions sounded in the distance, startling Gopalakrishnan and the man in the VLR stall into looking at each other. Firecrackers. Already the Diwali festivities had begun. *Soon Ramdas would be arriving in Paavalampatti for the harikatha. To celebrate the return of Rama to Ayodhya. But what did he have to do with such matters now?*

Tomorrow he would have to call Railway Raghu. He had no other choice.

He would do whatever the vicious old man asked him. Whenever the ticket, whatever the ticket, he would leave for Delhi with Suresh.

Hours later, Gopalakrishnan stood on the platform of Paavalampatti railway station and fidgeted with his Tayata bag. Making loud snorting noises of exasperation, he undid the zipper as if searching for something (yes, the bank draft still lay there, safe). He patted the bag's outside as if to remove dirt. To one side of him the train on which he had arrived from Thirunelveli Town went swaying by, continuing unhurriedly on its unfinished journey into the gathering dusk, its lit windows yellow in the gloom. Dense black clouds had advanced out of the east into an already leaden sky. The air felt thick and burdensome. From the corner of his eye Gopalakrishnan watched as his fellow passengers hurried down the platform. Only a few passengers other than himself had dismounted from the train at Paavalampatti. They included Ramu and his son. Gopalakrishnan had no desire to catch up with Ramu. Nosy man. He would be full of questions. Gopalakrishnan-Sir, he would say. Where have you been? What have you been doing? What is so urgent that you had to go to Thirunelveli the day before Diwali? Better to dawdle a little and let him go on ahead. Covertly watching the stocky shopkeeper, Gopalakrishnan pretended that a stone had lodged itself into the sandal of his right foot. He gave out more loud irritated snorts and shook the sandal as if to remove the stone, while Ramu and his son, weighed down by the heavy bags in their hands, shuffled along the platform behind the other passengers. Somewhere not too far away firecrackers sounded. All night it would be like this. *Btar, btoom*. All night long. But could anyone do anything about it? Not at all. Impossible. Gopalakrishnan felt a great desire to be backwithin the safety of the four walls of his home.

The red-painted carriages of the train went by slowly, so slowly. In the yellow open door of the last carriage, the figure of a man was silhouetted, the feet spread out, the two hands raised to grasp the bars running down each side of the door. He looked as if he were casting a benediction upon the village passing by. That image — the back-lit figure obscure and mysterious — struck Gopalakrishnan with startling force but he did not feel included in the blessing.

When the distance between Ramu and him had lengthened sufficiently Gopalakrishnan set off down the platform, trying to match the dawdling pace of father and son. Could they not walk faster? How long they were taking! Fortunately, at the exit the two turned left, presumably heading toward their shop. The other passengers had long disappeared. A humming fluorescent tube light washed the cement steps of the station in a harsh glare. Watched by the dog that customarily lay there, Gopalakrishnan followed Ramu and his son down the steps but then turned to the right, toward Meenakshisundareswarar Temple Street. The dog lifted its head off its paws as he went by and gave a yelp of recognition. He ignored it and hurried toward home.

Soon Gopalakrishnan came to the little maidan that lay across from the mouth of Meenakshisundareswarar Temple Street, along the railway tracks. Here had gathered, he saw, a small crowd ranging from children eight or nine years old to young men and women. The little crowd bubbled and churned with excitement around large cardboard boxes filled with fireworks that had been placed on the ground. The sounds he had heard in the station. Surely they were from here? Though there had been a pause in the fireworks, a smoke, accentuating the gloom of cloud and nightfall, still hung over the maidan, mingling with a sulfurous stench. The air had grown so acrid it made Gopalakrishnan's throat rasp and the tears come welling up in his eyes. Two of the young men — Gopalakrishnan was able to recognize them as Kumar and his friend Sriram because of the streetlamp under which they stood — had taken charge of the boxes filled with fireworks. They were handing out rockets and atom bombs to the oldest, flowerpots and snakes and whirlers to those a little younger, and sparklers to the very youngest. Gopalakrishnan was about to hurry past — best to get home before they started off again — when the lifting smoke uncovered something green and shimmering at the far end of the maidan. Sarala. In a sari of her favorite color. She was standing by herself, silent, as if preoccupied.

Suresh. Was he too here?

Gopalakrishnan's feet dragged to a halt on the road and he

searched the crowd, dark forms stirring restlessly beneath the smoke, for his son. He was still looking when a voice rang out: "Back! Move back now!" And another voice cried: "Remember! First the rockets! And then all together! Light up the night! The noise should break our eardrums!" There were cries of approval and laughter, and then the little crowd pushed back toward the end of the maidan where Sarala was standing. She disappeared from view behind it.

At the opposite end of the maidan a young man, faceless in the ever-deepening darkness, bent low. When the match in the young man's hand scratched into bright green flame Gopalakrishnan saw that he had placed a rocket, tail end first, into an empty bottle on the ground. With practiced ease, the young man took the flame to the fuse of the rocket and then, quickly, stepped back and away. There was a splutter and a whiz and a whoosh, a blur upward, a loud *phut,* and then a great umbrella of golden sparks showered down from the sky. Another whoosh, another blur in the gloom: this rocket showered down red and green and yellow sparks. Loud sighs of wonder and of fulfillment greeted the colorful rain from the sky, but were immediately drowned out by the rapid, sharp sounds — like a machine-gun firing — of the string bomb someone had lit even as he held it in his hand. Gopalakrishnan recognized the *tack-a-tack-a-tack-a-tack* from movies. At the very last minute the boy — he was really just that, thin and bony in a pale shirt too big for him — dropped the firecracker to the ground. It gave two or three final *tack-a-tacks* before expiring into silence. His shirt floating whitely around him, the boy strutted proudly to the cardboard box for more. Gopalakrishnan could not help frowning at the foolhardiness. If Suresh had done anything like that at that age, he would have given him such a talking to. Had the boy's parents not taught him anything? And then, all at once, the five flowerpots placed in a row burst into fiery life and arced their sparks into the air, and sparklers began spraying their light into the night, and whirlers and snakes began to spin and dart over the little maidan space that had been left for them. The whole maidan had erupted into a mad confusion of sound and light! Acrid smoke rose once again into the air. Gopalakrishnan gave up. How ever would he find Suresh in this madness? He hurried down Meenakshisundareshwarar Temple Street towards his home.

Already festive Meenakshisundareswarar Temple Street had grown even more so in the hours that Gopalakrishnan had been gone. The houses were bright with lights and loud with laughter and voices. Somewhere a voice was tunelessly singing a melody with no embarrassment whatsoever. Rows of little clay oil lamps with cotton wicks lit up the thinnais. Even the post office at the head of the street had not been ignored. Someone had placed a row of lamps along the edge of its thinnai. The ground in front of each house had been washed and decorated with a fresh kolam. One or two were extraordinary — multihued and intricate geometrical patterns conjured up out of rice flour by inventive hands. *Was this how it was when Rama returned home to Ayodhya after his exile? All the villagers put lamps in their windows to light the beloved son's way home. All of Ayodhya became bright and shining and joyful for his victorious return. This must have been how Ayodhya looked when Rama came back with Sita and Hanuman and all the others.* Gopalakrishnan had forgotten he did not agree with Vasu that Diwali celebrated Rama's return to Ayodhya.

From the maidan the fireworks continued to add their brilliant cacophony to the scene. Another rocket had been launched into the sky to rain down its golden sparks. More flowerpots had been made to spring to life and more atom bombs to detonate. The walls of Vasu's thinnai — wouldn't you expect it of a show-off like him? — were festooned with strings of red and green electric lights that blinked on and off. Gopalakrishnan could hear animated chatter coming from Vasu's house, but the voices were all female. Vasu's unmistakable voice was not among them. Then Gopalakrishnan remembered: it was the day, indeed the very exact time, of Ramdas's harikatha. Vasu would be there, in the room of the Bhajan Society in the temple. The pictures of Rama would have been taken down from the walls and arranged at the head of the room. Bright jamakaalams would have been spread out on the floor. All in honor of Ramdas. The thought was like a stone in the very middle of Gopalakrishnan's chest. *How he had prepared for the visit of this Ramdas. Day and night he had studied his books. They would all be there. And they would be wondering why he wasn't. They would think he was afraid of Ramdas.* A group of girls in colorful skirts came skipping down the street from the direction of the temple, their braided hair bright with oil. "Diwali greetings, Uncle!" one of them interrupted his cheerless thoughts as she passed. The stone in Gopalakrishnan's chest nudged a little. He smiled and said, "Diwali greetings to you too, child."

By now Gopalakrishnan had reached his house, which, unlike its neighbors, was dark, silent, forbidding as a tomb. Gopalakrishnan inhaled sharply. His was the only thinnai not made bright by lamps. *How could Parvati . . . ?* But then he saw that it was not wholly Parvati's fault. There were indeed a few clay oil lamps on the thinnai. In one of them a red dot still glowed faintly but in all the others the flame had sputtered out entirely. Perhaps Parvati had not poured enough oil into the clay lamps. Perhaps she had not prepared the cotton wicks properly. On a day like this Gopalakrishnan could not bring himself to blame her. He stepped past the perfunctory little kolam — barely five white lines of rice flour composed into the simplest of patterns — that decorated the front of his house and went up the steps.

The front door was shut but not locked. He pushed it open and passed through to the courtyard of the house, which too was dark. Where was everyone? Suresh was probably at the maidan watching the fireworks. But Amma and Parvati? Had they gone to the temple to hear Ramdas? Possible. Quite possible. Why should anyone give up hearing the great Ramdas? Gopalakrishnan vented his annoyance by going rapidly along the veranda around the courtyard and switching on lights. He then went into the front veranda of the house and switched on the single yellow bulb that dangled from the ceiling there, so that on this auspicious day before Diwali the house would not appear entirely without illumination from the outside. Through the veranda grill he saw once again how dark his thinnai was, how different from those of the neighboring houses. Really he should fix the lamps on the thinnai. But he could not do it. He felt completely drained by the events of the day, and he had not eaten since morning. He turned away guiltily and went back into his house, now bright with lights, and entered his room, his Tayata bag still clutched in one hand. He switched on the light and placed the bag on his bed carefully, as if it were a thing of great fragility. He took off his shirt, damp with sweat, and flung it on the easy chair. He switched on the ceiling fan to lift the great weight that was the air in the room.

And it was then that he saw it, flapping in the air set moving by the fan — a white sheet of paper, with a ragged edge showing it had been torn from a notebook.

The sheet had been placed on his desk amid the books, all those

Ramayana books he had been studying for the past many months. At one corner it was pinned down by one of the fat, red-bound volumes of the Ramayana of Kamban in the original Tamil. Even from across the room Gopalakrishnan could see the writing in black ink on the sheet as it fluttered up and down, beckoning to him to come over and pick it up. A note from Suresh? He knew in a flash it was so. He crossed quickly to the desk. The sheet felt smooth to his touch.

"Dear Appa" — the note, scrawled hurriedly in English across the page, began — "When you come back I will be gone. I am taking a taxi to Thirunelveli. Amma has told me what you plan to do. Why did you go to get your money? I don't want it. You cannot help me. What you have done is enough. What more do you want to do?" — what did Suresh mean? what had he done? — "You must not come to Delhi. You don't know about these men. They are goondas. Bad. If I stay they may come here. Then what will you do? What if they hurt you or Amma or Paati? I will phone call tomorrow. Don't worry about me. Suresh." And then the note continued: "I should never have come. I know it. You cannot help. ~~When have you ever~~" — Suresh had tried to blank the words out entirely but had failed — "I don't want you or anyone else getting hurt. I am sorry for everything." Finally *bad* had been circled and an arrow drawn down to the very bottom of the page — "Don't worry. Nothing will happen to me. Aloke has a plan. We know what to do. Everything will be fine. I promise." The black line under *promise* was thick, insistent, urgent.

Promise. Gopalakrishnan stared numbly at the English word as if he could not comprehend it. What did Suresh mean by that word? What was Suresh promising him? Gopalakrishnan could not understand it. He let the sheet of paper fall back to the desk, where the wind from the ceiling fan immediately snatched it up and blew it hard against the wall.

He too had made a promise to Suresh. That he would take care of all this. . . . What of that promise now?

Those words. The words Suresh had written and then tried to scratch out.

Suresh had so little faith in him.

The realization began as a dryness in the mouth. Gopalakrishnan sat helplessly down on his bed and stared at the sheet of paper trembling against the wall. He felt weak and helpless, as if some vengeful phantom he could not see had him by the throat. His stomach was a hollow pit of fear.

So many promises he had made to Suresh in his life. So many he had neglected to make. Or to keep.

Gopalakrishnan felt like crying.

Parvati.

Abruptly Gopalakrishnan stood up and left the house, barebodied and barefoot, not bothering even with his sandals. He headed up the street for the temple. It was night now. Only a few of the oil lamps lining the street still burned with a steady flame in the darkness; others were already extinguished or struggling weakly against their impending extinction. The dirt of the street felt hard and dry under his toes. Behind him, without his noticing, the little maidan of the fireworks had fallen silent. The voices in the houses too had quieted. But up ahead in the Bhajan Society room Ramdas's voice was still holding forth, expounding on Diwali and how the day celebrated Rama's return to Ayodhya. Through the open, lit door and the windows, Gopalakrishnan could see inside as he approached. He could see the people of Paavalampatti gathered in their fine veshtis and shirts and silk saris to receive Ramdas's precious words. *And he? What did he do? He came running, no sandals on his feet, no shirt on his back. Like a beggar.* He was almost in the room — he was at the very threshold and Narayan sitting cross-legged just within on the jamakaalam on the floor had turned at the sound of his approach — when his heart faltered and his feet refused. Instead of the Bhajan Society room, he turned toward the main entrance of the temple. As if in a dream, or a nightmare, he went up the stone steps leading through the tall doorway.

He stopped just within the temple, uncertain what he was doing there. Behind him, to one side, the two windows of the Bhajan Society room that opened into the temple enclosure cast white rectangles of light on the ground. Metal nets covered the windows and the shadows made by the nets patterned the rectangles with criss-crossing lines. Through these nets Ramdas's unrelenting voice pursued Gopalakrishnan, reaching for him over the whir of fans and the quiet murmur of gathered people. *If only he could shut that voice out.* The little portico of the temple, between the two sanctums of Shiva and Meenakshi, had been decorated for Diwali with clay oil lamps placed in rows on the ancient stone floor. Perhaps because of the harikatha in progress there seemed to be no one in the temple but him. In the two sanctums great circular brass lamps hanging from the ceiling glowed with numerous yellow flames. The hazy illumination provided by these lamps — Gopalakrishnan could smell the smoking oil even from this distance — revealed the squat black stone of the Shiva lingam and the idol of Meenakshi. Both had been washed and freshly clothed. Two fluorescent tube lights — one in the ceiling of the portico, the other beyond the portico on the far outer wall of the temple — also contributed their illumination to the scene. But such was the blackness of the still night air — so thick, so complete — that large parts of the temple enclosure remained shrouded in darkness. The neem tree that stood by the portico was a looming opaque hulk. In a far corner of the temple enclosure Gopalakrishnan could barely make out the well. And between tree and well he knew there was a large statue of Shiva's bull. Now the nandi was but a blot in the darkness.

He was alone in the temple. With God.

But, no, he saw immediately that he was wrong. His eyes had missed Sundaram sitting in his customary place against a pillar of the portico. Sundaram had almost merged into the pillar against which he was leaning, his long body folded into the slightest of shadows. He was gray against the gray of the pillar. On his head alone a little light fell at an angle, making it strangely luminous in the darkness. Gopalakrishnan remembered the story his mother had told him about Sundaram. *Sundaram in the temple like this. Day after day. What was he but an unanswerable question to the world? Staring with his enormous eyes at Shiva, the god for whom he was named, he sat there. Like an accusation.* The thoughts tumbled unbidden into Gopalakrishnan's mind, startling him, humbling him, even frightening him. *Accusation? Unanswerable question? Such strange thoughts. Such strange words.*

And then the rain that should have fallen and had refused to all these days at last yielded. The first sign was the falling drops caught whitely in the meager light from the fluorescent tube outside the portico. Soon the rain was hissing upon the ground. Gopalakrishnan abandoned his strange, disturbing thoughts and turned his head to look out beyond the portico at the water. The earth, dry and desperate only a moment before, expressed its gratitude by releasing its scent into the air. The wind bore this unsurpassable aroma through the temple portico, making the flames dance in their clay lamps. At first the wind was a cool relief against Gopalakrishnan's skin, clammy with perspiration; but then the rain grew stronger still, and the wind stronger with it, and a fine spray began lashing against the portico.

Gopalakrishnan stepped back to avoid it. He pressed against the wall of the Bhajan Society room, where, because of the angle, there was more protection from the rain. *Where was Suresh right now? Was he caught in the rain, drenched to his skin?* Through the netted windows he could still hear Ramdas. He had not been paying attention to the snatches of discourse that had fallen into his ears. Now he caught Ramdas's answer to a question he had not heard: "Rama went on a journey when he left Ayodhya. When Rama left Ayodhya he did not know who he was. When he came back he knew everything about himself. What he did right, what he did wrong, his divinity, his humanity — he knew all of it. When Rama returned to Ayodhya he returned to himself. He came back to himself. Other people may have other opinions. That is what I think. Rama's journey was ended when he came back to Ayodhya."

The words made Gopalakrishnan smile. All his months of study rose up in him at that instant. All the questions he could have asked, all the passages and examples he could have cited glowed radiantly in his head. And then he thought about Ramdas's words some more and his mind grew quiet again. More unfamiliar thoughts came to him, spreading an unforgiving light over the life he had led so far, so that things in him that he had never noticed before seemed perfectly visible now. He looked at Sundaram sitting there against a pillar. He looked through a window of the Bhajan Society room to find Parvati among the gathered people of Paavalamapatti. Clad in a sari of reddish brown color, she was sitting with Amma, her face careworn, distracted. *Soon he would have to tell her that Suresh was gone*. On the other side of Parvati sat Vasu's wife. And there at the head of the room, next to a large picture of blue-skinned Rama, was Ramdas himself in his black frame glasses and carefully combed long hair. The rain had made the audience restless; people were stirring, preparing to leave. But Parvati sat motionless.

All around Gopalakrishnan, as he watched Parvati through the window, the rain fell in torrents, as if to atone for all its days of denial. *So much to do. So much to set right. There was time yet. He would learn. He was not too old. He had no idea what he would do about the trouble Suresh was in. But he would not give up. There was time yet. For Suresh. And for him. There was no end to the journey.*

ACKNOWLEDGMENTS

Thanks . . .

to S. Muthiah, for *Madras Rediscovered*, his delightful introduction to the history of the city, a handy guide in the writing of this novel; and to P. S. Sundaram, for his translation of the Kamba Ramayana, from which the quoted passages in part one are taken

to Nirmal Selvamony and R. Radhakrishnan, for wise advice in the translation of Oothakaadu Venkatasubbaiyer's great eighteenth-century Tamil devotional song "Alaipaayuthey" (translated here as "Restless as the Waves of the Ocean")

to Laura Lyons, Cristina Bacchilega, and Mark Heberle, for doing one or two crucial things that cleared the time to bring Gopalakrishnan's story into the world

to Arindam Chakrabarti, for his wide-ranging conversations about the Ramayana, and for his patient translations from the Sanskrit

to John Zuern and Cindy Franklin, for reading a draft with their customary and exemplary sharpness of eye and mind

to Paul Lyons, for his enormous heart, wisdom about writing, and generous aid of all too many kinds

to the folks at Steerforth — Chip Fleischer, Roland Pease, Nicola Smith, Kristin Sperber, Pia Dewing — for their truly awesome professionalism, thoroughness, and dedication

to Jennifer Lyons, for her superb and savvy navigation of the depths of the publishing world, her unwavering faith

to my parents, K. S. Subramanian and K. S. Champakam, for their stories and memories, their vernacular knowledges, their indispensable affirmations

to Anannya, for patiently reading draft after draft, and for support beyond measure in ways beyond count

to Ujay, for bringing me again — and again! — to the end of words